THE
HOSTESS

Courtney Psak graduated with a degree in Communications and Journalism from Monmouth University, following with a master's degree in Publishing from Pace University. She started her career at magazines such as *Cosmopolitan*, *Self* and *Modern Bride*.

In 2015 she wrote her first novel, *Thirty Days to Thirty*, and sold thousands of copies while working as a project manager for Viacom in New York.

Courtney currently lives in Palm Beach, Florida with her husband and two sons. She is a member of the National Writers Association, International Thriller Writers, Crime Writers' Association and on the board for the Mystery Writers of America.

Also by Courtney Psak
Thirty Days to Thirty
The Tutor

THE HOSTESS

COURTNEY PSAK

HODDER &
STOUGHTON

First published in Great Britain in 2026 by Hodder & Stoughton Limited
An Hachette UK company

The authorised representative in the EEA is Hachette Ireland,
8 Castlecourt Centre, Dublin 15, D15 XTP3, Ireland (email: info@hbgi.ie)

1

Copyright © Courtney Psak 2026

The right of Courtney Psak to be identified as the Author of
the Work has been asserted by her in accordance with the
Copyright, Designs and Patents Act 1988.

All rights reserved. No part of this publication may be reproduced, stored
in a retrieval system, or transmitted, in any form or by any means without
the prior written permission of the publisher, nor be otherwise circulated
in any form of binding or cover other than that in which it is published and
without a similar condition being imposed on the subsequent purchaser.

All characters in this publication are fictitious and any resemblance
to real persons, living or dead, is purely coincidental.

A CIP catalogue record for this title is available from the British Library

Paperback ISBN 9781399748162
ebook ISBN 9781399748179

Typeset in Plantin Light by Manipal Technologies Limited

Printed and bound in Great Britain by Clays Ltd, Elcograf S.p.A.

Hodder & Stoughton policy is to use papers that are natural, renewable
and recyclable products and made from wood grown in sustainable forests.
The logging and manufacturing processes are expected to conform
to the environmental regulations of the country of origin.

Hodder & Stoughton Limited
Carmelite House
50 Victoria Embankment
London EC4Y 0DZ

www.hodder.co.uk

Prologue

Houses aren't haunted, just the people living inside of them. Their inner demons getting the best of them and at times taking over their reality.

That was what I always believed. It's what I had to believe. That my mind was simply playing tricks on me. Taking advantage of my damaged brain, still healing from the accident. Through my own post-traumatic stress, my head was spinning webs of lies and deceit, like a spider trapping a fly, injecting its venom, paralyzing me, eyes pried open in a bad dream that I couldn't wake up from. The worst was it would happen out of nowhere. I would be focused on my work when suddenly, out of the corner of my eye, I'd see a shadow. The flicker of an image from my past, my brother Danny running by the window, like watching an old home video.

I would shake it off, tell myself of course this wasn't Danny, my six-year-old brother from twenty years ago.

But the truth was much more horrifying.

What I saw and what I heard inside that house is still so troubling to me that I can barely get the words out to describe it. Despite living there in the present, I was still clearly living in the past. The past of someone else's life before their tragic demise.

I've heard of the phrase, *if these walls could talk*; I just never knew they could.

I didn't know what to make of it for a long time and, to be honest, to this day I still can't fully comprehend all that happened in that Hampton house.

All I know is, I could never go back there again.

Not after everything that happened.

Chapter One

Natalie

"Well, what do you think?"

I turn toward Luke, his hazel eyes bright with excitement as he anticipates my answer. He pauses at the entrance of the light gravel driveway for effect. The house itself is still another fifty yards away.

I manage a smile on my face and tilt my head. "It's perfect."

His hand leaves the steering wheel to find mine and he gives it a gentle squeeze.

"This is going to be fun."

I rub my thumb over the top of his hand. "For both of us," I say.

He sucks in his dimpled cheek, before cocking his head at the oversized summer home. "At least I don't think we'll suffer."

I let out a small laugh. He's right. The house is gorgeous. A proper Southampton estate. I count twenty-four windows all perfectly adorned with black shutters just in the front of the gray cedar-shake house.

"Sadie said the guest house is on the right." Luke points as he hunches over the wheel, peering out of the front windshield.

I turn and look out my passenger window of our newly purchased black Jeep Grand Cherokee. The perfectly manicured hedges give way to display a smaller, but still sizable, house bookended between its own private swimming pool and tennis courts.

"Whoa," Luke says, eyes the size of sand dollars.

I gaze up at the two sloping gables of the roof staring down at us like a pair of eyes.

I find myself clenching and unclenching my grip on the door handle. My pulse suddenly quickens and I'm drowning with an overwhelming sense of dread.

Luke seems to notice my breathing becoming shallow.

"You okay?"

I drop my head. "Yeah, I just need a minute."

He strokes my brown hair, softly pulling down on the strands of my pixie cut until he gets to the base of my skull. He gives my tensing muscles a gentle squeeze. Instinctively knowing how to calm me down.

"I know this has been a lot for you today. Just take your time."

"Thanks," I say, slightly embarrassed, even though I shouldn't be. Not with Luke. He knows how hard it was for me to leave our apartment today. Ever since the accident, I've been terrified of cars. I don't trust being in them and I don't trust others driving, which is particularly difficult when you live in New York City. It's made me agoraphobic over the last several months.

I used to be different. I had a bright, bubbly personality, some may say I was a social butterfly, even. I was happy and why wouldn't I be after everything I had overcome? I have a wonderful job as a nurse practitioner, and I'm married to the love of my life.

I turn toward Luke, his clean-shaven face slightly rounded just like when we met in college. Always getting carded at the bars because of his boyish looks. Now he's settled into his age. His dark hair is tousled and parted on the side, still holding off any signs of gray or thinning. His broad shoulders always give him the appearance of being in shape when he doesn't have the time to put the effort in. He's just blessed with naturally good genes. If things ended between us, I know he wouldn't be single for long.

I, on the other hand, feel uglier by the day. The accident did not help with things. The scars under my hair, raised and still sensitive to the touch. I'm not really meant to have a pixie cut—it's just my hair growing back. I'm finally in a place where it's no longer patchy. But I used to have beautiful hair. Long and silky. My favorite part of it was when Luke would pull it behind my ear before kissing me.

My bright blue eyes, which always gave me a striking appeal with my naturally long lashes, have dulled a bit. The signs of tragedy dimming them like a light switch.

I bite my inner cheek and look up at Luke, waiting patiently for me. I inhale deeply and open the door. Luke springs out like a jackrabbit to come over and help me. It's the most exposed I've felt in a while. Being outside in an open space like this, something I haven't done in so long, feels like I've stepped into another dimension. I can smell the salty brine of the air along with freshly cut grass. I close my eyes and find myself pretending to be back in our apartment to give myself a moment of calm.

I feel Luke's arm gently guiding me.

I can do this, I remind myself.

Right before the accident, Luke had landed this amazing job at a private equity firm. Not only that, his boss, Jim, the founder of the company, took Luke under his wing. In the last six months the opportunities with this position have accelerated faster than Luke could've ever hoped, putting us financially in a better situation, which we desperately needed after all the medical expenses.

Earlier this week, he and I discussed—or rather, he claims—that I'm stunted in my recovery because I don't leave the house.

"I'm better than I was before," I tried to explain to him.

"I know you are. You have come a long way," Luke said, his hand scooping crumbs off our linoleum countertop in our small galley kitchen. "But listen, I have this idea."

I remember stiffening.

"I found this rental in the Hamptons."

I stared at him confused, not quite believing it. "In the middle of the summer?"

"Yes," he said, almost not believing it himself. His fingers propped on the counter. "The price is very reasonable, and I know that the city has made you . . ." He trailed off.

"I know," I admitted, shifting nervously.

"I thought this would be a great opportunity to get you out of the city and give you the space you need to fully heal."

I didn't say anything.

"I just think this would be a nice escape." He paused. "For both of us."

My chest tightened at the implied statement. It's not just me who needs to recover. It's our marriage.

"So, what can you tell me about this place?" I tried to act more enthusiastic.

Luke's face softened to a smile. "Well, it's part of this estate in Southampton. The owners decided to rent out the guest house."

"So, we're on their property?"

He shook his head. "It's a big lot, so we won't be on top of each other. It's a separate house, not an apartment over a garage or anything. It's set very far back from the road. You could walk around the estate without a car in sight." He looked at me directly. "You need the fresh air."

"Sounds wonderful," I said, pretending to be excited. "I'm curious as to why it's only coming on the market now."

Luke shrugged his shoulders. "Just timing and luck, I guess. Plus, all these hurricanes off the coast recently aren't shaping up to make a good summer. But the weather is going to be beautiful this weekend and it's ours for the month if we want it."

Luke was right. The weather today isn't anything but pleasant. We step up to the wraparound porch, supported by Corinthian columns, with unobstructed views of the endless ocean ahead of us. White cumulus clouds float like whipped dollops in the sky to complete the picturesque scene.

My eye follows a boardwalk that edges the property and bridges over the thick covered dunes.

Off to the corner, I notice a gas firepit elevated on pavement stones with four white love-seat couches surrounding it, the dunes backdropping it into a picture-perfect scene. I even imagine myself and Luke snuggled up under a blanket on a cool night, the fire dancing in front of us, until my mind wonders what sort of creatures could be hidden beneath the brush.

The backyard, while spacious and well manicured with corduroy lines of freshly cut grass, still doesn't feel as private as I would've initially thought. There is a garden hedge squared off in the middle of the property that seems to act as a privacy wall, but it can't be more than a hundred feet, which on a property as large as this, doesn't do that much. Then again, it's obvious that the garden is meant more as a beautiful feature of the property, rather than to act as a divide.

I think about what Luke and I are paying for this rental and it's much lower than anything else on the market, despite being ten times nicer than anything else available. I wonder what the reason for that is. Are the pictures online for this property dated and we are in for a surprise? Or did something not work out with a previous renter? Then again, anyone—no matter how wealthy—can run into money troubles.

The taxes alone on this place have to be astronomical. Maybe they needed a quick fix.

I follow the porch toward the backyard, descending from a set of stairs, bringing me toward the pool. It's large and rectangular with an elevated hot tub pouring into it like a miniature waterfall. The white cushioned loungers lining the edge are perfectly even, as if they were brand new and being staged for a photo shoot. I suddenly have the feeling like I'm being watched. I turn toward the main house, but I don't see anything at first. I still can't shake the feeling. My eyes flick back up, scanning the windows until I notice the silhouette of a woman on the second floor. My body stiffens. After a moment, the figure steps back, the white curtain falling closed.

The thought of being here, knowing someone might always be spying on us, sends a deep shudder through me, but I have to push the thought away. We need this to work.

"Are you okay if I go get the bags from the car?" Luke asks.

"Of course."

Luke gives me a quick smile.

I look back up at the now-empty window and suddenly feel vulnerable and exposed. I turn, scurrying back up the steps to check the door to the back porch, praying that it's open, my hand shaking as I try to grip the handle. I feel a pressure building in my chest as I struggle with the door. I need to be inside right now, but I can't seem to get my feet to listen. All I have to do is walk around the porch to the front, but I can't seem to do that. It's as if I'm frozen in place, the panic in me rendering my body catatonic, unable to move.

I see a dark shadow on the other side of the glass door inside the house. It's approaching me, the outline I realize much larger than Luke. It comes up on me fast, ripping the door open angrily. My hand, still on the handle, jerks and pulls me inside, causing me to fall into the figure.

I let out a startled gasp, as I feel the strong grip of seemingly large hands on my arms, holding me in a tight lock, unable to escape if I wanted to.

The fear overwhelms me as I look up at the person in front of me. His face is slack with emotion. His dark brown eyes are deadened, as if there is nothing behind them. His thick, black eyebrows furrow angrily at me.

I find my footing, eager to back away, but his grip remains tight on me. I struggle again, about to let out a scream loud enough for Luke to hear, when finally, the man lets go of me and I step back, catching my breath.

I notice then he has got to be a least six and half feet tall. Taller than my five-six frame or Luke's even six. He appears older, early to mid-forties, but strikingly muscular.

He's standing there, his squared-off jaw tightly set, and there is the slight hint of a scowl like I'm an intruder in his house. Then it suddenly occurs to me that I might be. Maybe we have the address wrong. I swallow hard.

"I'm so sorry," I apologize. "We were looking for the Wilson residence. We are supposed to be staying in their guest house."

He crosses his arms, leaving his expression the same. "This is the Wilson residence." His voice is deep and scratchy.

"Oh," I say, confused. "I'm Natalie. My husband Luke and I were told by Sadie Wilson that we could stay in this guest house for the month of—"

"You shouldn't be here," he says cutting me off.

I blink in surprise. "I'm sorry. Was there some sort of mix-up?"

He appears angry with me for asking the question. "No."

"Okay," I try to keep my voice light.

We stare at each other for a long moment.

"Can I help you?" I hear Luke's voice behind him, as he comes in through the front door with our bags.

He turns back toward Luke, his expression still the same. Then he lets out a long-winded exhalation from his nostrils, as if frustrated.

He turns back to me. "Just get out," he growls, his breath hot on mine. Then he walks past me, slamming the back door shut.

Chapter Two

Sadie

I peer out the window from the second floor, trying to get a glimpse of the couple that just arrived. A flush of anxiety and anticipation courses through me. She looks so much like my friend Cassie, though Cassie had longer hair and more confidence. The woman I see below has short brown hair and worried eyes. She walks around the backyard curiously, but with an air of hesitancy. I wonder if she's one of those people with psychic abilities who can read the auras or energy of a place. I can only fathom a guess how much tragedy, death and heartbreak has washed up on this shore over the course of history.

I catch the woman staring up at me and, embarrassed, I shyly close the curtain, taking a step back and sitting on the white couch in my master bedroom. The room feels cold, but I'm always cold lately. Worse than that, it's like a chill that you feel deep inside your bones. It's as if the light inside me has been extinguished and with it the warmth of a soul is gone.

My eyes sweep the room around me. It's a minimalistic design that I picked out. Stark contrasts of white furniture, curtains and bedding against the dark wood of the floors. Jute rugs accent between the two. It just shows my lack of imagination. All this came from a page I found in a magazine and pointed to a designer to recreate.

Not that I have a lot of family pictures that I can display. Happy memories and grinning faces are not something that I've seen since I was ten. I've lived a life of trepidation, much like the woman lurking outside on my property right now. I recognize that look. I wore it all the time until I taught myself how to successfully hide it. That idea that you can't allow yourself to be happy, because you're waiting for the other shoe to drop. Even if you think you've done everything you can to put yourself in a position where you can one day smile, you can't always trust it. Once your heart has been broken, it's like a crystal glass that has shattered. You can never put it back together. Even if you think you can, it's forever distorted with jagged edges that no longer fit the way they once did, because tiny fissures have etched away who you once were.

It makes me wonder what sort of person she is. What she's experienced in her lifetime to make her always look so afraid.

She appears to wear her emotions on her sleeve, right now down to her clothes. Her T-shirt is too big for her tiny, frail body, and her jeans are torn. Her skin is deathly pale, and her shoulders seem to settle in a hunch. I myself do what I can to hide those feelings. I make a point of keeping up appearances. I get my hair highlighted every eight weeks; my nails done every two. I have a personal shopper who dresses me in mainly white and cream colors but occasionally I go for the bright and bold. Everything is tailored to my shape, which I keep up with tennis classes and gym sessions with a personal trainer three days a week.

Despite how different we appear on the outside, I'm hopeful that we will get along well or at least relate to each other somehow. God knows I could use a friend. My gaze falls to the empty bottle of Adderall sitting in the trash can of my bathroom. I flash to myself crushing the tiny pills on my makeup mirror before snorting them, then scrubbing my skin so hard in the shower that it was inflamed with a pinkish hue long after I was done.

The loneliness has been intolerable. During the day, I know I have the busy sounds of our maid, Shar, vacuuming; the cook, Marla, clanging pots and pans; and the groundskeeper, Riley, always with his whir of some sort of landscaping machine.

But last night, the house was quiet and that's when I heard the screams in my head. An inescapable pitch that was deafening to my ears. Sometimes I try to scream over it myself, but it's no use.

I hear a seagull squawking in the distance and I look out over the ocean and see a beautiful white sailboat gliding past. The water is flat and calm. It's a picture-perfect day. Still, I eye the beach every morning, waiting for the ocean to betray me and wash up my buried secrets.

The air in here suddenly feels stale and thick. I open the window to let a breeze in when I feel my shoulder seize up. I wince and gently massage it. The bandage is fresh over the stitches underneath. The doctor said I was lucky. It was just a minor flesh wound.

My thoughts slide to my husband, Tom, returning soon, and I'm scared. For him and for myself. I know that I can't keep this up forever, but I'm not ready to give up on him.

That night washes over me like a wave. I saw myself from above with no power to control what was happening to me. The searing pain of cold steel piercing my flesh, the look of horror at what he had caused. I shake my head. I just hope that Tom knows how much I still love him.

I know they will only hold him for a few days, so I need to figure out what I'm going to do. Guilt consumes me. I know it's not easy for Tom. I'm just hoping that he'll soon see the right path so we can move on with our lives. He just needs to find a way to be happy; we all do.

I think about all the sacrifices I've made for him. We had both lived in Los Angeles. I was a psychiatrist, and he a billionaire bad boy turned golf instructor. But I knew once Tom started to spiral, that fast and hard life of LA was not a healthy place for him. To get him away from all the bad influences in his life, we moved here from across the country two years ago. Giving up my practice so I could focus solely on his recovery. Our recovery.

I grunt and finally get the window open, letting in a cool breeze off the ocean.

It was a quick decision to rent out the guest house. I knew it would go fast. It's in a desirable location and it's a beautiful house. But the truth, really, is that I just don't want to be alone. Especially when Tom does return.

I peer once more through the voile of the curtain, the woman now vanished, and there is nothing but a quiet stillness that lies in her wake. A dead calm that creates an uneasiness in me.

I've been close to death my whole life. First my father, followed by my mother. When you go into psychiatry you spend most of your time with people who themselves are teetering on the edge of death.

In my field I've worked with an exceptional number of dark individuals, and I'm fascinated by how their minds work. How they rationalize the world around them, how they justify their actions and thoughts. These people work on a different plane of existence. It makes anything else I do feel like child's play when you can see how much worse a person's mental state can truly become if you put them in an unhealthy environment without stable and reliable people to depend on.

It's strange the attraction I have to it. Like a homing beacon I can't help but follow. It was likely what led me to Tom, my ongoing enigma. There was something about him I noticed when I studied him from afar. For some reason, with him I was blind to the darkness lurking beneath his surface. I never saw it coming, despite knowing deep down that it was always there, but refusing to believe it until it was too late. But no matter what, I'm still a hopeless romantic who believes true love and care can save a person. And I want to save Tom. We will find the man he once was. He's still inside him; I know it. I just have to coax him out. But for now, I look out the window at the guest house. I'm relieved to know that there will be someone else here, and I won't be left alone with him.

Chapter Three

Natalie

"Who the hell was that?" Luke says, his forehead creased in anger.

I shrug my shoulders. "I don't know. He was just in the house. I thought maybe there was some sort of mix-up and we were at the wrong address, but he told me we weren't . . ." I trail off in confusion, trying to make sense of the whole ordeal. "Either way he's not happy we're here."

Luke's jaw clenches. He puts the two oversized black suitcases he was dragging in off to the side. Then he walks toward me, his steps heavy with determination. He reaches for the door behind me and locks it authoritatively. "Let's keep the doors locked until we can figure out who that was," Luke says.

I agree, still feeling sore on both my arms where the man gripped me so tightly.

I close my eyes and take a moment, trying to forget about the recent unpleasant interaction and instead picture my own apartment. Somewhere that felt familiar and safe to me. But the smell of cleaning supplies overwhelms my nostrils. A concoction of ammonia and bleach, along with lemon furniture polish, it makes the place smell sterile—like someone just cleaned up a crime scene. When I finally feel calm, I open my eyes. I'm alone in the living room. It's a stark contrast of dark wooden floors and white fabric couches settled on top of woven jute rugs. The coffee table and end tables look as if they are made from the same color and material as the floor. It's clean and elegant, unlike our apartment on 42nd Street, which has an old leather sofa, faded and worn next to a used coffee table we had found on Facebook Marketplace. But where there is style in this wonderfully staged house with sweeping sheer white curtains framing the large windows, there is a lack of comfort or coziness. Already I am reluctant to drink coffee on the couches for fear of staining them. Luke and I are only starting to get used to this new idea of having a discretionary income, and there is something cold about this place that makes me feel like we will never belong here, no matter how successful we are. Still, I will try to make the best of it. I have to.

I'm startled once again by a loud banging on the door behind me. I jump, an obvious overreaction, but I'm expecting to see that terrifying man again. Back to harass us until we leave.

I'm taken by surprise when I see an elegant-looking woman, slightly older than me, in a cream-colored, long-sleeved top and khaki pants, accessorized with wooden jewelry, giving her a smart, sophisticated look. Her hair is perfectly highlighted blonde and rounded into a soft cut that falls just a little over her shoulders. She smiles sweetly, waving a manicured hand from the other side of the door.

I give a weak wave myself, before plastering on a smile and opening the door.

She stares at me, eyes wide like she's seen a ghost, but then she recovers. "Hi," she says, her voice soft and soothing. "You must be Natalie. I'm Sadie."

"Hi," I respond. I go to put my hand out to shake hers, but I'm taken by surprise when she pulls me in toward her, kissing not one, but both of my cheeks.

"It's so lovely to meet you."

"You as well," I say self-consciously.

I hear Luke's footsteps coming down the stairs. His face has softened into a more welcoming smile. "You must be Sadie," he says, descending the last step and making his way across the room. She extends both arms and Luke naturally goes in for a hug, though she doesn't try to double kiss him like she had me.

"Thank you so much for having us. This opportunity is a real lifesaver," Luke tells her.

Lifesaver. I can't help but cringe at his need to show others how desperate we are to escape from our own lives.

"So glad to hear it." She smiles. "Well, welcome. If you need anything, don't hesitate to ask."

"Thank you but I'm sure we'll be fine," Luke says happily, as if the memory of the man who tried to run us out of here moments ago was just a figment of our imaginations.

It wasn't, was it?

"I have a quick question," I say. Both Luke and Sadie turn to me. "There was a man here before, when we just arrived . . ." I start.

Sadie swats her hand. "Oh, that's Riley. He's our groundskeeper."

"He's . . ." I start. "A little intense for a groundskeeper."

Sadie agrees. "He may seem a bit—" she gestures with her hands as if fumbling for the words, before finally settling on mine "—intense, but I assure you he's no one to worry about. He's wonderful with the landscaping." She points out toward the rose garden that separates the two houses. "He does it all himself. A bit of a savant in that way."

Luke bows his head at me as if this answer is satisfying, but for me it isn't.

Sensing this, Sadie adds, "I'm sorry, I probably should've told him you were coming. He's wary of strangers. Here, let me show you around." She waves her arm for us to follow her. I see a brief sense of uneasiness come over her as she steps over the threshold into the house and walks through into the kitchen.

Luke gives me a reassuring look, but I can detect a slight widening in his eyes as if to tell me to drop the issue now. Then again, he doesn't know what Riley said to me.

But still, he's always doing that. Making me believe that I'm just paranoid all the time. I know there have been moments since the accident that I've given him reason to downplay my upset, but he was a witness to this encounter. Did I overdramatize how threatening the situation really was?

I can sense Luke's frustration with me lately. He's trying his best, but it doesn't help that we were likely already on the verge of breaking up before this happened. At least, that's what I think was about to happen. We had reached an impasse. He wants to change the course of our relationship by having children, while I am happy with how things are. I can't bring myself to take that next step with him and, more importantly, I can't bring myself to tell him why. While he knows I'm estranged from my parents, I never really explained to him how traumatic my childhood was. I never told him about Danny.

Sadie taps her gel-tipped nails on the island counter, making a clicking noise. Behind her is a gas range stove, equipped with two ovens and a griddle that are sandwiched between two large stainless-steel refrigerators, unless of course one of them is a freezer, which wouldn't surprise me. The window above the white farmhouse sink doesn't face the ocean, but rather the neighbor's yard, though the house itself has to be a hundred yards away with dunes far and wide between them.

"So, everything in here should be straightforward." Sadie bites her cheek as she looks around. "Let me show you the upstairs."

We follow her up the dark wooden steps, heels clacking all the way as she grips the white studded railing. Her body is arched and stiff, appearing almost as if she's nervous about something. We walk down a dark hallway and Sadie finds the light, clicking it on. Another jute runner lines the dark wooden floors, and we follow her to the first room on the left.

"This is just an extra guest room," she says, dismissively. "The main bedroom is down the hall."

Luke and I take a quick peek. Again, very much like the aesthetic of the house, there is a queen-sized bed with a white duvet, a jute rug and a dark brown chest, next to another door, which I can only assume is a closet. The light shines through the white sheer curtain of the window and I can faintly see that it overlooks the pool, which faces the direction of the main house. I hear Sadie's footsteps already further down the hall, as she points out the bathroom.

"Your main bedroom has a bathroom, so I doubt you'll use this too much."

I hurry to catch up, eyeing the white marble bathroom with a small sink, toilet and glass-door shower.

"Here we are," Sadie says as if announcing the main attraction. The room is excessively large. The vaulted ceiling extends an extra five feet with big, rounded windows reaching to meet it, giving an indulgent view of the ocean. The far wall has a fireplace surrounded by white wood paneling and a large flatscreen TV that rests above the driftwood mantel. I eye yet another jute rug underneath the white king-sized bed and wonder how that will feel under bare feet each morning.

I hear Sadie's voice echoing and meet her in the bathroom. It has floor-to-ceiling marble, a large jacuzzi tub catty-cornered between a glass-door shower and a toilet and bidet with its own private room. I turn toward the mirror, eyeing the double sinks and the vast amount of cabinet space underneath for everything. This place I realize is four times the size of our apartment. Yet still, wasn't that expensive, which gives me the feeling that something is terribly wrong with it.

Sadie pulls on the door of a wooden cabinet. "This is where all your towels will be." She opens it to reveal perfectly rolled plush white towels, stacked neatly on top of one another.

"Across the hall is your laundry room, which should make things easier."

I nod, thinking about our own laundry room in New York. It is in the basement of the building, always dark and dingy. I could never go down there alone, even before the accident.

Luke and I haven't discussed moving. First, we needed to pay off our debts and medical expenses. And I would've thought after paying everything off last month and my ability to start returning to work, that would've been the next step. But instead, he suggested this place. Which makes me realize that this is our trial. If we can't go through this together, we will be moving, but the question will be if that's together or apart.

Sadie leads us across the hall and flicks on another light to reveal the washer and dryer that look like they were recently purchased. She points to a shelf. "Here is the fabric softener and detergent." She smiles. "I had my maid come in to scrub the place top to bottom so everything should be fresh and ready to go."

They must've just come this morning considering how strong and lingering the smell of disinfectant still is.

"Thank you so much," Luke says. "Were there tenants in here before?"

Sadie shakes her head rather quickly. "I just wanted everything fresh."

"What made you list it in the first place?" I can't help but ask.

She shrugs her shoulders. "Just thought it would be nice to have the company."

There is something sad about her answer, a level of current beneath the surface that shows a sense of insecurity and vulnerability. A woman like Sadie doesn't strike me as a person who is lonely, but again you can't judge a book by its cover. "Well . . ." Sadie now swings her arms and claps her hands. "My husband Tom is unfortunately out of town at the moment." She twists her wedding ring, a large round solitaire, several carats with a platinum band, nervously with her thumb. Then realizing what she's doing, checks her gold designer watch. "But come join me for dinner tonight."

I can't help but feel as if it sounds more like a plea than an invitation.

"Of course," Luke says.

Sadie smiles. "Great. Well, I will let you get settled and I will see you around . . . let's say six tonight?"

"Wonderful," I add, trying to sound as enthused as everyone else seems to be.

Sadie gives a smile, baring her perfectly white and straight teeth. "Excellent, I look forward to it."

I smile back but feel as if her hospitality is disingenuous. Then again, I could be jumping to conclusions.

Luke and I stare at one another for a moment as Sadie's clacking heels fade away. He looks around, his arms outstretched. "I mean, it's not a bad place to recover."

"I am recovered," I say a bit defensively. "I'm even starting back at work this week. I have my first virtual appointment on Monday. Honestly, I think by next month I can go back full-time to the emergency room."

Luke shakes his head. "Nat, I'm glad you're feeling better. I know that you are. The fact that we got you into a car today is huge. I get that. But let's keep taking baby steps. The ER . . . He stops, trying to find the right words. "It's a very traumatic and chaotic place. Aren't you worried about getting triggered?"

The truth is, I do share in that same fear, as does my boss. He knows I am itching for normalcy and has agreed that starting slow with virtual appointments is the best option for now.

But there is a high that I get from the emergency room. There is a part of me that feels that the sooner I go back the sooner I will feel like myself again. There is no downtime in the emergency room. Something is always happening. I run on coffee and adrenaline. That feeling of saving a person's life, the race against the clock, that dopamine hit I feel when it is all over after we have done our job. It doesn't allow me to sit around in my own paralyzing fear. Because in the ER, you don't have time to think about yourself.

But he has a point.

"You're right," I admit to Luke as he leads me back into the main bedroom where we both start to unzip our suitcases, which Luke had brought up. "I'm almost done with my medication though, and Dr. Warton said after I finish the course we can assess if I still need it or not."

"Are you still having hallucinations?"

I look at him angrily. It feels like he's trying to undermine me. "It is a side effect of this medication, but I haven't had an episode in weeks."

"I know that," Luke says, sensing my growing irritation. "I just don't want you to dive into the deep end too quickly—that's all."

"I know," I say, feeling slightly defeated.

Luke wraps his arms around me, and my anger slowly thaws as I sink into him, smelling the fresh scent of his cologne on his shirt. It's the same one he's used for as long as I've known him. He wouldn't be Luke if he didn't smell like pine and musk.

"So, what should we bring tonight?" I ask, changing the subject and finding myself pulling away from him.

Luke checks his watch. "It's already three o'clock. By the time we are settled, it'll be time to go over. I'll just run out quick and grab a bottle of wine."

"We won't have to do this all the time, right?" I ask while trying not to sound too ungrateful.

"I'm sure she just wants to get to know the people she decided to rent to for the next month."

I agree. But I thought the point of this place was for us to focus on repairing the connection that Luke and I seem to have lost. And yet, part of me wonders if he's doing the opposite by looking for any sort of distraction that isn't about us.

I see a look of guilt cross his face and it's like he can read my thoughts. "Did you want to take a ride with me?"

I shake my head. "That's okay, we have a lot of unpacking to do."

A look of relief flashes across his face and is gone in an instant, but I can't pretend like I didn't see it.

"Will you be okay?" Luke asks instinctively.

I suppress the urge to go on the defensive. The drive here from the city was enough on my nerves, I wouldn't be able to summon the energy to do it again even if I wanted to. I know I should practice getting out more, but like Luke suggested, baby steps. It was enough for today. "The unpacking and organizing will keep me busy."

"Okay," he says, slightly dragging the word out in case I change my mind.

"Go on, I've got this."

"Anything else you want me to grab while I'm out?"

"Yes," I say. "Might as well have you do a grocery run."

We both head back downstairs. There is already fresh fruit in a bowl on the counter. I open the fridge to find a drawer with cheese sticks, yogurt containers and a half-empty milk carton.

"Strange," I say.

"What?" Luke asks, peering into the fridge.

I pick up a cheese stick and check the expiration date. "There's food in here, but it doesn't look like it was meant for us. Rather it's left over from whoever else was here before," I say. "But she just told us we are the only ones she's rented to."

"Maybe that groundskeeper, Riley, was using this place as his work kitchen," Luke rationalizes. "Now he's annoyed because he can't anymore."

I shrug. It seems like a reasonable idea. He did react like a child when its sibling has found their Halloween candy stash.

I make a grocery list on the personalized stationery sitting on the marble countertop. There is a stencil of the house in the header with the title The Overlook next to it. Luke is looking over my shoulder. I'm curious if he's noticed the header yet. The name of the house that eerily matches the name of the hotel in the Stephen King novel *The Shining*. I hand it to Luke, keys jingling in his other palm.

"Okay, back shortly." He gives me a quick peck on the cheek.

I smile as my eyes follow him to the door.

I take a deep inhalation. "Okay," I say out loud. "This is fine." I take another moment to walk through the kitchen and living room. I check out the kitchen appliances, drawers and cupboards. All seems to be in good shape.

I make my way back into the living room. There is a mahogany shelf along the wall full of matching books with white dust jackets and decorative glass vases. I stand back, arms crossed, looking curiously at it. It seems so impersonal, like it was staged for a photo shoot and left that way. Sure, this was the guest house, but nothing here gives me any insight into the people who own this place. Almost like they are going through leaps and bounds to hide who they are. Suddenly, I hear a loud bang and thunderous footsteps above me. I duck instinctively as if the ceiling is going to come down on me. I look up, not sure of what I heard.

Adrenaline-fueled, I run up the stairs two at time, eager to see what it was. But when I reach the top floor, it's silent again. All I can hear now is my heavy breathing. I walk slowly through each room, but there's nothing. The suitcases are still laid out the way they were left. But I know I heard something. I rub at my temples, frustrated. This is supposed to be over. I'm not seeing or hearing things anymore. I haven't in several weeks.

"Please, this can't be happening again," I say, willing myself to overcome this irrational behavior. I am almost in the clear. I just hope this new environment doesn't cause a setback. Since the accident and this medication, I've had audible hallucinations. Usually, faint whispering that I don't understand, or I'll think that Luke's called out my name, but he hasn't. But never anything this loud before.

I stare out the bedroom window when I hear it again, another crash and heavy footsteps, like running. I let out a scream. I think about Riley, the groundskeeper who had threatened me earlier, and I realize with horror that I'm not alone in this house.

Chapter Four

Sadie

I walk out of the guest house, trying to keep my pace steady, even though I want to run as fast as I can away from here. I let out an involuntary shiver as I see my shadow reflecting in the pool, and I quicken my pace.

When I reach the side of the house, I close the door hard behind me, startling Shar, my maid. Though she is in her sixties, since I hired her she has appeared to age significantly. Her black hair has become grayer, causing unruly strands that fray from her tight bun. Her skin has wrinkled at a rapid speed, her frame thinner than it once was.

She jumps, but keeps her head down, minding her work of dusting the furniture in the living room.

"Shar," I address her. "We are going to be having guests tonight. I want this place to be spotless, right down to every piece of glassware."

She looks exhausted as she only just finished cleaning the guest house, but still, she tilts her head slightly in acknowledgment.

"Good," I reply. "Thank you."

"Marla," I call to the cook as I walk across the hall, my heels clacking against the wood floor. When I reach the kitchen, Marla is standing at attention, a pen and pad in her hand.

I lift my chin in approval at her readiness. "We are having the new renters over for dinner. Can you please prepare a cheese and charcuterie board, gazpacho soup, salmon with asparagus and tomatoes as well as some sorbet for dessert?"

Marla is heavyset and her upper arm flaps like a chicken wing as she scribbles down the list. Then she straightens herself up. "Yes, ma'am," she answers. "I'll call Jonathan in to be the sous chef."

"Great idea," I tell her.

She grins.

I had found Marla in the Michelin-star French restaurant Chez Vivienne. She keeps her connections and will work there during the week after prepping my meals for the day. It's helpful that I can reach out to them when I need extra hands.

"You're a doll," I add, and she smiles brightly.

Nothing is better than young and ambitious people.

The idea of having a dinner party makes me feel lighter somehow. It will provide an opportunity to create more positive memories in this house. I like the idea of ridding it of the toxic energy that appears to sit in the atmosphere like a thick fog. Just a few nights of normalcy, before Tom comes back. A night where I can happily entertain guests and not have to worry about what I say or do. Not to stress about Tom's drinking and feeling his eyes monitoring me and my every move, deciding what to punish me for later.

The reminder of it causes me to feel a bit stifled again. I go upstairs to our front balcony. I need the salty breeze in my face. I jiggle the door, which is a bit rusted, and remind myself to be cautious of my stitches. When it finally opens the wind lifts my hair up and tickles my neck. I take in a deep inhalation then gaze upon the tennis court. Its chain-link fence was recently repainted in a fresh green, and the red clay of the court is smooth and even with newly painted white lines. I smile. Riley did a nice job. Tennis is the one escape

I have that makes me happy. It gives me time to forget about everything else going on in the world and just focus on the game. My only concern is getting that bright neon yellow ball over the net. I love the sound of the pops as it hits the wires of the racket. It reminds me of my first time visiting a country club. I'd see the rich women in their tennis gear, and I envied them. Wearing a tennis outfit was a status symbol. It meant you had the money to pay for country clubs and fancy outfits and lessons. It was always a dream of mine to one day be one of them. A smile creeps across my face just thinking about how far I've come.

Then I remember it was my friend Cassie, who brought me to my first country club. Visions of her flash in my brain and I try to will them away. The painful thoughts are too much.

My smile fades as I feel the tenderness of my shoulder. It reminds me that I need to cancel my tennis instructor for the next several weeks. I will make up a minor injury to avoid alarming him. I'll say that after a dermatology checkup, I had an irregular freckle that had to be removed, which would explain the stitches. Just a minor routine surgery.

Guilt crawls up my skin, causing me to look at my watch and pull out my phone. I want to go see Tom and explain everything to him, make sure he understands what happened last night. I pull the facility's number up, swallowing the extra saliva that has formed in the back of my mouth as I listen to the automated message and select the keys that will take me to the right department.

"Psychiatric floor," someone with a heavy-sounding voice answers.

"Hi," I stammer. "I'm Sadie Wilson. I'm calling in regard to a patient you have there."

"Name?" they ask while I hear clicking noises from them typing on a computer.

"Tom Wilson."

I wait a moment as they pull up his file. "How can we help you?"

"I'm his wife and I would like to see him."

"Let me speak with the doctor. I'll have to put you on hold," the voice says, slightly annoyed they will need to get up from their seat.

Before I can respond, I hear symphony music streaming down the line.

I bite my cuticle nervously, then realizing what I'm doing, quickly stop.

"Mrs. Wilson," a more self-assured voice answers and catches me off guard.

"Yes?" I say, my voice cracks and I clear my throat.

"I'm Dr. Turner. I'm treating your husband."

"Hello."

"Your husband is doing fine, though he's still a bit agitated," he says, treading lightly on the words. "We need to stabilize him a bit more before we can evaluate him further."

"I understand," I answer. "But would it be okay if I saw him?"

"I'm sorry, Mrs. Wilson. We need him to calm down before he can see anyone. You are more than welcome to call again tomorrow for an update."

A sense of relief washes over me. I bob my head, then realizing he can't see me, I add, "I understand," forgetting I already said that.

"Is there anything else we can help you with?"

"No, that will be all for now. Thank you so much." I hang up and sigh, perching on a nearby ottoman, my eyes slightly watering.

Has it all gone too far now?

But then an anger settles in me. *Don't forget this is his fault, he brought this upon himself.*

I'm startled by an eager knock at the front door. I didn't see a car come down the drive, which means it must either be Riley or the new renters, but I thought I saw them leave. I return back inside and go downstairs to answer it.

"Hello, Riley," I say, slightly embarrassed, blinking my eyes dry.

"Who are those people?" he asks, pointing toward the guest house. His eyes look bloodshot from lack of sleep.

I stiffen slightly, then push my shoulders back to show more confidence. "I've decided to rent the house out. They are the new tenants."

He lowers his head, narrowing his eyes on mine. "They shouldn't be here."

"And why is that?" I ask, challenging him. I feel small next to his tall stature, but I straighten my posture to firmly show I am not intimidated by him. I am the one in control here.

His eyes shift around before they fall back to mine. "You shouldn't have done that." His voice is now more of a whisper, so no one else can hear.

I furrow my eyebrows curiously. "And why not?"

His teeth clench and I can see his sunken cheeks flex in and out. He looks as if he's about to say something, but then thinks better of it. His shoulders slump, a silent surrender before asking, "How long will they be here?"

"A month," I answer defiantly.

He lets out a shaky breath. Riley is nervous. I've never seen him look that way before. Then again, this is likely about last night.

I think of when I first met Riley. It had been prefaced by an older gentleman, Wake Sterling, who explained his nephew was looking for a job. He had shown up at our door, a rotund man with a shiny head and a silver ring of hair slightly above his ears. It was unexpected, as if he had been going for a leisurely walk and spotted our moving vans.

He smiled appreciatively, his cheeks reddening and explained how Riley was a very talented landscaper who took pride in his work. A big estate like ours could keep Riley very busy and he lived for routine.

I asked why he wasn't already working at a landscaping company, and Wake explained that Riley was a war vet who had since been suffering from severe PTSD, and he hadn't been the same since being on the battlefield. He now had social anxiety and thrived when he worked alone. I agreed to meet him.

As soon as I looked into Riley's eyes, I understood what Wake Sterling meant, and even more so when he spoke. I treated him like I did all my patients. I tried to make him comfortable. I could sense that the outdoors was where he was the happiest, so instead of inviting him inside, I led him to the rose garden. I could tell he was fascinated by it. I told him my plans and asked his suggestions on how we could expand. He seemed excited about it. I got him talking about the work, which distracted him from the fact that he was talking to a stranger. We seemed to understand each other. Over the past two years we've had no cause for complaint. Wake was true to his word: Riley is an exceptional artist when it comes to landscape design.

Since his uncle passed away last year, I think he fears his opportunities for any other sort of job would be much harder to come by. They must've been before, even when his uncle was alive. Given Riley's condition, paired with his size and stature, I could see why most would be afraid of him. For me though, especially when Tom is around, it's nice knowing I have Riley to go to if need be.

But in this case, it's my house and I will decide who can and can't stay here.

Riley's eyes look down at his feet then intensely into my eyes, like he's trying to tell me something without saying it. It's the most eye contact I've ever gotten from him.

"I know I allowed you to stay over in the guest house last night, but I expect you to give the new couple their privacy moving forward."

Riley gives me another look and I feel a chill crawl up my spine, as if we both know what the other is thinking. I shake the thought away and clear my throat.

"There are a few shingles on the side of the house that need repairs," I tell him. "I'd like you to fix that today, preferably."

Riley nods and slowly steps off the porch.

I can sense that he's on to me.

I have the upper hand here and as long as I can maintain that, it will keep Riley in check. But if the dynamic of power switches, I know first-hand what Riley is capable of, and it sends a paralyzing fear through me.

Chapter Five

Natalie

I do another sweep of the house, but no one is here. I'm frustrated that I can't rationalize this noise. Most people would let it go, but I can't. My own mental state depends on it. I need to know if I'm better or if I'm getting worse. I have a fear that this might be something that I just have to live with forever. Never being able to trust myself, what I've seen or heard. Everyone thinking I'm crazy, because I am.

I shake the feeling away. "It's your meds," I remind myself. I come across the upstairs hall bathroom and turn the lights on. It's then that I notice a small pool of water on the floor, next to the toilet. It seems odd at first. Why would there be any water in this bathroom, if no one has used it? I bend down to touch the puddle, rubbing the wetness between my fingertips.

Then I think about Riley, the groundskeeper. If he was using the kitchen for his food, he was obviously using this for his bathroom.

I open the lid of the toilet. It looks clean. When I flush it, I hear it again. What sounded like a loud thundering crash was in fact the water pipes and the rushing water must've been the footsteps I thought I heard across the ceiling.

I breath out a sigh of relief. I wasn't crazy. These pipes just need to be fixed. I check under the sink for a towel and find one, already wet and crumpled, which is odd, but I use it to sop up the slow stream of water that is leaking from under the porcelain. I leave it there until I can tell Sadie tonight that they'll need a plumber in for that.

I'm satisfied with my discovery, about to leave the room, when something stops me. How does a toilet flush itself? If that was in fact the noise and I was the only one in the house, then how could that have flushed in the first place?

My finger shakes a bit as I raise it to switch off the light. I decide to dismiss the idea. It doesn't make sense, which means that I simply don't know enough about plumbing to understand the reasonable explanation, though I'm sure there is one.

I leave the room and decide to focus on the bedroom and unpacking our things. I glance out the window and while the pictures on the ad had displayed an expansive property, I notice how when you are on the second floor, there isn't as much privacy as you are led to believe. The guest house has large windows and I can only imagine how illuminated the main house is at night, allowing an unknowing spectator into your private space. My thoughts go back to Sadie, spying on me from her window when I was in the backyard. While she seems relatively harmless, I know nothing about her husband who could be into voyeurism for all I know. A wave of nausea climbs up my throat.

"Be reasonable," I say to myself as I pull my clothes from my suitcase in frustration. A swell like a rising tide builds up inside me. I'm already getting paranoid and I'm afraid of losing all my progress. "I shouldn't even be here," I say angrily now, tossing my clothes from my suitcase to the bed. I cross my arms and my head drops.

If only none of this had happened, then I wouldn't be stuck in this creepy house. I instead would be at the hospital, my second home, tending to patients instead of being one myself.

I look up, frozen in time as I pick my head up and stare out at the ocean view. The sun, a glossy gold, reflecting off the ocean like sparks of fire. Tiny little flames everywhere.

I'm brought back to that night of the accident and wonder if it all had gone differently, if I'd even still be with Luke. My recovery is the only thing that is holding us together right now. He's been great at putting our issues aside while I get better, but now it's time we address them again.

An ache forms deep in my chest. I remember everything from that night, surprisingly. The smell of the French restaurant, rich with butter and lemon sauce from the escargot that a neighboring table had ordered. It smelled delicious even though I could never muster the courage to try it. The atmosphere was buzzing with patrons, packed as usual. We were lucky to get a table at the last minute. We had entered and the maître d' had laughed when we asked if we could dine without a reservation. He had dismissed us to the bar and said we were welcome to wait. I was willing to go somewhere else. It was already late, and I was starving. I imagined Luke was too. But he'd insisted we stay, taking my hand and leading me to the one free barstool. I'd perched on it, my heels pinching my toes. I normally lived in scrubs, but I'd had a feeling tonight was a big night, so I'd dressed special for the occasion in a navy sundress with yellow floral designs. Luke had stood behind me in his blue suit and white button-down. There were times I saw him as so grown up and other times he was still the same Luke from college, only playing dress-up now. After a few minutes of waiting, we had finally made eye contact with the bartender, who had simply nodded his head in our direction.

"Two martinis, please," Luke had said, holding up two fingers.

I'd looked at him, surprised. That was certainly going to give us both a good buzz. We weren't big drinkers to begin with, and now he was ordering cocktails on an empty stomach.

It wound up being forty-five minutes and three martinis later before the maître d' finally approached us with an open table.

I was so hungry and just tipsy enough that I was tempted to snatch a piece of bread from the basket off a table we had passed.

Luke had stumbled a bit as well.

The waiter led us to a small table, too cramped to pull our chairs back properly to sit, wedged between the back wall and another table. Maybe the maître d' had taken mercy on our determination and had them add a table for us.

The waiter handed Luke and me both menus.

"The wine list, sir." The waiter with slick black hair and what I guessed was a fake French accent handed it over to Luke.

"We're fine," I said at the same time Luke ordered us a bottle of Burgundy.

"Very good, sir," the waiter said, my voice overruled.

After a delicious meal, Luke raised his glass in a toast. My stomach did a butterfly flip. I sensed he had some good news, but he had been reluctant to tell me, until now apparently.

I joined him, raising my glass, my elbow propped on the white linen tablecloth.

"I got a call this afternoon." A smile tugged at his lips.

"And?" I asked eagerly.

"I got the job."

I'd let out a squeal of excitement and leaned over the table to kiss him. "Luke, that's amazing. I'm so happy for you. I have to say though I was never worried. No one deserves that job more than you."

Luke smiled, embarrassed. "Thanks, babe."

"I was looking over the contract," he started. "It's a significant pay raise. Brings us up to a new tax bracket, if you know what I mean."

I smiled. "That's wonderful!"

I think of all the times Luke and I had to spend each month looking at our bank statements. We'd be going over our student loans and monthly expenses, trying to see if we were on track or if we had to cut out a dinner night out, or takeout orders. It would be nice not to have to analyze our expenses so closely. I relished the idea of freedom in just saying on a whim, "Let's go out to dinner," and not having to look up the prices on the menu before we go.

"I mean, you wouldn't even have to work anymore," he added. Then cleared his throat. "I mean, if you didn't want to."

My smile faded then. "Why would I want to quit my job?"

He shrugged his shoulders. "Well, we've been together forever; we're in our mid-thirties now."

I braced myself for what I knew was coming.

"I mean, all our friends are starting families. I was hesitant until we were more financially stable, but—" he leaned over and grabbed my hand "—now we are," he said excitedly. "Aren't you excited to start a family too?"

And there it was. My muscles froze. I didn't know how to answer. When we were younger, the topic had come up. I had merely said that I wanted to have a career first. Then see where life took me.

Luke had always wanted to have children. Now that his parents had passed recently, I could sense that his loneliness was growing, even with me here.

"Luke." I pulled my hand away. "I'm not sure. I'm just getting to a point in my career that I've been striving for my whole life."

I had contributed to our financial struggle when I decided to go back to nursing school for my nurse practitioner degree. Now that I had finally finished, it seemed counterproductive to sacrifice all that hard work and dedication, to leave now to have children.

"I shouldn't have said quit your job," he started. "I know how much you love it, and I appreciate how good you are at it." He wiped his mouth with his napkin. "What I meant was, taking some time off. Or at least shortening your hours. That's the beauty of your job, right? You can make your own schedule?"

It was partially true, but there was a lot that Luke didn't understand.

"Luke," I said, my voice dry from the wine. I could taste the tannins in the back of my throat. "I just . . . I just can't right now, okay?"

Luke stared at me then and didn't say anything for a long while.

I wriggled uncomfortably in my seat, the atmosphere suddenly becoming too stuffy and too loud. I could barely breathe.

"Right," he finally said, looking down. He pulled out his wallet, tossing it on the table. I could tell Luke was drunk. He had been celebrating after all, but his mood had shifted from lighthearted happiness, to moody and dark like a cloud passing over the sun.

We sat in silence as the waiter dropped off the bill and Luke signed the check. All his elatedness deflated from him like a balloon.

"The Uber's here," he said, checking his phone but still not looking at me.

I stood up and tried to catch up to him as he threaded his way around the tables to the exit. When I got outside, I couldn't see him. My stomach dropped. The air was just starting to get crisp, the signs of summer nights in the city disappearing as quickly as the leaves that fall off the trees. I thought he had left without me when I saw him standing between two parked cars. He was staring down at his phone, swaying a bit. Then he brought it to his ear. "Sorry, man, where are you?"

I could tell that he was trying to locate the Uber driver. Despite the map on the app, he was too drunk to comprehend it. Though to be fair, we aren't that familiar with Ubers. Another way to save our money was to keep to the places near our apartment or somewhere not far from a subway stop.

"Luke," I called out. I wanted to grab his arm, tell him that I was sorry for ruining the night. I didn't want it to become about this. I wanted it to be about his great new job. But the night had become as sour as the nearby garbage cans down the alley next to me. I looked down, just for a moment. Preparing for what I would say in the car. I wanted anything but the silence on the ride home. But the truth was, I didn't think I wanted children. And there was nothing I could say that could change the way I felt. There also wasn't anything that could be said to change the way Luke felt. One of us would be sacrificing something and I feared the resentment that would build from it.

I was still at a loss for words, when I looked up and saw Luke stumbling across the street. It had been quiet enough, but Luke clearly hadn't seen the black SUV that was barreling down the side street.

"Luke!" I called out in a desperate scream. Before my mind could catch up, I ran. Like my instincts as a nurse, my job is to save people. I had to save Luke. And so, I ran, pushing Luke as hard as I could out of the way, and the last thing I remember is hearing the sharp crack of my own skull against the car's windshield.

Chapter Six

Sadie

It's almost time, I realize, checking my watch. I put on some jazz, light a few candles and welcome the smell of herbs and spices maturing into an intoxicating scent that's rich and buttery. Within a few moments, the house feels transformed. Woken from its haunted sleep and now alive and welcoming. I wish that it could always be like this. Instead, I breathe in the moment and try to hold it in for as long as I can.

I check myself in the mirror; my hair is done up in a chignon, my makeup reset to evening wear with darker eyeliner and redder lips. I smooth out my white cocktail dress, seeing how it makes my sun-kissed skin appear to glow. I no longer look like me, I feel. But that's exactly what I want. I want to be someone else. Hopefully one day I can be the person I see reflected at me.

It makes me think of Cary Grant. A classic movie-star icon. Everyone in that day wanted to be him. Then I learned that his real name was Archibald Leach. His father was an alcoholic, and his mother was sent to a mental institution for clinical depression, though his father told him that she was dead. Then he joined the circus until a Broadway producer found him and transformed him into the person that everyone knew him as.

If he could make it happen, then so can I.

I run my finger along the top of the mirror.

"Shar," I call out.

I hear her shuffling as I examine the layer of dust piled onto my fingertip. I lift it up to show her. "I know your son and his cancer treatments have taken enough of a financial toll on you. You certainly can't afford to lose your job since no one will pay you as much as I do. So I'd appreciate it that when I ask you to clean this place top to bottom that you do. God knows what our guests would think if they saw this."

"Sorry, ma'am," Shar answers, her voice quivering as she smooths out the gray skirt of her uniform. "It won't happen again."

"Thank you."

I hear a knock at the door and quickly step out into the hall, leaving Shar in my wake; I see the image of two figures shadowed on the other side of the door. I open it, smiling brightly. "Welcome," I say, arms outstretched. I lean in, giving Natalie a double kiss. She stumbles awkwardly then hands me a limp bouquet of roses wrapped in cellophane. "Thank you so much," I say pressing a hand to my chest. I stare at Natalie a beat too long. Now that she is dressed up, the resemblance to Cassie is just uncanny.

Luke opens his arms for a hug, and I embrace him. Then he extends a bottle of red wine to me. "Oh, this is too much—you didn't have to do that," I say gracefully.

I lead them down the hall, admiring the woodwork and proud at how well this house shows. The dark, rich mahogany wood paneling gives a statement of generational wealth. A structure that over the years has been able to stand the test of time thanks to the money that continues to be poured into its upkeep. I stop short and turn, pulling open a hidden door built into the structure. My eyes crinkle as the edges of my mouth form a sly smile. I open the door and both Luke and Natalie crane their necks to see the oversized wine cellar, with bottles stacked so high there was not one, but two ladders angled along the shelves, wheels on the bottom to allow you to access both up and across the narrow tunnel.

"Very nice," Luke says, impressed. I take the bottle he's given me and slide it into one of the grooves of the shelf. I close the door, locking it and continue the tour down the hall, stopping at the kitchen. It's a similar aesthetic to the kitchen in the guest house. Both Marla and Jonathan are wearing their white uniform jackets. Jonathan chopping onions and Marla stirring the gazpacho with a wooden spoon. The two of them stop momentarily to give a small wave then continue with their work. I steer Luke and Natalie to the living room where I've hired Charles, a waiter—from Chez Vivienne as well—to serve dinner and drinks.

Charles is wearing his uniform from the restaurant. Black pants, a black vest and a white button-down. He's standing at attention next to the wet bar. I have the varieties of liquor organized by brand and color, illuminated under cabinet lighting. A bottle of white wine and a bottle of champagne chill in a sink full of ice. The glassware all lined next to it, pristinely polished and ready for use.

"What's your pleasure?" I ask.

"I'll take a scotch," Luke says slowly, as if considering his choice, but then finalizes his last word more confidently.

I run my fingertips gently over the selection. "Pick your poison." I flinch at my own choice of words. For Tom, alcohol—especially scotch—is poison and leads to dire consequences for me. But I refuse to get rid of it all. Part of the process is learning to accept these things around you and being strong enough to refuse them. Not to mention it's the only thing helping me get by these days.

As Luke approaches Charles to complete his order, I direct my attention to Natalie, still looking around and unsure of herself. She had cleaned up a bit, switching from sneakers to heels, and her T-shirt for a green silk blouse, but she's still in her torn jeans from earlier, and her pixie cut appears almost patchy, which gives her a disheveled look. It's a big difference from her husband, who is clean-shaven and freshly showered, based on the scent of soap I picked up on when I hugged him earlier. He's in a button-down, top button loosened for a casual but smart look, and dark, faded jeans. He's someone who seems to know his audience. Or someone like me, who knows how to dress as the person you want to be.

"What can I get you, Natalie?" My voice borders on being sing-song.

"I'll just have a club soda with lime," she answers.

"Of course." Then I wave over Charles.

"A club soda with lime." Then I stop and look at her. "Ice?"

"Please," she answers.

"And for me . . ." I lean my body to the side to peer around the waiter. "May I please have a glass of champagne?"

"Right away, miss," Charles answers in what sounds like a German accent.

"Is it okay if I drink?" I look self-consciously at her.

"Of course," she answers quickly. "It's not a problem for me. I'm just taking several medications after an accident I had, and it's not advised to drink on them."

That explains the short, patchy haircut, but my eyebrows rise reflexively, waiting for her to elaborate.

"A car accident. Well, I was hit by a car," she clarifies, her eyes darting to the floor.

Her insecure mannerisms indicate there is something more going on than just the recent accident. Something that's been ingrained in her for a long time. "I assume this was in the city?" I ask.

She bites her lip in agreement.

"I'm so sorry. The city is full of crazy drivers. I wouldn't be surprised if half the population of New York City has been hit by a cab."

Natalie's eyes flick up toward the ceiling as if considering this statistic.

"Well should you need anything, I'm happy to help."

"I appreciate that," she says. "I love your dress by the way."

I smile and smooth my hands over it. "Well thank you so much. You know if you ever want to borrow anything I'd be happy to loan you something."

I notice her look sheepishly at her torn jeans and I worry that I overstepped, implying that she doesn't own nice things.

"I mean, well," I stumble over my words. "I used to always trade clothes with my friend Cassie." Saying her name out loud causes the acid in my stomach to churn.

Luke joins us with his glass of scotch and rubs Natalie's arm encouragingly. It pains me to see it. Particularly when I think how long it's been since Tom has shown any sort of affection for me. But I also can't help but notice that when he did that, Natalie slightly flinched.

I lift my eyes quickly and smile, feeling as if I have to justify Tom's absence again. "I'm so sorry that my husband Tom is out of town, but he will be back this week, so we should do this again."

"That would be great," Luke answers.

"So why don't you tell me a little about yourselves," I say taking a sip of champagne that Charles just placed into my hand.

Natalie and Luke exchange looks as if to decide who should go first.

"Well, I work at a private equity firm," Luke starts.

I nod accordingly. "That's wonderful," I say, turning my head to Natalie, hoping Luke won't go into the details of his work. I'm not one for talking shop, especially when it's something as mundane as finance.

Natalie takes her cue. "I'm a nurse practitioner in the city. I work in the emergency room."

"Wow, impressive," I say, dipping down at the coffee table we are standing over. "Please, everyone, help yourself," I say toward the artistic display of cheeses and meats that Marla assembled.

Luke and Natalie settle on the white couch and I sit on a matching one opposite them.

"What does your husband do?" Luke asks, placing a piece of prosciutto into his mouth.

I falter, feeling slightly unbalanced, then quickly recover. "He's a golf instructor."

He hasn't been for the last two years, but they don't need to know that.

"That's fun," Luke says. "I'd love to get out on the course with him sometime this month."

"Definitely," I say. It would be great for Tom to have an opportunity to get out of the house and have some guy time. Since his overdose two years ago, we've lived like hermits. It's one of the reasons I'd like to screen Luke now. Make sure he's someone who can be trusted. I take another sip of champagne.

"So how do you keep busy? What do you like to do?" Natalie asks. I can tell by the way she phrased her question she thinks I'm a rich, bored housewife. If it were only that simple.

"Well," I say again sitting up straighter. "My husband and I are originally from LA. We moved here about two years ago. I used to be a psychiatrist. It was a bit of an intense job, so I've stepped back from it for now but will likely be picking it up again and opening my own practice here soon." I say it with such confidence that I almost believe it myself.

"That must've been very interesting," Natalie says. "We deal with a lot of mental health issues in the ER and we have a psychiatrist there that we always seem to keep busy."

"I did that as well." I nod. "Then I switched to a physician's office."

"I give you a lot of respect. I thought my job was hard, but while I deal with the physical trauma, you have to deal with the mental, which is much harder."

I look at her appreciatively. It's been a long time since someone has acknowledged how hard I work. "Thank you," I say genuinely. "It can be quite a challenge."

"Excuse me, miss," Marla says softly. "Dinner is ready."

After a three-course meal and breezy conversation, I can sense that Luke is feeling a bit out of place. I do feel sorry for him. Natalie and I have connected on our former roles and are exchanging stories.

After the uneaten sorbet has fully melted, Luke checks his phone, then takes his cue and stands up.

"Thank you so much for dinner, but I have to get going. I have some work I must finish and submit to my boss by tomorrow."

Natalie stands up too, and a sudden surge causes me to stand up as well. "I understand." Then I turn my attention to Natalie. "Would you like to stay for a nightcap?"

Natalie and Luke exchange glances. He nods at her encouragingly.

Natalie bites her bottom lip, unsure, but then gives in with a smile.

I feel a relief wash over me. I don't want the night to end just yet; the atmosphere is warm. I know that as soon as they leave, the cold and loneliness will return. I will be left with nothing but my thoughts and the memories of this evening dissipating like a dream after you wake up.

I give them a moment to say goodbye to one another and make my way into the kitchen.

"Marla, the meal was spectacular."

"Thank you." Marla smiles appreciatively.

I turn to Jonathan. "As always, your help is greatly appreciated." I pull out some money from my dress pocket that I had been saving for a tip and hand it to him.

Jonathan smiles, taking the money and putting it in his pocket. "My pleasure."

I hand another couple crisp bills to Marla. "For the extra work tonight." I wink.

"Thank you, ma'am."

"Marla, you can call me Sadie, please," I insist. "Oh, can you use some of the leftovers and arrange a dish for Riley? He's been looking rather thin lately. He spends so much time here and living alone all the way out by that marina, I don't think he's had a decent meal in a long time."

Marla smiles. "That's really sweet of you—of course I'll make him a dish."

I rest my hand on Marla. "Thank you, and again thank you for all of this. It turned out wonderfully."

I return to the living room, picking up the now-empty bottle of champagne and let out a disappointed sigh. "Charles?" I call and the waiter appears seemingly out of nowhere.

"Yes, ma'am?"

"Another bottle, please." I hand him the empty one along with another collection of bills that I reserved for his tip.

"Right away." He disappears as quickly as he had appeared.

I catch myself as I stumble over to the couch, falling back into the white plush cushions. I realize suddenly just how drunk I am. I look up at the large mahogany built-in shelves that line the walls with various books, vases and pieces of art. I'm still impressed that I get to live in a house like this. I never thought it possible before. I lean my head back and close my eyes for a moment. Then quickly snap back into focus when I hear Natalie's footsteps approaching.

"So do you entertain a lot out here?" she asks, sitting down next to me.

I shake my head. "I don't really get much of an opportunity anymore," I admit.

I think back to when we used to live in LA. I enjoyed the buzz of people's chatter and laughter, the music in the background, the scent of delicious appetizers. Now, with Tom, it's almost never a good idea. But I don't want to think about him, not tonight.

"Do you have any kids?" Natalie asks me.

"No," I answer.

Charles returns with a fresh glass of champagne and a glass bottle of sparkling water that he tops off Natalie's drink with.

"Thank you." She smiles to Charles.

"I didn't really have a good childhood," I admit, turning to Natalie. "When that's the sort of experience you have, it's hard to think that you'll somehow be any better than your parents."

"I know what you mean," Natalie says, staring into her glass. "Sometimes in life we have to be happy with just us, right?"

Her smile falters and I realize I'm right. I knew something else was going on.

"So is it you or him who doesn't want children?"

Her eyes widen in surprise.

"I'm a psychiatrist, remember?"

Her mouth rises to a slight smile at my cleverness. "I don't."

I'm beginning to like this girl. We have a lot more in common than I would've expected. Perhaps this is the beginning of a wonderful friendship. Without thinking, I raise my glass. "To us."

She cocks her head, unsure at first, but then smiles and clinks my glass. "To us."

Chapter Seven

Natalie

I wake up gasping for air as if I had been holding my breath. There are beads of sweat trickling from the base of my neck. My chest feels tight, the muscles beneath my ribs aching. My head sweeps around.

Where am I?

It takes a few moments for my equilibrium to balance out, for everything to come into focus in the darkness, the edges of my vision blurry. Once I hear the pounding surf of the waves from the open window, I remember. I'm in Southampton, staying in a guest house. I'm okay. I'm safe. I settle back against the pillow, trying to reason what woke me in the first place.

A flutter of my eyelids brings the dream back into the forefront of my brain.

I'm sitting in the corner of the funeral parlor, making myself as invisible as possible, scratching my palm with my nails so roughly it's drawing blood. I glance up at the other people in the room. There are hushed tones being spoken all around me. Eyes meeting mine before quickly turning away. Heads shaking in sadness. The front of the room is surrounded by bouquets with grieving messages on them. The smell of those flowers, fresh yet sour at the same time, settles in the back of my nostrils. My mother's eyes throw daggers at me. Without saying it I know she'd rather it was me in that coffin.

That's when I wake up. I choke down the tears stinging my eyes.

I stand up out of bed, the jute rug rough on my bare feet—as predicted.

Luke rolls over. "Babe, since you're up can you get me some water, please?" His voice is slurred, and I can't tell if it's because he's half asleep or still a little tipsy from Sadie's.

I nod at first, but then realize he might already have closed his eyes again. "Sure," I answer.

I enter the hallway. The moonlight shines through an open window, creating harsh shadows that cut like knives. My body contracts into itself. At the end of the hall, I see him. I see Danny.

I see his mop of dark brown hair, his frail childlike body always seemingly too small for his clothes, his arms and legs sticking out of the openings like twigs. His shoulders are hunched like a scared animal sensing its predator watching.

A dry, hoarse sob escapes my throat, my chest heaving. He's so real I could almost touch him. I close my eyes hard, rubbing them until I see white spots behind my eyelids.

"You're not real," I say in a harsh whisper, willing myself to make my brain work properly. "You're not real." I wrap my arms around myself, morphing into a rocking motion.

In a moment of truth, I open my eyes again. The hall is dark once more, the moon now obscured by darkening clouds. A clash of thunder rumbles, the house giving a slight shake.

This was only because of the dream, I tell myself. I'm half asleep. Even if I hadn't had my brain injury, I likely would've had this experience, I convince myself. But I feel something churning in the pit of my stomach, something that knows what I saw felt more real to me than any dream-like state.

A creak of a door opens and shuts, causing my spine to erect. Luke likely going to the bathroom, I tell myself as I quicken my pace down the hall. Afraid of proving myself wrong. Then I might have to admit that my hallucinations aren't gone just yet. That I'm not getting better. I've never hallucinated anything that was a full-fledged person. It was always shadows and blurred figures. But this, this was Danny. My dead brother from over twenty years ago. My feet pound the steps, my anger building up. I will not let myself regress now. Not after all I've been through. But the reality is, my condition is out of my control. It isn't like a broken arm suffering atrophy. As if all I have to do is a little physical therapy, and it will be better in no time. Yet I was treating it like that. Like the brain was a muscle that I just had to exercise. The more rationalizing I do, the more I can physically fix my problem. What if my sheer willpower could overcome this? Doctors can handle the clinical side of things, but the mental strength of the person can't be studied as it's beyond comprehension. Like a mother who gets an adrenaline surge so great, she can lift a car to save her baby. That's the type of strength I am trying to summon.

I turn on the tap in the kitchen as I watch raindrops pelt the window so hard it sounds like coins falling from the sky. I take a moment to splash the cold water on my face, the icy liquid contracting my pores and awakening me from my fog-like state. I tear away a sheet of paper towel, dabbing my cheeks. A bolt of lightning strikes somewhere in the distance, lighting up the sky to momentary daylight.

I open random white cabinets looking for the water glasses, when I finally find them on my third try. I fill up both, placing them on the white marble of the countertop. I turn around slowly, anticipating that I might have another hallucination. The hairs on the back of my neck stand up. No one is there. I let out a breath I didn't know I was holding. I stare across the open floor plan, searching for any sort of movement. But the white couches almost illuminate in the dark. The sheer curtains, still.

"You're going to be fine," I tell myself, walking toward one of the coral-shaped lamps on the end table by the couch. I turn it on and light and relief flood me.

I'm rattled by the thought of Danny. I haven't thought about him in so long. Some memories are too painful to bring back up. So instead, I tried to bury them deep within the crevasses of my mind as a means of survival. I did that because otherwise it would cripple me. Before I had the guts to leave home at eighteen and never come back, I was the shell of a person. I acted like a normal teenager, which my mother deemed evil. Wearing makeup, cute clothes, liking boys, going to parties; I might as well have been snorting meth with a bunch of deadbeats and robbing stores for money. Then again, she had made up her mind about me long ago. Nothing I ever did would make it right. She would never forgive me.

I worked my ass off at school, knowing it was my only way of getting out. I got a full ride to NYU. I went into nursing because I wanted to help people. I wanted to save them in their time of crises, the way I never could for Danny.

I remember the day I packed up my room. My parents went off to work without so much as a goodbye. I would be taking the train to the city and moving myself into my dorm. Before I left, I looked around my room one last time. There wasn't much in it, despite how much time I had spent in there. The walls were still painted pink, likely from when it was a nursery for me. My bedspread was white lace, something out of the Victorian ages. I'd argued about it, but I'd learned that if I wanted to change something I was going to need to buy it myself and the money I earned through my hard work as a cashier at a clothing store would be better off spent on other things. No one saw my bedspread but me. I never had friends over at my house. I likely wouldn't have been allowed anyway.

I remember stopping off at Danny's room before I left though. It was still exactly how it was the day he died. Left like a shrine. The walls were a light blue, and he had a navy-blue bedspread. There was a shelf full of books and trucks still on the floor.

The only thing added to the room after the fact was his teddy bear, which sat in the middle of his bed, its head cocked to the side as if about to fall over. I stood there for a long time, tears streaming down my face, burning every detail into my brain. I stared at the closet, where Danny and I would hide, sneaking treats I stole for us from the kitchen. That rush of feeling like we were getting away with something. I looked at the bed, where I taught him how to roll his body into a somersault. Or the corner by the window, where I crouched down the night he died. I'd snuck in, my knees to my chest, willing him to appear in his bed sleeping like all of this was a bad dream. I wanted to forget, but at the same time not. Wanted to remember the good memories too. The ones that I could cherish, even though they would be tarnished forever.

I knew I'd never go back to that house again. I already had plans to secure student housing in the summers through internship programs and any other jobs that I could do for the school. I knew I'd never see my parents again.

I think about a time around ten years ago when I was in the city on my way to work. I was in my nursing scrubs looking down at a text I had just received when I bumped squarely into someone.

"Sorry," I said, looking up, my mouth dropping when I saw it was my own father.

His skin was dry and patchy, eyes deep set and heavier than I remember, his chin sharpened when his lips pursed together. He looked at me squarely in the eye, our gazes fixed on one another for what felt like an eternity. Then he kept walking. I'm not even sure if he realized it was me. I remember staring at him as he walked away. Curious if he'd turn back with even a hint of wonder, or the slightest bit of regret that he didn't acknowledge me. But he kept walking. That same hurried gait that I inherited from him. I watched as he crossed the street, getting farther and farther away until he was swallowed up by the crowd.

I don't want to be thinking about Danny. The pain is too great even when I'm in my strongest state, let alone now.

It should've been you, I hear my mother's echo in my ears and I shut my eyes tightly, willing the voice to go away.

I tread back upstairs with a feeling as if I am being watched, but every time I swivel my head, I see nothing.

This is just my imagination, I assure myself.

I crawl back into bed next to Luke.

He stirs a bit.

"Did you forget something?" he murmurs.

"What do you mean?" I ask. "I went downstairs and got you water."

He sits up as I hand it to him, looking half asleep and confused. "I thought you were already in bed. I thought I heard you come in and then were about to get into bed but then left again."

I let out a shaky breath. "That wasn't me."

The sunlight strobes in the next morning, the warmth of the sun hot on my face, the traces of last night's storm gone, except for the droplets of water on the sill from when I had forgotten to close the window. I push myself to sitting. I had slept well after that. The adrenaline rush of my dream or hallucination had sent a crash through me that I had felt deep in my bones. Still groggy, I sit up in bed, my eyes squinting and my nose scrunched. I turn back toward the bed to find that Luke's side is empty. I rub my neck in a slight stretch, checking the time. It's almost ten. My eyes widen in surprise. I haven't slept that late in a while.

After brushing my teeth, I throw on a white terrycloth robe hanging from the back of the bathroom door. It's soft and plush like it's never been worn before. I pull the collar around my neck, slightly rubbing it against my cheek.

Instinctively, I open my makeup bag and pull out my medication. I stare at the white bottle with the blue top. The name Seroquel is printed across the front. Going through the motions, I grab my water off the nightstand, about to take them, when suddenly I stop myself. I stare down at them in my hand, the white chalky residue spreading across my palm. It was given to me to handle my increased anxiety after the accident. I had such a fear of leaving the apartment, afraid that I would get hit again. My thoughts stray back to Danny. His childhood mop of brown hair that fell over his blue eyes, his crooked smile with a missing tooth, on the verge of losing another. I stare at myself in the mirror, the white of my eyes glassy.

I need to know if I'm better, I think to myself.

I drink from the water glass, then put the pills back in their container. *Just for a few days*, I think. Just to see if the hallucinations are me or the pills.

When I reach the kitchen, I find Luke sipping on coffee. His hair is still a mess from last night's sleep and his eyes are bloodshot. I feel slightly relieved that he hadn't gotten up that much earlier than me.

"How are you feeling?" I ask.

He opens his palm to reveal an aspirin, then pops it in his mouth and swallows it down with a sip of his coffee.

I wince. "That bad, huh?"

"The worst. I have to stop drinking scotch."

I want to ask him, then why did he, but I know the answer. I had seen Sadie's insistence, handing him drink after drink like she didn't want us to leave. She had seemed nervous, maybe even afraid of being alone.

"Were you able to get your work done?" I ask him.

He reaches for his laptop on the counter behind him and places it on the table. "I need to do it now," he says, lifting the screen and typing in his password. "So, what did you think of Sadie?" His eyes are still on the screen.

I take a moment to consider my answer as I pull a slice of bread out of its packaging and place it in the toaster.

"I like her," I answer, locating a mug and pouring myself a cup of coffee, while I wait for my toast. "At first I didn't know what to expect, but despite all that money she seems really down to earth." I shrug, remembering her comment about having a bad childhood. Something I could definitely relate to. "I could see myself being friends with her."

"She was awfully chatty with you."

"Sorry, we didn't leave you much room to get a word in edgewise."

He shrugs. "It's okay. I'm not going to be here that often and when I am I'd rather be with you." He smiles sheepishly.

"What do you mean?" I ask.

He looks at me confused. "I have to go back to the city and work."

I blink at him.

"I can't take a month off of work," he says, now registering that was exactly what I had thought. He eyes me nervously. "You knew that, right?"

"I didn't think you were taking off, I just thought since you pushed so hard on this, that you were going to be working remotely."

He closes his laptop. "Babe, this is a new job, I've been there less than a year. I can't just take a month and work remotely."

I exhale deeply out of my nostrils as I close my eyes. I guess I shouldn't have assumed, but it would've been nice if he had clarified with me. Then again it would force him to admit what he was really doing. Taking a break from me. Maybe this isn't a trial about us finding each other again. This is a trial separation. A deep ache forms in my chest. How am I supposed to fight for us, when I'm still fighting against my own health?

"Why don't you have your friends come stay with you during the week?"

I smear the toast with strawberry jam then cut the bread in half, taking a bite to consider my thoughts. "Because my friends have jobs and kids. They can't take off in the middle of the week. Besides, they don't need to babysit me."

"No one has to babysit you," Luke says cautiously.

I try not to get upset, but it feels like he's been trying to find excuses to spend less and less time with me.

"You okay?"

"It doesn't seem like you want to be with me." My voice is weak and pathetic-sounding.

He raises his fingers to his temples. "Of course I want to be with you. I just don't know what you want me to do, Nat. I've been doing nothing except working and trying to help you get better."

"And you hate me for it," I mumble.

"I don't hate you for it—you saved my life!"

I step back. So, does he now feel obligated to be with me because of that? I don't want to be considered a charity case to him.

"I'll be fine here."

"Nat . . ." He trails off.

"Really, I have Sadie next door for company and to keep an eye on me."

He stands up, taking a step toward me, but I back away. "Really, I'm fine."

He lets out an exasperated breath. We stand there in stunned silence for a moment.

"I'm sorry," Luke says now, his words weighted with guilt. "Let's just forget it, okay?"

We eat our breakfast in silence, the atmosphere so tense it feels like my childhood again. I try to change the subject. "Oh, we need a plumber to look at the toilet in the hall bathroom upstairs. The pipes connected to it are broken and it's leaking."

"I'll take a look at it." Luke stands up and puts his plate in the sink.

"You don't have to do it this second," I tell him.

He shrugs his shoulders. "If I do it now then I won't forget."

Then I realize we are both looking for a distraction.

"Have you seen any tools here in case I need them?" he calls out from halfway up the steps.

"I think I saw a toolbox in the hall closet on the top shelf. I'll take a look."

I follow him up the stairs and point toward the toilet, grimacing as I remove the towel and bring it to the laundry room. I stop off at the hall closet and pull out the toolbox. I open it up to see random items haphazardly shoved in it: a Phillips-head screwdriver, hammer, box of nails and zip ties.

I come back, standing over him with it, and place it down. "Not much there, but here it is in case you find something you need."

"Thanks," he calls, his head still down, looking for the root of the problem.

I'm standing there awkwardly when I turn my head and remember the guest room. I glide across the hall, flicking the light on. I walk over toward the window, seeing its layered views from the ocean to the beach, lowering my eyes all the way down to the pool, directly below the window.

When I turn back around, I notice what looks like a piece of paper, on the dresser. I approach it, realizing now that it's a photograph. Fairly recently taken. Luke and I don't have any printed pictures in our house aside from our wedding photo. It's one of those things I mean to get around to, but then never do.

I pick up the picture and examine it. It's a tall brown-haired woman, mid to late thirties. She's sitting at a table holding a big ice cream cone. Her eyes are bright, lighting up at whoever is taking her picture. I can't help but think that she looks a lot like me.

I stare at it for a long, hard moment, wondering who this woman is and why there is a picture of her here in this house. Could she be related to Riley? The thought of him having a girlfriend seems far-fetched. He didn't seem like much of a people person.

I hear another loud bang that causes me to jump, before I remember it's the toilet.

"I think we have a ghost in here," Luke calls out, causing me to freeze momentarily, thinking about last night.

"What?" I try to keep the shake out of my voice as I slowly put the picture back down on the dresser and walk toward Luke, who's still leaning over the toilet in the bathroom.

"The toilet. It's called ghost flushing. When water leaks out of the tank and into the bowl, it triggers a flush." He bends his head. "I don't see where the source of this leak is down here." He points. "We just have to keep an eye on it. Might even be coming from the shower."

I crease my brows. "Why the shower? Who would've been using it?"

"Maybe when the cleaning service came in."

"Right." I remember now Sadie mentioning that.

My shoulders sag in relief. So, I'm not crazy. There was a reasonable explanation for the flushing.

"I'll have to run to the hardware store and change the flapper. Won't take long." Luke stands up. "I better take a shower."

As Luke steps into our new bedroom, I find myself drawn once again to the spare room and the photo on the dresser.

I pick it up, running my fingers over her face. We have the same facial features. Her cheeks when she smiles seem to rise into the bottom of her eyes like half-moons. Her teeth are bright below her bow-shaped lips, chin sharpened.

A loud thud startles me, causing me to drop the picture. Did someone throw a rock at the window? Leaving the picture where it is, I make my way to the window. I can't see anything, so I pull the frame up, letting in a blasting wind gust. I stick my head slightly out, looking down, when I see it. A gray dove is struggling on the grass, its wings spasming. I let out a sigh. The bird must've flown straight into the window and injured itself badly.

I notice Riley coming around the corner of the house. He's carrying a plastic garbage can full of trimmings from the hedges. He holds a pair of cutters in his right gloved hand. Odd for him to work on a Sunday, I think. I see him notice the bird, flapping around helplessly. He puts the cutters down, crouching his whole body as he makes his way toward it.

He picks the bird up delicately in his hands. It struggles weakly. Then in one quick motion his left hand grabs the bird's neck and snaps it.

I jump, banging the back of my head on the open window. The noise brings his gaze up to me and I stare down at him in horror as he tosses the bird into the trash can and continues with his hedging as if nothing had happened at all.

I quickly slam the window shut.

I walk into our bedroom and hear the shower running. I try to scrap the image of that poor, helpless bird in Riley's hands out of my mind. I decide to start making the bed, pulling up the sheets and duvet. I go to pull my pillow off when I see something.

A pebble maybe? I lean over and pick it up in my hands to examine it. Bile suddenly starts to rise in my throat. I drop the object and burst through the bathroom door to throw up. I start to shiver, my legs weak after I've emptied my stomach.

Luke opens the shower door. "Hey, are you okay?"

"It can't be real," I say to myself. "It can't be."

"What?"

"Nothing," I call to him. "I'm fine."

I remember the image in my palm again, feeling the sharp edges. What I had in my hand was unmistakable. It was a baby tooth. The same one I remember on the hood of the car, covered in blood, the day that Danny died.

Chapter Eight

Sadie

I wake the next morning mortified, the night playing over in my head. My stupid behavior. I shouldn't have drunk that much, especially when I knew Natalie wasn't drinking, but I couldn't help myself. I was terrified at the idea of being alone again with my thoughts. At least I did have one night of reprieve, only I feel the slight tinge of an oncoming headache.

I hope I didn't screw things up. All I want is for her to like me. I remember my comment about her clothes and wince. Hopefully when I mentioned swapping clothes with friends before, she realized that was what I had intended. Doing things that friends do for one another.

But then I had to go and pry my way into her marital issues using my psychiatry background as an excuse. That was stupid; it just made me look like I'm nosy and looking for gossip, though I wouldn't have anyone to gossip to.

I crawl out of bed and look out the window. Their house seems quiet, and I decide I'm going to give them space today. I don't want to be too on top of them as this is their vacation as well, but I also don't want to come on too strong.

The sun is bright and stings my eyes. I squint at the shoreline, scanning it for anything that might be out of place. Then, I pull the curtains closed, but they are light-filtering, so it doesn't do much.

The narrow wooden planks shift beneath my feet as I pull a bottle of water from the mini fridge I keep in our bedroom, underneath the sideboard that has a coffee maker along with several snacks like fruit bars, should I decide I don't want to leave my room for the morning. I drink the water eagerly, some of it dripping along the sides of my mouth. I use my other hand to wipe it away. I start the shower up, leaving my pajamas strewn on the floor, and step inside, hoping to wash away the stain of last night's humiliation. I hope this is not starting to become a routine of mine.

After applying an under-eye mask and a brightening serum, I put on my makeup and dress in a cream-colored silk button-down with matching beige shorts. I let out a breath to regain my composure, satisfied at my transformation.

I assess myself in the full-length mirror once more, the evidence of what it took to get me here reflected behind me. My makeup scattered across the countertop and several outfit changes are tossed to the floor, which I'll have Shar come and clean up. I adjust the sleeve of my blouse to cover the patch of gauze. There will be no workout training sessions this week, but I'll make a point of trying to walk along the beach later. My heart stops when that night flashes again in my mind, the pounding of the rough waves on the shore, the lightning flashing in the sky, the look of disbelief on Tom's face, my blood-curdling scream.

I see my phone resting on the end table, still charging, and I pull the wire out, dialing the number of the facility again.

"Psychiatric floor," the same voice answers.

"Hello. This is Sadie Wilson; I'd like to speak to Dr. Turner," I say as I head downstairs to make myself some coffee.

"Patient's name?"

"Tom Wilson," I answer.

"Just a moment."

I pull a mug from the cabinet, place it under the machine and put in a coffee pod.

The music fortunately doesn't play as long this time before Dr. Turner comes to the line. "Mrs. Wilson," he answers.

Before I can say anything further, he adds, "Today seems to be a good day. Your husband can see you."

"Thank you so much." I'm relieved Tom is willing to see me, but still anxious as to what he'll say. Will he believe me? I certainly need him to. If not, then I'll just have to make him understand. "I'll be there shortly."

I hang up the phone, turning around with my coffee when I see Shar standing in the darkness of the hallway.

I scream, dropping my mug, breaking the porcelain, brown liquid splattering across the floor.

"Oh my God, you scared the hell out of me." I put a hand to my chest, my nerve endings fried as she reaches for a tea towel and bends down to pick up the shards of glass.

I walk away in a huff of anger. She always seems to be sneaking around every corner, always watching me, waiting for me to slip up.

I pull into the hospital parking lot in front of a sterile white building shaped like a T with small windows. I grip my purse to my chest and take a deep breath. My hands are shaking. I step out into the thick heat of the day. The air sits idly like smog. I slowly make my way across the parking lot until I reach the automatic sliding glass doors that open with a whoosh, blasting me with cold, refreshing air. I find myself frozen in place, afraid to move any farther. I see someone inside give me a look of annoyance when I realize that until I step off the sensors, the doors will remain open. I give an apologetic smile and continue, one foot in front of the other, until the doors behind me close.

I am greeted with an antiseptic smell that hits the back of my throat, bringing my hangover that I had been keeping at bay back to the forefront.

"May I help you?" a woman behind a desk in white scrubs calls to me with her head cocked to make sure I know she is talking to me.

My mouth opens but I can't seem to get the words out. She raises her eyebrows at me impatiently until I finally manage to move my tongue.

"Sadie Wilson to see Tom Wilson."

"ID, please."

I hand it over and she takes my information down. She looks to be one of the head people around here, with an authority and familiarity suggesting that she's seen and done it all. Don't mess with her, is the permanent look on her face.

She hands back my driver's license and I smile, but she doesn't seem to notice as she grabs her phone and makes a call. "Just one moment." She points to a set of plastic chairs lined along the wall.

The other faces in the waiting room appear just as grave as mine. Then again, anyone in a hospital waiting room is not excited to be there.

"Floor seven," she calls out and I see again that she's referring to me.

I take the pass that she's printed out, apparently having taken my picture with her computer, which I was unaware of. I find the elevators. My finger lingers for a moment before I finally press the number seven. The elevator soon begins to rise, but I feel my heart sinking, or shriveling rather, in my chest.

All too quickly the doors open and there is another nurse sitting behind a desk. She looks up at the sound of the doors pinging open.

I put on my brave smile. "Hello, I'm Sadie Wilson."

Before I can say who I'm here to see, she tilts her head, directing me on as if she already knows who I am and who my husband is.

"Right this way." She stands up and I follow her down the hall, but instead of bringing me into his room, she leads me to an office with several desks in them. She gestures for me to take a seat and, confused, I do so.

"You will need to leave your items here," she explains.

I nod, now remembering how this works, and hand over my cell phone and purse.

"Anything else on you that could be considered a weapon?"

I shake my head no.

"Good," she answers. "The doctor will be with you in a moment."

I look around the room. This must be the doctor's office where they do their clinical work, but there are no personal items in sight. No family pictures. Just awards, certificates and diplomas to verify the doctor's license and practice.

"Mrs. Wilson?"

I turn my head to see a tall, thin man with soft eyes smile and extend his hand. I shake it, noting his firm handshake and rough calluses.

"I'm Dr. Turner. It's nice to meet you in person." His smile is welcoming, and I can imagine it's a practiced move he's been doing for his whole career. A job of trying to make people feel comfortable and safe.

"You as well," I answer. "So how is he?" I cut right to the point.

Dr. Turner reaches for his rolling desk chair and sits across from me. He sits upright but casually crosses his ankle over his knee. "He started off agitated when he got here. He claims that he didn't do it and is determined that it never happened."

I nod gravely. "As I had said to the police when they showed up, he had likely been on a hallucinogenic. Not his first time. I don't think he meant it. It's just that sometimes he gets these random urges."

Dr. Turner rests his chin on his fist.

I try to keep my anxiety at bay as I explain, worried I'm going to trip myself up. "This has become more prominent in the last two years, although it's never escalated to this degree before. I don't think it was his intention to try to harm me. I think he thought I had done something to upset him, and something else inside him took over."

"And what is it that you think he was angry with you for?"

I give a weak shrug. "I think he felt I was being a buzz kill. He was high on something, and I was trying to settle him and get him to go to bed. I slant my head curiously. "It usually comes out when he drinks."

"What does?" Dr. Turner props his elbow on his armrest, his finger on his temple.

"My husband has DID," I start. Then I add, "Dissociative identity disorder."

Dr. Turner merely nods.

"I am a licensed psychiatrist, so I know how to diagnose a person. He's completely normal for the most part, unless of course he's under some sort of influence and then . . ." I trail off. "He will start becoming irrational, acting solely on reflex. When that happens it's as if he blacks out. He has no memory of what he's done. I have records that I can email you of his discharge papers from when he overdosed on fentanyl two years ago. It's what prompted us to move here from LA. And if it helps, I can show you the gambling debt he acquired under his personal account with again no memory of it. I also have a court order by a judge that grants me guardianship."

"I see," Dr. Turner says, seemingly more convinced. "If you could send me that information it would be extremely helpful when we make our final evaluations tomorrow." Dr. Turner stands up. "I'll bring you to him."

I swallow, my stomach churning that this is the end of our conversation, and I'll actually have to face Tom.

Remember, make him understand, I think to myself.

"Of course."

When I walk in, I feel my legs buckle. It's almost impossible to reconcile the image of Tom with this person in front of me. He is alone in a white box of a room, devoid of any items that aren't deemed necessary. The TV is on, but it's muted. He's in a hospital gown, staring out the window. The lighting makes his skin almost appear gray. Whether or not he heard us come in, he makes no acknowledgment of it.

"We gave him some Klonopin for agitation," Dr. Turner says softly to me.

From his side profile, Tom looks as if he's aged ten years. His face is unshaven, his dark hair unkempt with two cowlicks in the back of his head with no product to contain them.

I bow my head to Dr. Turner again to let him know he can leave us be. He steps out but doesn't close the door.

"Tom," I say softly, as if trying to coax him from wherever he is in his mind, trying to bring him back to reality.

He turns then, his expression grim. His eyes are a dark shadow of someone who has no fight left in them.

Good, I think to myself. *He knows what he did.*

"I didn't want it to come to this." I gesture with my hands out to the suffocating hospital room we are in.

He turns away from me.

I swallow. *Stay in control.*

"Are you sorry?" I ask with trepidation.

He swallows, his eyes fixed on the floor.

"You know, we could be happy again," I tell him hopefully. "If you just allow it."

He looks at me now with a blank stare, like he has no idea what I am talking about.

"I love you so much, Tom," I start and I truly mean it. "We need to find a way to put the pain behind us and move forward."

When he doesn't respond, I feel myself start to tear up.
I can't lose him.

"I promised you for better or worse, and we will see our way through this," I say encouragingly. "You may not love me today, but I know that you will love me again. One day, once you realize everything I've done for you."

He continues to stare at me with no sort of emotion on his face.

Finally, knowing that I'm not going to get much further than this, I wipe the tears from my eyes, nodding in surrender, and turn to leave.

"You can't," he starts, which causes me to turn around. My chest lifts in hopefulness that he's willing to take the next steps forward.

But when I turn, his expression is not that of someone who's about to say *you can't leave*, *I love you*, or even *I miss you*. Instead, he is holding the same helpless look of a broken man, only this time his eyes seem darker, a shadow over his expression. I can sense the anger behind them. Like a person about to die but they will go out fighting. "You can't love someone who's already dead."

The words hit me like a sucker punch. I leave the room, stricken as I try to keep it together. I gather my things from the nurse and race back to my car as fast as I can before I break down into a heart-wrenching sob.

Chapter Nine

Natalie

I'm glad I never told Luke about the baby tooth. There was a part of me that wanted to scream, tell him to hurry out of the shower and look for himself. But after I emptied my stomach and stopped myself from shaking, I went back to the bed. It was empty. I remembered that I had dropped it once I knew what it was, but as I searched the floor and under the bed, I never saw it again. It was just my imagination—it *had* to be. What had been in my hand was likely some sort of rock or pebble. How it got under my pillow I can only imagine. My mind was running away from me again. What I really need to do is not overthink everything. It's nothing but me blowing things out of proportion, which only makes it all worse. Today is all about Luke and me. No ghosts or hallucinations are going to distract from that.

By the time Monday morning rolls around I have settled into the noises of the house, the creaks here and there. Without the Seroquel, I feel like I have more of a handle on myself. Luke was up early; it was still dark when he left. He kissed me on the cheek as he said *I love you*. Yesterday we had spent the afternoon on the beach, and it was lovely. Both of us are aware that a bigger conversation needs to be had, but yesterday was exactly what I was looking for: a reconnection. Just a husband and wife spending a romantic day on the beach with a picnic.

I started to realize yesterday just how needy I've been since this accident. Luke was right: this could be a good thing for me. A real way for me to start being more independent. If I want to actually be better, rather than just say it, I need to start doing it.

My alarm goes off at nine a.m. I have my first virtual appointment at eleven. I fling the covers back and tiptoe to the window, peering down at the crystal-like pool. The water is so still it looks like glass. I smile, putting on my royal-blue one-piece bathing suit and grabbing a pair of goggles. A swim is just what I need, I think. It was time to start exercising more. Now that I am away from the crushing fear of the city and its congested traffic, I have felt calmer. I have room to breathe here. Instead of letting this place be what causes my regression, I am going to make this experience what finally heals me. I owe it to Luke to at least try.

I step out onto the back porch, a slight chill in the air. There is an eerie stillness this time of the day. Even the ocean appears flat and calm, the dunes quiet. The sun has risen over the icy blue ocean, clouds hovering and creating darkened shapes against the water.

I hear a car pull up and notice Sadie's maid entering the house.

The pool is colder than I would've expected, sending a chill from my tailbone to the nape of my neck as I enter the water to my waist. I quickly duck under the surface, blowing air from my nose as I sink deeper. When I look up it's as if I am peering through a water glass, everything a little bit distorted, like I had sunk into some sort of alternate universe.

Once I pop back up, I inhale deeply and start to do laps. Each stroke feels like me fighting back at the world.

Everything that has stacked up against me over the years, I slice at it with my arms cutting through the water like a knife, smooth and pristine. A clean cut, a clean break. I continue with the rhythm, losing track of my laps, just swimming until my muscles burn, then right before I reach the edge, I flip my body into a somersault before pushing off the side of the pool, gliding to the surface before continuing my freestyle in a synchronized motion, like some sort of dance. I can feel my heart pumping in my chest, but I can't bring myself to stop. I want to keep going until my lungs burn. Until I lose all strength in my body. My mind just keeps pushing and pushing. I barrel through the exertion until a tight grip snags at my wrist.

I gasp, pulling water into my lungs. I explode to the surface, coughing and terrified at what still has my wrist in a lock. Once the water is out of my lungs, I let out a scream. The grip quickly loosens, and I pull my arm back, pushing my body away from the edge.

"I'm so sorry!"

I look up to see Sadie's terrified face. Her hands are over her mouth. "I didn't mean to scare you like that," she says as I slowly make my way to the side of the pool and pull myself out. I sit on the edge, still coughing a bit.

Sadie fumbles, not sure what to do, so she grabs the white towel I had brought out that was on the lounge chair and hands it to me.

"Thanks," I say, dabbing my face.

"I had been trying to get your attention for quite some time." She points sheepishly at a woven picnic basket filled with pastries sticking out of it like a bouquet. There are muffins, Danishes and croissants.

"Sorry," I tell her, then smile at the basket. "That's very sweet—you didn't have to do that," I say, standing up.

"I wanted to apologize for my behavior the other night."

I look at her confused. "What do you mean?"

"I got a little carried away. The champagne kind of snuck up on me."

I shrug my shoulders. "It happens, no worries."

"Still, it wasn't the impression I wanted to give the first time meeting you," she tells me, her eyes gazing down to avoid mine.

"Seriously, don't overthink it," I try to assure her.

"I was hoping you like pastries. Of course, if you want something else that's fine. I also know it's late in the morning—you might've already eaten."

I know she's trying to be nice, but her desperation is like a thick scent coming off too strong.

"It's perfect, thank you." I smile at her. I glance back at the guest house, then tap my phone, which I placed on the white lounger to check the time—ten-fifteen. "Would you like to come in for some coffee? I have an eleven a.m. appointment, but I still have a bit of time."

"I had thought maybe the patio by the beach." She points, seemingly uncomfortable here. "But if you have an appointment . . ." She trails off as she eyes the house nervously, biting her lip. Then she smiles as if afraid I might refuse otherwise.

"Sure, I'd like that."

She follows me to the porch, where I stop to dry my legs, wanting to avoid dripping water all over her house. "I'll be just a minute," I announce. I want to say make yourself comfortable, but it feels strange saying that, as it is her place. She can get as comfortable as she wants.

When I come back downstairs after changing, Sadie has already prepped the coffee machine. I can smell the grinds, a nutty caramel percolating as I reach the kitchen. For a second, I pause, second-guessing my outfit—a black V-neck T-shirt and khaki shorts—next to Sadie's well-tailored clothes, not a single hair on her head out of place. There is an air about her that suggests someone who is always put together. But I can sense through her eagerness to get my approval, a level of insecurity that I have to admit I also see in myself. Sadie cares a lot about what people think of her and I'd be lying to myself if I haven't felt the same.

Without knowing I'm here, she allows her feelings to be displayed on her face. She looks distraught. Her brows are furrowed in anguish, and one hand is over her mouth as if she's trying to stifle a cry. The other arm is wrapped around her waist to either keep her from keeling over or to give herself a supportive hug, I'm not sure.

I clear my throat awkwardly and watch as the transformation occurs in front of my eyes in an instant. Suddenly her smile is bright, her spine straightened. Other than the slight shine in her eyes, you wouldn't know anything was wrong.

"Coffee's almost ready," she says quickly, turning her back to me as she reaches into the cabinet to pull out plates and two mugs.

When she turns around, she looks me up and down. Part of me wonders if she's going to ask again if I want to borrow anything of hers, but instead she flicks her gaze to the table.

"What would you like?" she asks, pulling out a chair for me.

I sit. "It all looks so good. What would you recommend?"

"The croissants are to die for," she tells me. "Chocolate or plain?"

"Plain," I say. Before I can reach for it, she already has a hand on it. She places it on a plate then sets it in front of me. I see her pick the other plain one to put on her plate.

"How do you like your coffee?" Her voice is behind me now as she pours some into a mug. "Oh, I can get that," I say, pushing back in my chair, the wooden legs scraping against the floor.

"Nonsense, I'm already over here," she says.

"Just black," I tell her, extending my hand as she gives it to me. "Thank you, but you don't have to wait on me."

She finishes pouring her coffee, black as well, and sits down next to me. "It's no problem." Then she looks over my shoulder behind me. I turn as well.

"Sorry, just looking to see if Luke was here. I didn't want to be rude and not offer him any pastries."

"He went back to the city this morning to go to work," I explain. "He'll be back on Friday."

"Oh." Her voice is cheery.

"Tom will be back tomorrow," she says almost cautiously. "It looks like it's just you and me then."

There is something about the way she says it. Does she mean for today? But she said Tom was coming home tomorrow. Does she mean her and I, against him?

I take a bite of my croissant and manage a closed smile. When she mentions Tom's name she seems . . . I'm not sure . . . apprehensive. I noticed it at dinner the other night as well. When I tried to ask about him, hoping as well to get Luke into the conversation, she would completely deflect and switch topics.

I decide to be blunt now but keep my voice light. "Tell me more about your husband."

My suspicions are confirmed when Sadie's shoulders tense and it's as if her whole body goes rigid.

"Is he intense, like Riley?" I decide to come out with it.

Sadie almost laughs at this. "No, no nothing like Riley. Riley suffers from PTSD."

I chew my croissant as I consider this. I knew something seemed a bit off kilter. I remember his eyes when he first stared intently at me. They were eyes that had seen things. Things that would change you forever. It made sense now.

"Tom was never in the military. In fact, he was a cushy rich boy, who liked to have fun. Maybe sometimes too much fun."

Her voice becomes more wary, as if maybe she shouldn't have shared that with me.

"Oh," I realize. "So, is he recovering?" I insinuate that Sadie means he's a recovering drug addict or alcoholic. It's not uncommon; wealthy people with lots of money and time on their hands tend to fall down the rabbit hole of partying too much.

She sucks in a breath, and I realize that he's not recovering and still very much suffering from it. Sadie nervously pulls at a stray hair to put behind her ear and I think I notice the hint of a gauze patch under her sleeve. Could it have been caused by him? I want to ask, but it seems inappropriate. Still, it makes me apprehensive about being here alone during the week. First Riley and now Tom. Two strong and seemingly unstable men.

If Sadie, his own wife, seems to fear him, then what exactly is he capable of doing to me?

"So how did you and Luke meet?" she asks, changing the topic.

I wait to swallow. "We met at a college dorm party at NYU. We both went there. My friend Katie was dating this guy Jake and Luke was his roommate. Both Katie and Jake were actively trying to set us up. We were both painfully shy at first and they kept inviting us to dinners, which would wind up being the four of us. Eventually it worked and Luke asked me out on his own."

"Was it love at first sight?" Sadie says, eyes to the ceiling in a romantic way, but it sounds patronizing.

"No actually," I admit. "He says it was for him, but I don't know, I guess my insecurities kept me from thinking that a guy like Luke could have interest in a girl like me."

Sadie frowns and tilts her head. "What on earth would make you say that?"

I give an involuntary laugh.

"You deserve whatever man you choose." She sips her coffee. "Don't let your mother's words of you not being good enough paralyze you from doing what you want."

I fall back into my chair. "How did you . . ." I ask but I can't finish the sentence.

"I'm a psychiatrist," she reminds me.

"Right." I nod. "Wow, you sure know how to read me."

She shrugs. "It's what I do, or did, rather." Her eyes trail outside, staring out over the ocean, taking in the memories of another life.

"So how did you and Tom meet?" I ask.

She sips her coffee. "I took a golf lesson from him." She eyes the clock. "You mentioned an appointment at eleven. What time do you have to leave? I'll make sure I'm out of your hair and give you time to get ready." She starts to slide off her chair.

"It's just a virtual appointment, and I'm the doctor so to speak."

"Oh, so you're back at work?"

I nod. "My boss wants me to take things slow after the accident so I'm handling virtual appointments."

"What sort of appointments?" she asks curiously.

"Pretty much anything that doesn't involve needing a physical examination. I can treat eye or sinus infections, upper respiratory issues, mental health issues like anxiety and depression . . ." I trail off, the irony not lost on me that I can treat someone with the same issues as I have.

"That's wonderful," Sadie's says brightly, but she looks nervous. Almost as if she's worried that I can see through her.

"Oh, I meant to ask," I say, pushing my chair back and standing up. "I'll be right back." I run up the stairs and retrieve the picture of the woman that I had found in the guest bedroom. I return downstairs and place it in front of her on the table.

Sadie jumps back, startled. "What's this?" Her voice is slightly uneven.

"I'm not sure. I found it in the guest room. I figured it belonged to you or whoever was in the guest house last. Do you know who she is?"

Sadie swallows hard. "Cassie."

This was the friend she had mentioned swapping clothes with, I remember. And now given how similar we look, I can see why Sadie gave me sort of a double take when she first saw me. But I pick up on the way she says her name now. It's weighed down with sadness. I decide not to say anything and wait for her to continue.

"We used to be best friends." She sighs. "She must've left the picture behind." Sadie's eyes appear watery.

"Was she here recently?" I ask.

"Yes." She bites her cheek. "But in typical Cassie fashion she shows up in your life as quickly as she leaves it, without so much as a goodbye."

The same distorted face I saw earlier returns in Sadie and she quickly drops her head and stands up. "I've got to run," she says warily. "Thanks for the coffee."

As she leaves I think again about how similar Cassie and I look and can't help but wonder if Sadie is hoping that I can replace her friend and be her new "Cassie."

I lose track of time when I look outside and notice how dark it seems. I check my watch. It's only five, but when I look outside, I see dark thunderous clouds rolling in. It's about to storm at any moment. It was apparently like this all last week: sunny skies during the day and storms rolling in at night. It's supposed to clear up and we're going to have nice weather by the end of this week, at least according to the local news.

My eyes are heavy. I had back-to-back virtual appointments all day. It took more out of me than I had anticipated. It's my last FaceTime of the day, with my boss no less, who wants me to check in with him.

I stand up to get myself some water, my voice dry from all the talking I have had to do today. When I turn around to face the living room I jump, seeing Riley's oversized shadow peering in through the window of the French doors.

I let out a scream and grab my chest, spilling water all over myself. But Riley doesn't react at all. Instead, he eyes me for a moment through the glass then he walks off.

My heart is still beating out of my chest as I run to the door realizing that I hadn't thought to lock it since Sadie left this morning. What if he had tried to come in? How would I have stopped him? Sadie claims he's harmless, but how sure is she of that?

I hear a beeping noise on my laptop when I realize it's my boss phoning in. I quickly try to settle my nerves and click accept. He pops up on the screen of my laptop. "Dr. Warton." I smile, trying to keep myself looking energized.

"How did you do today?" His voice is light and encouraging. I consider Dr. Warton the father I never had. He's in his mid to late sixties with a widow's peak at the top of his forehead where his gray hair is slicked back. His face is worn with age spots and wrinkles, but his eyes and smile could still light up a room.

"It was great. I'm excited to be back," I tell him, trying to keep my voice from shaking. "Nothing too serious, just a couple of respiratory issues and a sinus infection."

He bows his head, while focusing on something offscreen. He writes something down and then draws his attention back to me. I wonder if someone has asked him to sign off on something or if he is taking notes of our conversation. Knowing him well enough, I am sure it is the latter.

"I hadn't meant to send you so many on your first day," he starts. "The day just really picked up more than we were expecting."

I raise my arms. "It's how the job goes," I tell him.

He smiles. "And how are you feeling?"

I straighten up a little more. "I'm good," I tell him. "Happy to have something to focus on other than myself."

Now I know the reason he requested a FaceTime instead of a standard call. I can see his eyes assessing me, to see if I'm lying.

"The openness out here has been very helpful. There isn't a car in sight, which allows me to take the necessary steps I need. I went to the beach this weekend and went for a swim today," I tell him brightly.

He shakes his head in approval. "Very good. Are you still taking your medication?"

"I'm taking my seizure meds," I start. "Even though I haven't had an episode in almost a month now. But I don't want to risk it," I say.

"And the Seroquel?" he prompts.

I let out a sigh. "I have been having some hallucinations with it. Likely just a trigger from the change of environment, but I decided to not take it yesterday and today. I must admit I feel much better, and I haven't had any episodes," I lie.

He purses his lips at me. "Okay." He seems to give in. "Just be sure to regulate yourself. Any further hallucinations, you let me know."

"Will do," I answer.

"Is there anything else?" he asks.

"No, I think we're good. Thank you, Dr. Warton."

"Have a good night, Natalie."

"You too, sir," I say as I shut my laptop. I quickly jump back up and peer out each window around the house. No further sign of Riley. Was he trying to intimidate me so I will leave?

I triple-check that the front and back door are locked and lean against the wall. I feel emotionally and physically exhausted. I extend my arms into a big stretch, feeling my muscles already sore from this morning's swim. A crack of thunder causes me to jump. I hear what sounds like scurrying upstairs. An animal of some sort? But wouldn't that sound likely come from an attic and not the second floor?

There is no way that Riley got in somehow, right? I climb the stairs with trepidation. A shadow seems to dash behind a door, or did I just think I saw that? I put my hand nervously on the door, slowly opening it, not wanting to see Riley on the other side. But as the door gives way to the guest room, I don't see anything except darkened shadows from the lowering sun. I relax my shoulders and retreat into the hallway, opening up each door. Nothing. It's got to just be my hallucinations. It's been a long day. My mind is tired and playing tricks on me. Even Riley's earlier appearance might've been a figment of my imagination. All I want to do is take a hot bath. My skin is still itchy from the pool this morning, like it had been doused with too much chemical cleaner. I can already smell the scent of the bubble bath formula I packed, feeling instantly calmer. I decide to forget about Riley and let the rest of the day wash over me. This was a long but productive day.

When I walk into my room, I take a moment to look out the window; the clouds over the ocean are ominous and the rain has picked up significantly. I'm about to turn away when I see a dark figure, looming on the wooden boardwalk that descends to the beach. I think I'm seeing things again but as I squint I realize clearly that it's Sadie. She's still in her well-tailored clothes from this morning, leaning on the post of the railing as if she needs it to support her weight. Her head hangs heavy, and her shoulders are heaving as if she's crying. I can't pull my eyes away from her. A moment later she stands up straighter, as if she's moved on from whatever she is crying about, and she makes her way toward the beach. I'm growing more concerned now as I watch her cross the threshold of the beach, etching closer and closer to the waves that are now lapping at her expensive clothes. She stops for a moment, her shoulders upright, then continues to walk straight into the surf.

    I think about Sadie in the kitchen earlier. She had clearly been distressed and upset. Alarm bells start going off in my head. Sadie is trying to kill herself.

Chapter Ten

Sadie

I stare at the picture of Cassie that Natalie gave me earlier.

My throat constricts. Another person in my life that I considered family.

I wonder where Natalie found it exactly. When Cassie had left, I had torn through that place with a fine-tooth comb, then sent in Shar to clean. Surely this couldn't have just been sitting on the floor or a dresser haphazardly.

Did Shar get wind of our altercation and leave it there on purpose?

I run my thumb over the image of her face. That bright smile of hers, always so infectious. It makes me want to cry.

Why did it have to be this way?

My mind flashes to when it all went downhill. It had only been two weeks since Cassie came back into my life and I still can't believe how much had gone wrong so fast.

"Sadie!"

I heard Cassie's voice on the other end of the phone, knowing instantly that it was her despite the fact she'd called me from a number I didn't recognize.

"Cassie?" I still checked even though I recognized the sheer shrill of her voice.

"Of course, it is," Cassie said in a way that suggested her presence should always be obvious. She wasn't wrong.

My throat constricted with a mixture of relief and hurt. "What happened to you? You fell off the face of the earth. I haven't heard from you in forever."

"I know," Cassie said, her voice guilt-ridden. "I was going through some stuff. Can you forgive me?"

I bit my lip. Of course I could forgive Cassie. No matter how much time had passed, she was my best friend, my sister. "I could've helped you, whatever it was," I said, feeling bad that she couldn't come to me about it.

"I had to deal with it on my own." There was silence for a moment, then she switched gears, her tone back to upbeat. "I've missed you. How've you been?"

"Wow, how long *has* it been?" I asked, trying to think back.

"Over five years, less than ten. I know it's been a long time."

I still regretted what I said to her back then, I couldn't help but think. What else would have made her cut off contact with me as suddenly as she had? She went as far as ignoring my calls, until her number was finally disconnected. I thought back to the night of my wedding. She'd acted happy for me, but I knew she had been faking it. She was sad. Her own life—no job or boyfriend—had nothing but a bleak future, and she must've seen me as leaving her behind. She'd asked what she would do without me, and I'd told her I'd always be there, but maybe it was time for her to focus on her own life, her own happiness. I had meant it in the best way possible. We'd both had rough childhoods and when my life had started to get better, with Tom, she'd started to cling to me like a lifeline.

I remembered her expression had changed then. She'd put on a brave face for my wedding but after that, I'd assumed that's what she'd done—tried to focus on her own life. Yet, I knew she thought I was abandoning her when I was doing anything but. This was my chance to make it up to her, I thought.

"So how are you, Cassie?" I said with a warm smile on my face, because no matter the circumstances, I loved hearing from Cassie.

She'd never lived a conventional life, but that wasn't really her fault. Her mother had carted her around the US for the better part of her childhood. It just so happened that she'd landed in class with me in second grade and we'd become fast friends. When my father died, and the scandal came out about his second family, there was gossip all over town. Kids who I thought were my friends were regurgitating rumors they had heard from their parents. Saying that it was my mother who was the homewrecker and not Laney. That my mother knew about her the whole time but was too pathetic to let go. That I wasn't even my father's child.

Kids could be cruel. It was Cassie who had gotten suspended for cursing out a group of boys with language so foul that I didn't even know what half of it meant.

She'd always defended me. Maybe because she saw herself in me. Cassie didn't even know her father and her mom never stayed in one place for too long. So, it could've been that Cassie didn't care what people thought about her because she'd be off to the next town in a matter of time.

But for me, it meant everything.

"I'm your family now," she'd told me once, grabbing my hand as I hid in an abandoned tree house behind the soccer fields of the school. I had run off during that time between lunch and recess, but she'd known exactly where to find me. "I promise no matter where I end up, I'll always come back for you." She had then picked up a rusted nail half hanging out of a piece of plywood, meant for supporting the tree house, and pulled it out with a force so great that she flew backwards with a loud thud.

"Sisters for life," she had told me, piercing herself with the nail along her palm until it drew blood. She'd reached for my hand, and I had done the same, despite knowing it wasn't the best idea. We both got infections because of it. But I was so touched by the gesture that it didn't matter. I had someone in my life who saw me for who I was. Not as someone who wasn't good enough, like my mother kept insisting. It was always that we were never good enough for my father, but she never clarified to me whether I was good enough for her.

Cassie had kept her word, at least for some time. Like clockwork, she had moved a few years later, but we found ways to reconnect. She would send me letters about a summer camp she was attending and how I could convince my mom to let me go. When I went off to college, Cassie came back to be there for me when my mom died. Then when I graduated, she convinced me to backpack through Europe with her. It was a whirlwind of a summer, some of the best memories of my life.

"I'm doing great," she said now, cheerfully. "I was wondering if we could get together sometime. I miss you."

"Of course," I said. "I miss you too. Where are you living now?"

"Well, I'm sort of in between things," she started.

And there it is, I realized. The real reason for the call was Cassie needed a place to stay. It hurt that it took her needing something to get back in touch with me. It hurt because I truly missed Cassie. I missed how present and in the moment she always was. She shone her light on you, and you felt like the most important person in the world. Cassie was like my sister. And like any sibling, no matter what happened in life, you always looked out for one another.

But I had to think of Tom as well. Cassie was usually not the best influence. I couldn't afford a setback with him. But then again, people change.

God knew what sort of predicament Cassie had landed herself in. It seemed almost fun at first, hearing about her wild stories when we were young, but now that we were getting older,

I hope she wasn't still doing that. Her whole free-spirit aura at this age would feel sad and tiring, like a good TV show that runs for too many seasons. The protagonist facing the same problems every time. At some point the audience wants to scream: *haven't you learned your lesson yet?* But then there was a reason another season came out. Because no one wanted the story to end. Maybe Cassie didn't want her adventures to be over.

"So, tell me about you," Cassie pushed. "It's been almost a decade. I'm sure you have some juicy updates for me."

I sighed. "I don't know, Cass; my life is pretty boring without you in it."

"I'm flattered." Cassie laughed. "But seriously what's new?"

"Well, when's the last time we saw one another?"

She hesitated.

"The wedding, right?" I flashed back to mine and Tom's wedding day. Cassie as my maid of honor, fluffing my dress for me. Her hands on my shoulders as we look into the mirror. "The best girl won," she had said.

At life? At marriage? I could only assume. Cassie and I were always competitive with each other, or rather Cassie was the competitive one. She wanted anything I had. It was a bit childish, but her mother always felt guilty about moving her around, so she gave her everything she ever wanted, which made her act a bit spoiled.

I tried to think of what to say. My life had certainly changed, in some ways unimaginable and in others, disappointing.

While it had, from a financial perspective, been everything I could ever dream of, it still felt hollow.

The first few years of marriage seemed great, and then, within the last two years, Tom had really started to spiral and I'd had to double down.

I realize now, all of it manifested in how I answered Cassie on this simple question. In the past seven years, what had I done with my life?

"Well, we moved to Southampton," I started.

"I saw your house in the *Wall Street Journal*. You bought it from, like, the Rockefellers or Vanderbilts? Or something like that?"

"Yes," I answered, remembering that our purchase was a big enough deal to make the papers.

I smiled, proud that it seemed I'd been able to accomplish something in the last five to ten years. I was able to impress the notorious Cassie Dune.

"So why don't you give me a brief run-down of your life," I pressed. I knew that Cassie wanted to come stay with us, but I needed to know that she wasn't the same Cassie anymore. Most people mature with age, but I was worried about Cassie. Tom and I were very fragile and she could come in like a gale-force wind and blow us both away.

"Um," she fumbled a bit. "I have a son."

"A son?" I said, surprised. "How old?"

"Six."

I couldn't hide the shock in my voice. "You have a child, who is six, and you never told me about him?"

"I didn't want you to judge me."

"Cassie." I felt my heart break. "I can't believe you'd think that. I think it's wonderful you have a son," I said. I heard the relief in my own voice. If Cassie had a child, then she had responsibilities. She had another life in her hands. Surely she couldn't be the same person she once was.

"Did you want to come visit?" I finally asked.

"Yes, please. We can be there as soon as tomorrow."

My heart breaks thinking about Cassie now, our relationship officially done forever. I lie on the floor of my bedroom. It's dark and the wood is cool against my hot skin. I've been crying all afternoon. It's all getting to be too much. I wonder why I fight it. Why do I try so hard to be someone I'm not? Who

I'll never be no matter how much I try? Everyone I have ever loved has betrayed me in some way. In the end, what else is there if you have no one who cares about you?

All I wanted was a better life for myself and yet, I somehow managed to screw it up beyond recognition.

I think of Tom's cruel words. *You can't love someone who's already dead.*

The words hit deep like an ice pick through my heart. Maybe he is right. Maybe I am dead inside, but then who killed me? Who made me this broken? It was him.

I look at my phone and see another missed call from the hospital, likely confirming that I'll be there to pick him up tomorrow, but I can't go. I can't bring myself to face him. They'll be forced to hold him until someone comes to sign the discharge papers. Like me, he has no one else. Not anymore. Maybe it's time for him to wonder how that feels, when everyone you have ever loved abandons you and leaves you to rot. But then, my heart smooths over the rough edges of my anger like sandpaper. No matter what, I know I can't let him suffer forever.

I drag myself to my writing desk in the corner of the room and I pull at the drawer where I find our personalized writing pad, a sketched image of our house in the header and the name of the house, The Overlook, inscribed on it. I should've known when we bought a house called The Overlook that it was a bad omen. Nothing good would come of it here. I sigh and pick up a Montblanc fountain pen.

Dear Tom, I begin to write.

When I am done, I breathe a sigh of relief. I stand up and go into our closet where I open the safe. I fold the letter and place it on top of our passports. He will find it soon enough and he will know what I have done. He doesn't have the code for the safe, so I know I'm in control if or when he finds it. There is just something cathartic about writing it all down. It clarifies my reasoning and paints a clear picture of just what exactly brought me to this breaking point.

A loud roar of thunder shakes the house. I edge toward the window. My eyes are swollen and my cheeks still wet with tears. I stare out at the ocean, the waves crashing loudly. I think about the last time we had a hurricane and how the storm called to me. I need the feeling of that rush again. My head cranes toward the guest house. The lights are on in the living room.

My eyes flick back toward the picture of Cassie that is on the floor, and I put it in my pocket before heading downstairs and out onto the back porch. I fight against the wind and rain that has started to come down hard, pelting my skin. I check the guest house again and see the lights in the bedroom flick on, Natalie's silhouette small compared to the oversized windows.

I start to cry again but I keep going until I reach the steps that lead to the beach. I lean on it, supporting almost all my weight. My legs feeling as if they'll collapse beneath me.

My childhood with Cassie flashes before me like watching a movie trailer.

Her hand in mine, telling me she was my family, right until the end of our friendship. The final scene full of shock, sadness and regret.

I realize as I replay my life in sequence, recalling memories of my father, my mother, my husband, it's Cassie who my heart breaks for the most.

It's all too much to bear, I think. I push myself off the post and drag myself down onto the sand.

I step onto the beach, wet and heavy like walking through quicksand. An angry mist sprays my face as the waves start to pull at my legs, my clothes already soaked and sticking to my skin.

I look out at the ocean, murky and foaming, ready to take its revenge on me. It seems fitting, deserving even. Getting washed up and spat out just like life does to you.

The piercing screams return to my head, no matter how loudly the wind roars in my ears. I've made up my mind. I give one last glimpse behind me and I see Natalie, her silhouette pressed against the window, watching me.

I go further out until my head is submerged under the water. That's when I see Cassie's face looking back at me, eyes wide with terror at what I'm doing.

Then she fades away as a wave knocks me over. I feel a sharp pain as my skull slams against something sharp. Then, I give in to the fear. I let myself be free and let the ocean take me away. For the first time ever, I feel at peace before everything goes dark.

Chapter Eleven

Natalie

"Sadie!" I cry through the window, though I know she can't hear me. I turn and sprint down the stairs as fast as I can, skipping the last two. I burst through the back door, leaving it open, and run as hard and fast as I can.

"Sadie!" I start to call again, the wind carrying my voice away as rain pelts my face.

I reach the edge of the boardwalk and stand briefly at the top of the steps, trying to locate her in the surf. A gust of strong wind almost blows me backwards.

My stomach churns with every second that I can't spot her.

Then I see a light shade of blonde hair floating on the surface of the water like seaweed.

I sprint down the beach, never taking my eyes off the hair, even as it starts to slip below the surface.

I run in, battling the force of the waves that start to topple me. I lose my footing but try to keep my eyes on Sadie the whole time.

A wave catches me off guard, knocking me down and causing me to spin. I panic, unable to figure out which side is up or down. My feet find the bottom against a sharp rock, and I push myself to the surface, taking in a deep inhalation.

"Sadie!" I call again. I think I spot her now. I dive down. The water is murky and churning with sea foam. My eyes burn with salt, but I see the outline of a body. I grab her, pulling her head to the surface, but there is no gasp for air as I would've hoped. She's not breathing and there is trail of blood pooling from the side of her head.

"Sadie!" I drag her by the arm, swimming as hard as I can, allowing the waves to now work in my favor as they carry us back to the beach. I grab both her arms and pull her as far from the water as I can before dropping down next to her, my clothes heavy and wet over my skin. I feel for a pulse, tilt her head back and perform CPR.

"Stay with me, Sadie," I call to her while giving her chest compressions. Despite my heart beating out of my chest, my body is steady and performs each motion like I have done a thousand times before.

"Come on," I say, softer now as I continue, worried as I realize that in the excitement, I didn't think to bring my phone with me to call 9-1-1. I can't risk running for a phone and giving up breathing for her.

I curse under my breath.

Suddenly, Sadie retches the water up from her lungs. I roll her to her side, so she doesn't choke again. Then I slowly sit her up and rub her back.

"You're okay," I say softly, my body flooding with relief.

She turns looking at me, eyes wide not with horror but rather with anger, it seems.

I don't say anything. I just look at her.

Then, seeing the recognition in my eyes that I knew what she was doing, I see her face fall in dismay. Her lips tremble as she turns back toward the ocean. Then her face crumbles into her hands.

I give her a few minutes to pull herself together and reflect on the enormity of what she just tried to do to herself.

I give her a quick physical assessment.

"Come on," I finally say, my body cold from the heavy rain and wind. "Let's get you inside." I pull her up, surprised at how light she is. Her body falls into mine like a fawn learning to walk for the first time. Her legs are shaking.

I steady her, then slowly walk her back to the house. When we get to the porch, I reach for the door to open it, relieved that it's unlocked. The house is dark and cold. It seems like a completely different atmosphere from the one Luke and I experienced just the other day. No music playing, no conversation, just an eerily quiet house. I find the remote for the stone fireplace sitting on the mantel and turn the gas on. The fire ignites immediately behind a wrought-iron grate. I sit her next to it.

She is staring off in the distance like she has no idea where she is. I check to see if her pupils are dilated, but she doesn't look like she's drunk or on anything. She's just in shock.

"I'm so sorry," she says finally, her voice shaky. "I-I don't know what came over me."

I'm relieved, glad that she seems to regret it.

I sit next to her, waiting for her lips to stop trembling, for the shock of what she's done to subside a bit. She turns and gives me a look of surprise, as if she didn't realize I was here.

I find a blanket in a wooden chest and wrap it around her. Her blue lips are still quivering.

"Do you have any gauze so I can clean up your head wound?"

She seems taken aback when she reaches up along her hairline and touches the wound, wincing, then she notices the blood come away on her hands.

"The cabinet under the sink in the hall bathroom."

I hurry down the hall, remembering where it was from when we were here the other night. I pull open the cabinet and find a full and extensive medical kit. As if Sadie is prepared for situations such as this. My mind going back to the gauze I spotted earlier on her arm.

I pull out the entire basket and return quickly next to Sadie to examine it further. I clean the wound and assess that, while she did get pretty banged up, enough to render her unconscious, it's a minor flesh wound that won't require stitches. I finish cleaning her up while we both shiver from a deep, bitter chill.

"Let me get you a change of clothes," I tell her, standing up. "Are you okay with me getting them for you?"

"There are two terrycloth robes in the hall closet upstairs," she tells me.

I bow my head and retreat down the hall, my bare feet thumping off of the wooden planks until I reach the foyer, where I find the grand staircase that curves up to the second floor.

I strip down in the hall, wrapping myself up. The tension in my body releases the moment the warm robe wraps around me. I go back downstairs, holding the other robe out to her. She strips off the blanket and begins to peel off her wet clothes. I instinctively hold the robe out and up, averting my eyes to give her some privacy. I let go when I feel the tug of her arms through the sleeves.

"Thanks," she whispers.

I look down at her wet clothes and I notice the picture of Cassie I gave earlier to her slip from her shorts pocket. I wonder if it had anything to do with her decision to drown herself, or if it just happened to still be there from when I gave it to her this morning. Maybe this has more to do with Tom and his upcoming return?

A bolt of lightning strikes out in the distance and the lights flicker for a moment, followed by a rumble of thunder.

A smile touches Sadie's lips. "Do you like storms?"

"Sometimes," I admit. "Not often though."

"I've witnessed several hurricanes here. One was so bad that we had to evacuate, but I didn't." She looks past me and out the window, her eyes glazed over as if she's somewhere else. "I sat in one of those Adirondack chairs." She motions toward the chairs perched at the top of the boardwalk that overlook the beach.

"I sat there for hours, watching as the air stilled, the sky remained bright, and the ocean looking almost as calm as a lake. I watched the birds fly above me, all in a hurried motion, away from the impending doom just lurking on the other side of the horizon. Then I waited patiently as the storm clouds brewed and the wind kicked up, the trees bending in unnatural ways. It was in sync with the ocean starting to angrily churn, the tide so high it scraped at the dunes, threatening to spill over and wash me away with it."

She turns to face me now, like she's about to tell me a secret. "I got a strange thrill at being that close to danger." A smile crinkles around her eyelids. "It's such a rush, the feeling of excitement that builds inside you. Like when you are riding a roller coaster, the gears grinding up that first hill before it gives in to the inertia and spills you over. You let go, with a sense of freedom. Whatever happens now is out of your control, but you accept it, and it creates a sense of peace. It's only then that I feel what I take to be true happiness. Something about flirting with danger—it somehow never makes you feel more alive."

I take this all in, wondering if maybe this wasn't a suicide attempt, but rather the result of an adrenaline junkie. The calm, collected Sadie I met two days ago, seems like a far-off concept from the person in front of me right now. Like a violin string, too tightly wound, which is starting to fray from the pressure.

"Let me make you some tea," I offer.

"Right," she says, face flushed with embarrassment. Then, she follows me into the kitchen, taking a seat at the counter. She is still staring off into the distance as I attempt to locate the mugs, only to find everything I need is arranged in a similar fashion to the guest house, which is becoming less and less of a surprise. Her house is merely a grander version of where I'm staying. The only difference is, at least on the downstairs level, everything is opposite. The living rooms seem to both face the backyard but angle toward one another.

As I prepare the tea, I run through in my mind the checklist of assessments I need to do on Sadie. Physically I know she is okay now, as I looked her over once I was able to revive her. Now it's the matter of a psychiatric evaluation and I'm curious how open she's willing to be with me.

"Please don't take me to the hospital," she says as if reading my thoughts.

I turn around and she has managed to climb herself onto a stool against the white marble countertop located in the center of the kitchen.

"You need to get checked out," I tell her. Although I can't drive and it would involve calling an ambulance to get her.

"But you're capable of that, right?" She gives me a hopeful look.

I ignore her silent plea and hand the mug to her. She looks down into it, as if the answers to her problems will be in there, or maybe she's just seeing a reflection of herself. She shakes her head, wet strands tangled and sticking to her face.

"My mother killed herself," she says before taking a cautious sip.

"I'm sorry," I say, knowing that if I leave it at that, she'll fill in the silence and I'll be able to get a better understanding of what this was all about.

"I can't believe I almost followed right in her footsteps." She shakes her head.

"Why did your mother kill herself?" I ask, noting the family history of suicide.

"Because of me," she admits in a whisper.

I try to keep my expression even. "How so?"

"My father was a pilot, who traveled a lot. My mom stayed home with me," she says, setting the scene. "When I was ten, he died in a plane crash. He was flying a private plane for an overly demanding client who insisted on leaving in bad weather, even though my father knew better."

"That's terrible," I say.

She shrugs her shoulders, matter-of-factly, and takes another sip. "We were sorry too, at least I was until I found out the truth."

I look at her perplexed.

"It turned out that dear old Daddy had an entirely different family in another state and we didn't know anything about it, until of course the will came out." She laughs. "I had three other siblings. Turns out I was the oldest. I had a brother who was five, a sister who was three and a two-and-a-half-month-old sister, who were mothered by another woman: Laney."

"Wow," I say unable to keep the shock out of my voice.

"He was gone a lot, but when he was home, we were his world." She smiles up at the ceiling, reliving a private moment before her face sours again. "At least that was how he acted. Like he was so upset to be away, and so happy when he could return home to be with us." She shook her head. "Turned out it was all a charade."

"So, what happened to your mom?" I ask.

"Well . . ." She picks up the mug, holding it to her lips but not drinking it. The steam rises above her top lip. "After we found out that his will left nothing to us, we learned our real worth to him. My mother went into a deep depression. She told us that we clearly weren't good enough for him. That he had to go and start an entirely different family and had been too much of a coward to tell us. It turned out that Laney knew about my mom and me all along, and the joke was on us, apparently."

I wait silently for her to continue.

"Unlike my mom, I was angry. I was angry with my father for lying to us. I thought it was all his fault, but my mother acted like it was ours. All she could focus on was that we weren't good enough. I never understood that, and I got angry when she would say it." Sadie's eyes start to form tears, and she eagerly blinks them back. "Instead, I helped my mother go further into a depression. I would get mad at her and as a result she shrunk more into herself." Her voice starts to shake, and she takes a sip, the tea sloshing in the mug as she slams it on the counter too hard. "The day I went off to college, my mother took a bunch of pills."

"Oh, Sadie," I say, outstretching my hand, teetering on the line of patient and friend. She grabs it like a lifeline, squeezing hard.

"That's when I realized what my mother meant this whole time. She hadn't been good enough for my father, and I hadn't been good enough for her. I wasn't a good enough reason for her to stay alive, because I was a bad daughter who didn't understand her."

I lean in now, hugging her tightly, feeling her embrace me back.

"I'm so stupid," she chokes out and rubs her eyes, embarrassed.

"No, you're not," I assure her.

"What I just did was so dumb. It doesn't change anything. It doesn't make up for what happened."

"So, you regret your decision?"

"It went too far." She extends a hand to me. "Thank you for being there to save me."

"Of course," I say, relieved I was there too.

She hesitates for a moment, the dark smudges of eyeliner under her eyes make her appear helpless and vulnerable. "Please don't make me go to the hospital. It was dumb of me, but I promise I don't intend on doing that again."

"What made you come to the decision to do this now?" I ask—my final evaluation question.

She swallows hard and I can hear the gulp in her throat.

"I have spent my life acting as if everything that happens to me is my fault. A trait I inherited from my mother, clearly." She shrugs. "But, when you pulled me out of the water, I can't explain it. It was like I had this revelation. These horrible things that happen to me aren't my fault. I just need to take back control of my life."

I look at her, trying to work out if she's lying to me or if she's being truthful. Granted, I don't know her well enough, but I see myself in her. I know deep down how she feels. I had that same epiphany as well. I left my parents' house that day and never looked back.

"This is all because of my father," she says, leaning back, her shoulders stiffening. "He's the reason that I'm the way that I am. I was a happy and trusting child until his betrayal. It destroyed me, destroyed my mom." She looks up at me now. "Am I wrong for never wanting to feel that same pain again?"

"Of course not," I tell her.

"I know this may sound strange," she says. "But do you mind staying over in this house tonight? I don't really want to be alone right now."

I nod eagerly. If I wasn't taking her to the hospital, I was going to insist on staying with her through the night. She needs to be monitored to make sure she means what she says and she's okay. Not to mention the severe concussion that she just got. "Absolutely."

She smiles, relieved. "Thank you. You are such a good friend," she says, extending her hand to me. I hold it and give it a gentle squeeze.

"Do you ever feel haunted by your past?" She looks at me. "Like no matter how much you try to run from it, it always catches up with you?"

An involuntary laugh escapes my throat. "You have no idea," I tell her.

Chapter Twelve
Sadie

I come out of my shock like I had just stepped out of a cold plunge. What was I thinking? I almost died out there.

Thank goodness for Natalie. She really came through for me.

My stomach rumbles loudly and Natalie looks at me.

"Would you like me to order us some food?" Natalie asks.

I feel suddenly famished. I want something that I haven't allowed myself in a long time. Carbs. I turn and look at her. "I would love some spaghetti," I tell her. "Can I make us some?"

"Sounds great," Natalie says, relief on her face that I have an appetite.

I stand up, almost feeling lighter. By releasing the burden off my shoulders, I feel as if I've cleansed myself of my sins and out of the ocean came a new person.

I open the cabinet and pull out a pot and begin to fill it in the sink with water. I look at Natalie. She's about to say something but thinks better of it. "Go get your things," I say. "I promise I won't do anything drastic."

She considers this for a moment. "I'll be right back," she says.

I nod, opening the pantry to find a box of pasta and a jar of sauce.

Once I hear the front door close, I run upstairs. I feel salty and sticky and could really use a shower. I quickly wash myself, trying desperately to scrub off . . . I don't know what . . . guilt? Mortification? Everything that I have put myself through, this poor woman through. Someone I wanted so desperately to like me and instead I come off like a complete lunatic.

You're losing control, I think to myself. *You've got to keep it together.*

When my skin can't take the scalding hot shower any longer, I redress my bandages, thinking about all that has happened in the last few days, let alone the last two weeks. I know that Natalie has seen the bandage on my arm. She hasn't asked me about it though, which makes me think she is assuming Tom had something to do with it. I'm glad she didn't question me. If I had to tell her Tom stabbed me, that would really drive her away. Obviously, she wouldn't want to stick around on the property of a violent man who just got out of the psychiatric ward of a hospital.

But I know Tom better than he knows himself and, trust me, this will never happen again.

I need to fix this. Make sure Natalie knows that everything is all right. It's all about keeping up appearances, I think as I change into a blue loungewear set. I pull my wet hair into a bun and apply some fresh makeup, trying to cover my puffy eyes. Trying once again to mask the real me and stuff her deep inside, but traces of her are still there, the pain obvious behind my eyes.

I come downstairs, turning on the stove to boil the water. As I wait, a chill runs up my spine and I decide to go back by the fireplace, slightly tripping over my wet clothes. I glance down to see the picture of Cassie.

I try to push her out of my mind, but it keeps coming back, like some sort of purgatory; she won't let me forget her betrayal, never.

My mind finds its way back to Cassie, when she first arrived two weeks ago. The beginning of the end.

"You're here!" I called, seeing Cassie perched on the steps that lead to the beach. Cassie had said she'd come in the morning, but it was almost four. Typical Cassie time. You know not to hold your breath for her.

Cassie was wearing a fiery red sundress with large black sunglasses, her brown hair waving furiously in the wind. Her arms waved eagerly until I'd climbed the steps from the beach to greet her as they wrapped tightly around me.

"I've missed you so much!" she cried, rocking my body back and forth. I smiled, my arms around her tiny frame.

I pulled away when I saw a small boy behind her, standing awkwardly, looking down at his feet. His brown bowl cut shone in the sun.

Cassie, seeing my expression turned. "Owen." She waved an arm. "Come here and meet mommy's oldest friend Sadie."

I bent down to reach his level. "Hi, Owen."

"Hi," he said, without looking directly at me. Instead, he assessed his surroundings, focusing on the house behind him.

Cassie stepped back to put an arm around him. "This is my son," she said it with a smile, but her voice was weary, as if expecting some sort of judgment from me.

"I had assumed as much," I admitted.

Cassie bent down to Owen. "Owen, did you want to get your bathing suit out of the car and go for a swim?"

He nodded his head and smiled. Cassie pulled the keys to her blue Subaru from the back pocket of her jeans and hit a button several times until the car made a beeping noise. "It's in the back seat," she called to him as he started to run to the car.

Cassie then turned back to me, her expression serious.

"I still don't understand how you couldn't tell me," I said.

"I was afraid of what you might think."

I looked at her, confused. "What do you mean?"

She shook her head.

If she wasn't going to give me answers, then I was going to be blunt. "Who's the father?"

Cassie shrugged her shoulders and again I wasn't surprised. Like mother like daughter.

"You're judging me, aren't you?" Cassie said a little defensively.

"No, of course not." I closed the gap between Cassie and me. "It's that I'm hurt that you left me for all those years. We've been through so much together; I'm just upset that you couldn't talk to me, and you had to go through it all alone."

I looked over at Owen holding a pair of yellow swim trunks in his hand as he made his way back toward us. "I would've helped you; you know."

"I know," Cassie said like a sulking teenager. "I'm making excuses. The truth is, I was scared, and I didn't know what I was going to do. All I know is that I . . ." She trailed off.

"Mom, where can I change?" Owen held up his trunks.

"Why don't I show you both where you will be staying," I said, glad to finally have a use for the guest house.

We walked across the lawn, the wind strong but the sun still hot. I could feel it burning my skin. "Make sure to put on sunscreen," I said as I opened the French doors of the back porch.

"Whoa, look at this place," Owen said, his jaw practically on the floor. "It's huge."

Cassie gave a slightly embarrassed laugh.

I pointed to the door under the front hall steps. "There is a bathroom right here where you can change," I told him. Then I looked to Cassie. "There are beach and pool towels in this hutch right on the porch."

She looked back at it. "Thank you, Sadie," she said sincerely, squeezing my arm. "Look, I know I haven't been the best friend I always promised to be, but I intend on making that up now." Her eyes lifted from the floor to me.

I nodded, understanding. "No more secrets," I told her.

"No more secrets."

I hugged her tightly, her arms locked around mine, making up for all that lost time. All those hugs we didn't get to have, all those moments that could've become wonderful memories, lost.

"Well, let me give you some time to get settled and you can come over when you're ready."

Cassie nodded and I saw myself out.

I spotted Tom sitting on the back porch in a pair of jeans and a white linen button-down. He looked relaxed in a wooden rocking chair, his ankle over his knee, a cigar in his hand and a glass of scotch on the armrest.

I felt my back go rigid. Tom was drinking again, and something about the way he had been watching us made me realize this wasn't his first glass.

I climbed the porch and stopped next to him. The cigar smoke bothered me, but I forced myself not to swat it away. "Are you going to be okay?"

He brushed his hair to the side, fixing it from the wind, and stared at me through his tortoiseshell reading glasses. I noted the book he had on the side table next to him, George Orwell's *1984*. I had tried to persuade him that it probably wasn't the best book for him to read, but he insisted he wanted to be educated on the classics.

"Am I going to be okay?" He stubbed his cigar out and stood up. "I guess we'll see."

I pull myself from the memory and head into the kitchen, just as Natalie is opening the French doors. Her face relaxes when she sees me in the hallway, her panic subsiding.

"I was just about to put the pasta in," I tell her. She follows me into the kitchen. She has changed into a sweatshirt and mismatched yoga pants, but it doesn't seem like she has showered. A duffel bag is strapped across her body, and she swings it off herself, placing it down in the hall.

"Can I help you with anything?" she asks, awkwardly. Suddenly going back to formalities as if she didn't just pull my unconscious body from the ocean.

"You've done more than enough." I laugh, pointing a ladle at her and motioning toward a stool at the counter. "Just make yourself comfortable."

She agrees, perching herself on the stool closest to me.

We sit in silence as I pull out two pasta bowls, not sure where to go from here. I'd spilled my life to her, all jumbled and haphazard. I can only imagine what she's thinking right now.

I hear my timer go off and I grab two potholders off the counter and gently pour the boiling water through the strainer I have in the sink. The steam blooms like smoke in the aftermath of an explosion.

"Can I ask you something?" I say after we are settled with our bowls of pasta.

"Sure," she answers, twirling her fork.

"When we first met," I start, "I got the sense that something bad had happened to you, and not just the accident." I hesitate for a moment to gauge her reaction.

She bites her lower lip as if bracing herself.

"And just now," I press on, "you alluded to it again when I asked if the past still haunts you."

She drops her head, as a look of trepidation washes over her.

"You don't have to tell me," I say quickly. "I just wanted to know . . ." I trail off, trying to think of the right words. "How do you deal with it?"

She gives a slight laugh, as if she feels she is hardly dealing with it, so to speak. She wipes her face with a napkin and sets it back down on her lap.

"One of the reasons that this trauma is hitting you now is because it happened at a time in your life when your young mind was incapable of processing it all. Not only that, but your environment doesn't seem like it allowed for it either. That happened to me as well. Now that we are mature, our repressed memories are resurfacing in the hopes that we can address it properly and let it go."

"That makes a lot of sense," I say. My mind is churning this over. "I don't know why I didn't think of it. I'm a psychiatrist, yet it's as if a few years out of practice has made me rusty." I look up at her. "Then again, maybe you just need to hear things from someone else."

There is silence for a few minutes, nothing but metal utensils scraping against porcelain plates.

"I guess I sometimes feel alone in it all. Like no one else understands what I'm going through."

"I understand more than you know," Natalie says.

I look at her surprised.

Something changes in her expression as if contemplating whether or not to tell me. "I know what you mean when you say you feel you are the reason your mom killed herself," she begins. "Because my parents blame me for the death of my brother." She pauses. "They are convinced I killed him."

Chapter Thirteen

Natalie

There's a catch in my throat, as if trying to stop me from saying the words out loud. They are words that I have never uttered to a single person before. Not even my husband.

"Are you okay?" Sadie asks me.

I swallow a thick pool of saliva that had been building in my throat. Whether my accident had shaken the memories loose from my mind, there was no more ignoring it. The problem was it was right in front of me now. Showing up in apparitions that I can't escape from. I had to tell the truth. Like Sadie, I need to tell someone. Maybe then I will be free of the hauntings of my childhood and be allowed to live my life.

I was in the back seat of my parents' station wagon. My father was driving and my brother Danny was seated next to me, holding his teddy bear. I was eight years old; he was six. It was a rainy day, I remember. The drops of the rain were coming down so hard you could hear them thumping loudly on the hood of the car. Danny was a good kid. He was bright and funny, almost always happy with his mop of brown hair and splash of freckles across his cheeks. I was quiet, more reserved. I don't know now if it was an early onset of hormones or not, but my demeanor had switched from reserved to moody, or rather I'd just started talking back. I was in this stage in my life, where I felt more mature than I was. I wanted to be cool; I wanted to wear makeup and dress up. I wanted to be grown up.

My parents were strict. I just wanted to be girly. My mother, on the other hand, was the opposite of everything I wanted to be, which was what made us constantly battle one another. I don't think my mother ever wore makeup. Her wardrobe was relatively simple. I had never seen her get dressed up fancy. She said things like that were frivolous. My mother was practical, to a fault. Her hair was dark brown, cut at shoulder length. She let it dry naturally after a shower, and fortunately for her, it dried straight. But I remember she always had gray in her hair, and she never did anything to fix it, so she always appeared older than I would've thought. One time I had said that my mother was seventy when she was only forty-one. She thought I was being facetious, but I really didn't understand age at that point and how to judge someone based on that.

"She's going to be a wild one," I had overheard her say once about me. There was no joking manner in the way she had said it.

But Danny, he was my mother's favorite. Her bright, shining boy who represented that age of innocence still. He wanted to please her, and it didn't take much because he was their prince who could do no wrong.

I had loved Danny too. Everyone seems to forget that. My favorite memory was when I would sneak into his room after we were supposed to be in bed. I'd have several books in one hand and a flashlight in the other. His eyes would light up in delight as he lifted the spread, and we'd camp under his quilt. I was teaching him how to read, each of us taking turns on each page. When we messed up a word or didn't know what it was, like the game Mad Libs, we would replace it with another word, like unicorn, which would cause us to break into fits of laughter. She didn't know it, but I remember hearing my mother on the other side of my brother's door, laughing too.

Eventually she'd step in and tell me time for bed, but not before I would turn back to Danny with a smirk on my face and our eyes communicating that we would do it all over again tomorrow.

My father, however, didn't seem to have much to say. By that I mean, not in his marriage, not in the way he parented, or even in conversation in general. He was just always there, as if sitting back and observing his family like he was simply watching a play. All of us acting it out in front of him. I never once remember my mother asking for his help or his opinion on anything, and he seemed content in this role. He was a good-looking man. He had a thick head of hair, an all-year-round tan and a bright smile. He was in advertising and commuted to the city. He also traveled a lot, but none of us seemed to notice whether he was home or not. It all seemed the same to us.

I never would've considered my father a happy man. He stayed inside himself, becoming successfully invisible. And that seemed to work. My mother didn't notice him smelling like perfume when she didn't wear any, or pouring drink after drink, so long as he was sitting there in silence. In fact, I don't know if she even noticed him at all.

That rainy day had been the first time my mother had asked my father to do something. She'd gotten violently ill the night before and she needed my father to drive Danny and me to church, because none of us could ever miss church. My father begrudgingly brought us, even though this was likely the first time he had ever gone to church with us, or ever.

Danny and I weren't interested in what the priest had to say. For the most part we didn't know what he was talking about. So, we played games quietly with one another. I spy, thumb war, anything that would keep us entertained. Our giggles weren't as subtle as we would've hoped, which led to sharp-toned hushes from our father, who became increasingly irritated with us. So much so, that he left us there, several times, his breath smelling thickly like cinnamon when he'd return. I had always thought it was a mint of some sort, but when I smelled Goldschläger for the first time it had triggered something in me that ached deep in my chest.

By the time church had gotten out, he was downright fed up.

"Just wait until your mother hears about this." His tone was directed at me. Everything was always my fault. I was the older one; I was supposed to be the more responsible one. It had been pouring down with rain, but he wasn't going to waste any more time with us than he had to. Grabbing both of our hands, he pulled us through the torrential rain into the car where we were instructed to buckle ourselves in.

Despite my father's frustration, Danny and I didn't seem to notice, or care much. We continued to play, until one accused the other of cheating. A fight broke out between us. I told him to stop acting like such a baby when he started to whine. I pulled the bear that he had left in the car before church out of his hands. This made him wail in a pitch so loud that my father snapped his head back, reaching for me to rip the bear from my grip. But he hadn't been paying attention to the road. He didn't see the red light he ran. He couldn't stop because the downpour of rain had created a slick river running down the road, which caused us to hydroplane. I reached out for Danny's hand, both of us terrified. There was nothing any of us could have done as a fully loaded dump truck slid as well, slamming into Danny's side door. Our car was crushed like an accordion, before we were flipped upside down.

Then suddenly, everything was quiet. I had my eyes closed and I was afraid to open them. I knew then, deep inside myself, that something was terribly wrong. That this was a moment that would change our lives forever. I just didn't know yet what that meant.

I heard the groan of my father slowly coming to.

"Danny," I barely whispered. We were all still suspended, hanging upside down. I couldn't turn my head, but I wouldn't have wanted to. Our hands dangled loosely above our heads. I remember seeing a smear of deep red that wasn't there before, and a single tooth sitting in a pool of it. Then everything went dark.

Chapter Fourteen

Sadie

That night I feel itchy in my own skin. Restless, but at the same time still comforted by the fact that when I look over, Natalie is there, pretending to be asleep on the couch in our bedroom, a throw blanket tossed over her.

I hate to admit it, but when she told me her tragic story, I was happy. I've never met anyone before with a past like mine. I had plenty of them as my patients, but in there, you must keep the lines very clear.

There was that one time though, where I allowed things to get blurry. I think about Jason. He was sixteen trying to get emancipated from his parents.

He was troubled, but not in the way most people think. Rather he was smart. Too smart. He knew how to manipulate people, including me.

He had everyone believing he was someone he wasn't. He had fed me story after story relating to his father's double life and his depressed suicidal mother. I remember listening to his narrative on the edge of my seat. I felt like he was reaching into my soul, showing me the emotions that I should've had when dealing with the exact same issues. He gave me hope for my own situation. He was bright and optimistic about his life, and I remember writing to the judge with the utmost praise for him. To emancipate him from his family would be the best decision the judge could allow.

It wasn't until after that I found out it was all lies. We had our last session, and I learned that Jason had done his research on me. He knew about my past, and he fed it right back to me.

He'd forged emails from his father's account, creating the exchange of an affair, through a false email Jason himself was on the other end of. Jason even went as far as drugging his mom, calling an ambulance and claiming she'd tried to kill herself after she saw the emails.

He showed me the scars, then, on his body, admitting to causing them himself. But doing it properly, so as to not make it obvious they were self-inflicted. Then he'd call the cops on his father, claiming he had attacked him.

I cursed myself for getting swindled. It was my job to do more of a thorough background check, not just with him but with his family. It was then that I would've known right away his parents weren't who he claimed they were. They were good people, who just didn't know how to handle their unruly son. That's when I lost my job and my license.

I should have been infuriated and I was, but I found myself also admiring him. He had his reasons, and he executed them perfectly. The last I heard he had invented a gaming app that he had sold for millions.

I think of what Natalie told me tonight. I wonder how much of it is true. It wasn't so similar to my story that I would have my suspicions, but upon hearing my story and suffering an accident like hers, could she have just made it up? Like a bad recurring dream that she's somehow made her reality?

I can tell that my fretfulness is keeping her alert, so I try to meditate, to make my mind as blank as possible so that I can rest.

But every time I close my eyes, I see Cassie.

I eventually fall asleep, but my mind slips into a dream, replaying the slow churn of Cassie's presence getting more and more dangerous in our lives.

That second day, Cassie, Owen and I had settled on the beach. The day was beautiful and calm with only a soft breeze. A large fishing boat sped past in the distance, leaving a white foam ripple in its wake.

I was catching up with Cassie while Owen was building a sandcastle with a new bag of plastic molded buckets that I had picked up at the local dollar store before she got into town.

Despite my plea for Tom to find something else to do today and for the next few until she left, Tom appeared at the top of the steps, his bare chest covered with white streaks of sunscreen and a towel over one shoulder. It was as if he was testing me. Making his presence as prominent as possible just to watch me squirm with unease.

I noticed Cassie turn and stared a bit longer than she should've behind her glasses.

I wasn't blind. I knew Tom was a good-looking man.

Tom's muscles were still toned and tan. He kept himself in good shape. His teeth were pearly white, but that was because of his veneers. They give him a star-like quality.

"Hey, Tom." Cassie smiled brightly, standing up with her arms outstretched.

"Cassie." Tom grinned, and it was as if he had shed his former skin and stepped into someone completely different. As he hurried down the steps to greet her, he winced jokingly at the hot-baked sand burning his soft bare feet.

"Toughen up, big guy," she mocked him playfully.

"Who's this?" He looked over at Owen, who continued with his castle.

"This is Owen." She walked over to him and bent down, whispering in his ear to look up and say hi.

"Hi," Owen said, his eyes squinting from the sunlight.

"Yours?" Tom asked.

"Stop it." She pushed on his chest. "Of course he's mine. It's not like I picked him up at a store or anything."

"Never quite sure," he had said teasingly.

"Oh, hush." She touched his chest again to give him a playful shove. I forced a smile through my teeth. *Surely, she can't still be doing this*, I thought and wondered if she was doing it purposefully. For Tom, I knew what the intention was. It was to hurt me.

"Oh." Cassie picked up a foam board from behind her chair. "Can you teach Owen how to boogie board?"

"Sure." Tom shrugged, a little taken aback, but of course I knew he'd do it in order to keep up with the lighthearted vibe he was constructing. "Owen, have you ever taken a ride on one of these before?"

Owen looked up from his sandcastle. He shook his head.

"Do you want to learn?" Tom picked it up to show him.

Owen shrugged, indifferent to the idea, and there was a shimmer of hope in me that the suggestion could just die right then and there.

"Come on." Tom cocked his head. "It will be fun."

Owen stood up in agreement. I watched as Tom and Owen made their way into the ocean. Tom with his hand on Owen, guiding him over the waves, while the other hand grabbed the rubber strap.

"Aw, isn't this so sweet?" Cassie said after watching Tom prop Owen on the board and explain to him how to read the waves.

I nodded and smiled tightly, but there was an ache in my heart.

A large wave rose from the ocean and Cassie and I both stood up, nervous that it was too big for Owen. But Tom lined him up and pushed him anyway. He rode the wave, staying on top of it even as it crashed down.

Owen smiled broadly as the three of us cheered him on as he rode his first wave all the way to the beach.

"Great job, Owen!" Cassie called.

"That was amazing!" Tom yelled from the water. "Do you want to go again?"

Owen agreed more eagerly this time.

"Then let's go." Tom waved him back into the water.

"This is so great," Cassie said, smiling. "Owen really doesn't have a decent male figure in his life, and I think it's wonderful that he gets to do some boy stuff with Tom."

I shouldn't have been upset. It was a great thing for Owen to have a father figure in his life. I just didn't want it to be Tom.

"Are you seeing anyone?" I tried to press.

Cassie shook her head.

"Any recent relationships?" From what I could remember, Cassie never in her life had a serious relationship. I hoped that wasn't still the case. For Owen's sake she really did need to start getting her life in order. Stay in one place and keep the people in Owen's life a constant.

Cassie of all people should have known how hectic and frustrating that life is. It was hard for her. Then again, we all tend to repeat our history, don't we?

"I did just get out of a bad relationship," she admitted, settling in the blue beach chair next to mine.

"What happened?"

"He was like every other guy I date." She rolled her eyes. "I keep making the same mistakes over and over."

"What do you mean?"

"I thought he was a decent guy, came from a rich family, charming—you know all of that." She circled a finger in the air. "Then his drug habits just started getting worse.

He'd come home from the office coked out and just angry. I had to teach Owen how to hide and sneak around, just to avoid being in his eyesight. The slightest things would set him off and then he'd get violent."

"Why didn't you leave?"

Cassie shrugged. "I tried. I called the cops but with his slew of lawyers he didn't stay locked up for long. That's when I knew I just had to walk away for good."

"Jeeze, Cassie," is all I managed.

"I know," she said as if asking me to spare her the therapist spiel. "I need to stop repeating the same mistakes and create a more stable, happy life for Owen. I know. That is my plan," she started. "My first step is connecting with family." She reached for my hand and grabbed it.

I smiled.

"I would love it if you and Tom were a part of Owen's life."

Instinctively I pulled my hand away. Cassie looked at me strangely and I hit my hand pretending that I was swatting at some sort of bug.

Part of me was flattered that she wanted me to be part of Owen's life.

My jaw was so tight I worried that my teeth would crack under the pressure.

Cassie didn't really know about my life with Tom behind closed doors. No one did, because I knew people would judge. But the truth was, you can't judge the inside of another person's marriage. Everyone has their faults. There is no such thing as the perfect couple. It's just a matter of tolerance, how far you are willing to go before you or the other one snaps.

Tom and I had been in this locked-horns situation for some time now and neither one of us was done with the other yet.

"Mom, I'm hungry," Owen said as he came out of the ocean, standing over Cassie so closely that he was dripping water all over her legs. She seemed unfazed by it.

"I'll go back and make you a sandwich," she suggested, standing up.

"I'll come with you," I said.

"You boys have fun," Cassie yelled to Tom who was coming out of the ocean. "We'll be right back."

I followed Cassie up the steps, feeling Tom's eyes on me, wanting to see if he was successful in getting a rise out of me.

"Do you have any peanut butter? Sorry I'll go grocery shopping and stock up this afternoon."

"It's no problem. I already did it for you."

Cassie looked relieved. She hugged me again. "You're a good friend."

I led Cassie into our house, coming quickly around the corner, when I ran directly into Shar.

I jumped in surprise as she stared at me, horrified. "I'm sorry, ma'am."

"It's fine," I said a bit too harshly and continued on my way to the kitchen, my hands trembling as I opened the door to the walk-in pantry to the left of the stove.

As I returned triumphantly with the peanut butter and a loaf of whole-wheat bread, I stopped dead in my tracks. Cassie looked at me as if she had seen a ghost.

"Who was that?" she finally asked.

"My maid," I answered flatly. "Here's the peanut butter." I spilled the contents onto the counter and turned away, avoiding her gaze as I opened another cabinet for a plate.

She continued to stare at me.

"I know what you are going to say," I said, stopping her. "And I don't want to hear it."

Finally, she put her hands up in surrender and started making Owen's sandwich.

The silence remained between us, the tension in the air thick with unanswered questions and unwilling answers. I left the mess for Shar to clean up and was relieved when we stepped back outside, the grass brushing some of the remaining sand off of my feet. The breeze carried the floral scent of the rose garden. I heard Cassie's steps fall in line with mine until they didn't. I stopped and turned to see where she had gone.

"Well, hello," I heard Cassie say flirtatiously behind me as we walked back to the beach.

I saw Riley, bent over the rosebushes, pruning them. He stood up awkwardly, his knees covered in dirt. His height towered over Cassie's small frame.

I hadn't really needed or wanted a garden. I wasn't exactly the nurturing type. But it had already been here when we moved in and with Riley's interest in it, I knew it wouldn't fall into ruins. The lone cement bench was underneath an arbor in the middle of this two-hundred-square-foot space, lined with tall hedges like a small maze. It sat between the two houses and provided a bit of privacy to avoid being able to see wholly into the guest house. I'd never thought much of it, but occasionally I'd find myself sitting on that bench. Hiding from Tom, or from the world really.

"Well, aren't you a tall drink of water." Cassie laughed, lowering her sunglasses to check him up and down.

Riley smiled nervously.

"You work here?" she asked, even though the answer was obvious.

He nodded, lowering his head to the ground.

She smiled. "Well, I'll be keeping an eye out for you, gorgeous. Might need that strong pair of hands." She blew him a kiss, then wiggled her fingers at him in a flirtatious wave.

"What are you doing?" I whispered harshly to her when we were out of earshot.

"What?" She shrugged her shoulders. "Just having a little fun."

I rolled my eyes as my heart sank in my chest. Cassie would never change, no matter what she said.

"I mean it, Cassie, leave Riley alone."

Chapter Fifteen

Natalie

"Coffee?"

I open one eye to see Sadie standing over me with two mugs in her hands. The sun is backlighting her, giving her an almost angelic appeal.

"Thanks," I say, yawning and sitting up. "What time is it?"

Sadie turns her head, looking at the clock on her nightstand. "Eight. I wasn't sure if you had more appointments today and didn't want you to oversleep."

"My first appointment is at ten," I tell her. "But thank you for waking me. I do have prep work to take care of."

I sit up and swing my legs off the white fabric couch that I slept on. It is against the window across from Sadie's bed. I haven't slept much since I was keeping an eye on her. On top of checking in with her regarding her concussion, every creak I heard in the house woke me up with a surge of adrenaline, worried that Sadie might try to harm herself while I was asleep. I had just laid there, awake, watching the gray light creep through the gap in the white curtains.

At least I didn't have any hallucinations this time.

But as I look at her now, she seems to have slept very soundly and appears in a good state this morning. She's already showered and is ready for the day, wearing a white mid-length dress. The only disheveled thing, really, is her room. Her clothes are strewn across the floor and there is makeup all over the bathroom counter. I notice some liquid foundation has spilled over and it surprises me that someone as put together as Sadie doesn't make more of a point of tidying up after herself. Of course, I know she has a maid, but even I don't think I could let things get to this level of disarray. Then I have to remind myself of the events of last night. Clearly Sadie wasn't in a frame of mind to worry about what her house looked like.

Sadie sits down next to me, handing over the mug. "Thank you again for saving me last night. I didn't realize just how low I'd gotten."

"I'm glad you're okay. And I appreciate you for telling me about your family. I'm sure that wasn't easy for you."

"Telling a friend does make it easier."

Are we friends now? I guess so, and despite the events that brought us to her kitchen last night, it was helpful for me to unburden myself as well. Our tortured pasts have created a sort of kinship between us. A bond that I've never had with anyone before. Sadie and I live in very different worlds, but somehow beneath the surface, we really aren't that different.

"I'm here if you need anything." I smile.

"Thanks again for not telling your husband about last night."

I nod regretfully. When Luke had called to check in, Sadie urged me to let it go to voicemail. She explained that she didn't want anyone to know what happened. It was a mistake she vows never to make again.

"Let's just consider that what happened tonight never happened, for either one of us," I had told her.

"Right," she had said, her eyes narrowing on mine. She understood that if I was going to keep her secret, she needed to keep mine. For starters, it wouldn't look too good that I didn't have Sadie checked into a hospital. But also, Luke didn't know about Danny. I had never told him because it was too painful. I still didn't want to bring myself to tell him. He would try to fix me, when I can only fix myself. What I needed was someone who would just listen and leave it at that. While he had the best intentions, Luke didn't understand that. You can't when you come from a loving family. That's why telling Sadie last night was cathartic. Despite her psychiatry background, she's not trying to fix me. Only understand that this is a part of what makes me who I am.

After listening to Luke's voicemail, I had texted back, assuring him I was okay and having dinner with Sadie. I would talk to him tomorrow. I knew otherwise he would worry.

I look at my phone and reread his text from last night.

I'm glad to see you two are getting along and looking out for each other.

Looking out for one another—he had no idea the extent of it.

Sadie's maid arrived and is already cleaning last night's dishes that are in the sink. I tried to clean up, but Sadie put a firm hand on my wrist, stopping me. She was insistent that it was Shar's job. Still, I can't help but wince an apology as I place my empty coffee mug next to the sink. Knowing Sadie's no longer alone, I leave her house, eager to swim before my appointments. Now that there is someone else in the house, it gives me the assurance that Sadie won't be able to try anything if she has any more suicidal thoughts, though somehow, I doubt that will be a problem.

Most of the time, I'm wary of suicide victims when they tell me they won't try again. But it seems different with Sadie. It is almost like she needed to get it out of her system and now she has no inklings of ever doing it again. I almost wonder if maybe it was less of a suicide attempt and more of a cry for help.

I slow my speed when I see Riley coming around from the back of the guest house. There isn't any sort of equipment in his hand and I'm wondering what he's doing. He hasn't noticed me and I catch him looking in the window again.

So, I wasn't crazy. He did peer into the house last night.

"Do you need something?" I ask, startling him.

He turns around but doesn't answer me.

Then with heavy, determined steps he keeps his narrowed eyes focused on me as he walks with a look of resolve. I think about how forcefully he had grabbed me on that first day. I flinch as if bracing myself, but he walks right past me, continuing toward the front of the property.

I'm too stunned to call after him, so instead, I hurry into the house. I go to grab a banana out of the fruit bowl when I'm surprised to find they are all gone. I look around in confusion, wondering if I somehow moved them somewhere else without thinking. I even check the fridge.

I did tell Luke to get bananas, didn't I?

Then I realized that I didn't, but that was because there were already some bananas in the fruit bowl.

Technically, the bananas were Riley's. Did he take them back? If so, how did he get into the house? I specifically remember locking it. Then my insides roll nervously as it hits me; he likely has a key.

The idea of it makes me uneasy. I make a note that maybe I can talk to Sadie about it although her insistence on him being harmless makes me fear she won't do anything. I need to figure out how I can better secure these doors. I look out the window, scanning the property for Riley, but he's nowhere in sight.

I settle on an orange instead, then go upstairs to change into my swimwear.

My phone rings and I see that it's Luke.

"Hi," I answer.

"How was last night?"

"It was great," I lie.

"I'm glad to hear it."

"We have a lot more in common than I would've expected," I admit, knowing he'll want me to say more.

"That's a relief," Luke says. "To be honest, I was worried you were going to lock yourself in the house the whole time, but the fact that you went out and socialized on your own, that's huge. I'm really proud of you."

"Please don't patronize me." It comes out of my mouth before I even realize I've said it.

"I'm not trying to." His voice fades in frustration. "Is there nothing I can do right?"

"I'm sorry, it just feels like you treat me like a child sometimes."

"These past six months, they've been hard for both of us. I'm trying to compliment how far you've come. Stop making me the enemy."

"I'm sorry," I admit. I'm so afraid of losing him, yet all I seem to do is push him away. "It's just that I told you, I'm in a good place now. I think the break from the city has helped," I say though it's only partially true. Some aspects are, but then at the same time I think the change of environment is what's causing my hallucinations to return. No longer just shadows and quiet auditory whispers, but full-fledged people, and ghosts.

"Good," he says, a bit distracted. "I have another meeting I'm running to right now, but I just wanted to check in."

"I'm fine," I say. "Everything going well on your end?" I want to leave things on a lighter note.

"So far," he says, preoccupied yet again. "Anyway, they are all going in now, so I've got to run. I love you."

"Love you too," I say, thinking about all the unsaid things that are waiting in the wings.

I hang up the phone, my heart weighted down like an anchor.

I come in after my swim, creating a mental checklist in my head of the patients that I have this morning and the reason for the appointments. I'm not paying much attention as I climb the stairs until I reach the upstairs hallway and notice that the floor is wet. I check my own legs, pretty sure that I dried off well outside before coming in. I follow the trail of water that seems to come from the hall bathroom, across the carpet and into the guest bedroom. I look up, wondering if there is a leak in the ceiling given the extensive amount of rain we've had lately, but I don't see anything. When I turn on the bathroom light, I can already feel the humidity of the room, like someone had just stepped out of the shower. My body tenses when I notice that is exactly what happened. The glass of the shower is fogged up. The only explanation is that Riley must've been in to take a shower. I look down the hall.

"Is anyone up here?" I call, my skin crawling like I'm prey looking for a predator.

Silence.

Enough of this, I think to myself. I'm going to get dressed and quickly tell Sadie about all of this before my appointments. Riley cannot be coming into the house showering and taking food.

I'm about to angrily turn the light off and storm out when I notice something on the shower door. It's starting to fade, but it's still there. Someone had dragged their finger against the fogged glass. I step in closer, tilting my head, trying to decipher the fading image. It looks like waves with two stick-figure hands sticking out of them.

Like someone drowning.

Then underneath it, the numbers 6666.

I shiver involuntarily.

I turn back toward the mirror, which is also fogged up, and stop dead in my tracks, my eyes wide like saucers. Because the words spelled out on the mirror in childlike letters are not as complicated to understand. They are a direct threat.

I run out of the house, my towel wrapped around my shoulders, as I hurry barefoot across the lawn to Sadie's house.

I bang loudly and urgently on the front door.

Shar answers, giving me a puzzled look at my appearance, still in my bathing suit.

"I need to speak to Sadie, please."

"Natalie?" I see Sadie coming down the steps, looking at me with concern. "Are you okay? You look upset."

Damn right I am.

"I need to talk to you about Riley."

At this point the maid has retreated to the kitchen and Sadie waves a hand for me to come inside. When I stay right where I am, she joins me on the porch and closes the door behind her.

"What about him?"

"I think he's been using your guest house for his own personal use. The kitchen was full of snacks and fruit when we first got here."

Sadie nods listening intently.

"Then when I went for a swim, I came back inside and found that some of the fruit was gone and someone had just used the guest shower."

She cocks her head at me confused.

"Like literally just used. The bathroom was still humid, and the floor was wet."

Sadie's eyes widen in surprise.

"Not only that," I add. "But he had written a message on the mirror that he obviously wanted me to see."

"What did it say?" Her arms are crossed as she leans forward, intrigued.

"Get out."

Sadie furrows her brow. "That seems so absurd," she says in a way that shows me she's not accusing me of lying. "Why would Riley do that?"

"I think that he used that guest house more than you might've known and he's mad that we're there." A breeze picks up and I feel a chill run up my spine. I wrap the towel tighter around my shoulders. "Can you please talk to him? And ask him to give you his key, at least until we leave?"

"Of course," she says, worried. "I wasn't even aware Riley had a key, but I wasn't ever too concerned before. That had to have been terrifying. I'm so sorry." She reaches for my hand now. A stack of diamonds on her ring finger catches the light. "Do you want to stay here in this house until Luke gets back?"

She's being earnest and I appreciate it. Part of me would like to, but I really need to start practicing my independence, which I could do so long as I didn't have to worry about a groundskeeper breaking in all the time.

"I'll be fine," I tell her. "Just talk to him for me, please?"

"I'll do that right now," she says, following me off the porch. "I'll go find him." She puts her hand in front of her eyes to block the sun. "Wait isn't it Tuesday?" she asks.

"Yes," I say.

"Riley isn't supposed to be here on Tuesdays."

"He was here though—I caught him peering into my windows when I was walking back from your house earlier."

"Oh my gosh," she says. "I'll let you know as soon as I find him."

I hurry back to the house, slamming the front door with a loud thud.

"If anyone is in this house, I suggest you leave now," I call out.

All is quiet.

I do a quick sweep of all the rooms to assure myself no one is here anymore. Then finally I take a quick shower, locking the bathroom door as I do so.

I emerge ten minutes later, dressed, and do another check of the rooms.

I find Sadie coming up the back porch.

I open the door to greet her. She shrugs her shoulders and shakes her head. "I don't see him anywhere." She puts up a hand, reassuring me. "But don't worry, I will talk to him."

"Thank you," I tell her.

She checks her watch. "I have to run into town, but I will call him. Do you need anything?"

I shake my head.

"Let me know if you change your mind." Sadie smiles. "Oh, let me give you my phone number."

We exchange numbers. "I am really sorry about all of this," she says again. "Hey, maybe we can grab coffee, sometime in between your appointments this afternoon."

"I'm pretty much back-to-back all day," I explain then immediately feel guilty as I watch her smile fade. Don't get me wrong, I like Sadie, but she's a bit much and after last night I could use the break. "Perhaps tomorrow?" I suggest.

She smiles. "That would be great." She waves as she steps off the porch and I close the door behind her.

I stand in silence for a moment, waiting to hear something, anything. Part of me wonders if maybe it was a figment of my imagination. I take a deep inhalation, climbing up the steps. I don't know what would be worse. If it's still actually there or if my mind made it all up.

I clench my jaw and tighten my grip on the railing, wondering if I've made a fool of myself.

At the top of the stairs, I hold my breath, again waiting to hear something. But it's silent. I take the next few steps to the bathroom, my eyes closed, afraid to look. But I know before I open my eyes that it's real. I can already feel the humidity still hanging in the air. I turn on the light and stare at the mirror. The message is not only still there, but it looks even more sinister now as the letters bleed and fade away.

Chapter Sixteen

Sadie

I walk away from Natalie's house, my blood boiling. What the hell did Riley think he was doing? He's going to ruin my chances at a friendship with Natalie. Our heart-to-heart last night has finally put us in a good place. What is this new obsession of his with the guest house? Does he know something I don't? Either way, he's not getting away with this. I'll threaten his job if I have to. He needs to know who's in charge here.

My phone rings and I know that it's the hospital. I take a deep inhalation and this time I answer it. It's been three days, the standard amount of time the hospital will hold someone for a proper psych evaluation.

"Hello," I say casually.

"Mrs. Wilson. This is the Metropolitan Hospital calling. We will need you to come in and sign the papers for your husband's release."

"Right," I say with a slight shake in my voice.

"Do you feel uncomfortable or unsafe picking him up?" the woman on the other line says, lowering her voice into a less annoyed and more serious tone. "We would understand if you did. We would just appreciate another contact if that's the case."

I feel my heart contract again. Natalie is here, I think. I won't be alone. She'll be here to help me. A strength rises back up in me.

"I'll be there shortly."

I hang up, about to leave when it occurs to me that Tom will need fresh clothes. I go into his drawer, pulling out a pair of green athletic shorts and a black T-shirt, when I hear something hard slide to the back of the drawer. Curious, I reach my hand in, feeling around for what it might be. My fingers grip around a chunky piece of plastic and when I pull it out, I stare at it in surprise. It's an iPhone. Ancient-looking, like something out of the early 2000s. Why would Tom be carrying around a phone like this, unless... is this a burner phone? But who has he been calling with it?

I try to turn it on, but the battery is dead. I look at the charging outlet and realize I'm going to need to find the right converter for it.

I'll have to deal with this later.

I return to the hospital, the phone still in my blazer pocket. I'm dying to ask him about it, but then I stop for a moment. I'm a psychiatrist for God's sake. I can't just go in there like a jilted housewife. I know how to handle a crisis. I will need to wait for the right time, or he'll just shut down. Besides, I don't know for sure it's a burner phone. The last thing I should be doing is throwing accusations around right now.

I pick my head up then, stepping through those sliding glass doors with more confidence than the last time.

Tom will not hurt me again; I won't let him. If I do, then he wins, and I can't let that happen. I've worked too damn hard to lose it all now.

I'm prepared to do whatever is necessary.

I reach the seventh floor and the same woman from before is at the desk.

"Mrs. Wilson," she says. "Glad to see you back. The doctor is in his office. He'd appreciate if you met with him first." She gestures this time as I now know the way to go. I nod and continue down the corridor where I see Dr. Turner at his desk filling out some paperwork. The room is fairly dark except for a desk lamp hovered over his papers.

I clear my throat and Dr. Turner picks his head up. "Ah, Mrs. Wilson." He smiles and pushes his chair back to stand up, the metal legs scraping against the linoleum floor. "Thank you for sending over that paperwork. It proved very helpful in our assessment." Then he lowers his eyes. "Based on what you've given me, if you feel unsafe and would prefer twenty-one days on psychiatric evaluation, with these papers we can accommodate that."

"I appreciate that," I say, fighting the internal voice telling me to delay it. "But I don't think any longer will be necessary."

The truth is, I need Tom to know that I am on his side and by pushing his stay, it will come off as a punishment. We need to work on our marriage to get it back to where it used to be. I need him to know that if he listens to me then everything will be okay again.

Dr. Turner looks down at his feet while he sucks in his cheeks, disagreeing but knowing that it's ultimately my decision. "Okay." He leans back toward his desk and pulls out a brown file. He opens it up, handing several papers over to me. "These are the discharge papers," he states, putting his hands on his hips. "There is a plan for him to see a psychiatrist weekly, and we would like to see him a week from now for a follow-up."

"Understood," I say.

"In there is also a prescription for Klonopin, which will mellow him out should he become agitated."

"Thank you, Doctor."

"I know you yourself are a psychiatrist, but I want to reiterate, because it's your husband it's likely best for him to see someone else."

"Oh, of course," I placate, pulling on the sleeve of my linen shirt.

"And as I'm sure you are aware, but I want to make clear," he starts, apologizing for having to go through the motions with me. "When the other personality takes over, be sure not to agitate him. Don't accuse him of not being who he claims to be; just address him in whichever way he wants and keep him calm. That should hopefully alleviate the agitation that could lead to aggression."

I nod and smile, making it clear that I know all of this.

"Very good," he concludes. "Let's go get your husband."

The car ride home is silent. I had turned on the music, just to provide some sort of distraction, but Tom turns it off almost immediately.

The three-day stubble on his chin has grown into a thin beard, with a hint of a reddish tint against the sun. His auburn hair is now wet and matted down from his shower this morning. His eyes are bloodshot like he hasn't slept in days, yet I know he's been sedated.

I reach over and put my hand on his knee.

"It's going to be okay," I tell him. "I love you and we are going to get back to that place we once were."

He looks down at my hand. He doesn't put his hand on mine, but he doesn't try to pull away either.

Every human needs affection. They need love. And if he can't give it to me, I'm at least going to give it to him.

I turn and see him staring back out the window. His profile is still the same from the first day I laid eyes on him.

In an instant I am brought back to that country club, the smell of the pro shop's leathery yet musky scent, like there was a diffuser somewhere in the store made to smell like wealthy men. Cassie had been dating a guy with a membership, at least two decades older than her.

"I booked us a tennis lesson," Cassie said when she called me up one day.

"I can't just go there with you," I said, feeling self-conscious. Although Cassie knew, like herself, I idolized the rich and their fancy country clubs, I had nothing to wear. I could just imagine the looks I'd get wearing old gym shorts and a ratty T-shirt to a tennis lesson.

"I've got his membership card," Cassie said confidently. "He told me to enjoy myself and I'd like to buy you a new tennis outfit from the pro shop."

I remember coming out of the changing room in tennis whites, feeling like a whole new person. I was only twenty-four and the idea of being able to live this type of life seemed damn near impossible.

"Wow, you fit right in." Cassie smiled at me. She was wearing a matching tennis outfit, only hers was hot pink. I remember wanting to tell her that she stood out enough; she didn't need bright colors to do so.

That's when I looked over her shoulder and spotted Tom for the first time. He was at the checkout counter filling out paperwork, wearing a blue golf polo with a silver name tag and navy-blue shorts.

Cassie noticed my far-off look and turned around.

"Holy shit, that's Tom Wilson."

"Who?" I had no idea what she was talking about.

Cassie quickly grabbed my arm and pulled me toward her. "Tom Wilson. The guy is, like, a billionaire."

"He seems too young to be one, and why would he be working here then?"

"He's twenty-five. He's the one whose parents just died last year, and the press accused him of killing his father."

I turned to her, wide-eyed, convinced she was making it all up.

She rolled her eyes at me. "Have you been living under a rock?"

Unlike Cassie who buried her nose in tabloid news, I was studying every psychology book and case study I could get my hands on. Although I'm surprised this missed my radar.

"He didn't do it," she assured me. Then looked back behind me. "At least they can't prove it."

I shushed her, then pulled her into the changing room. "Explain."

Cassie lowered her voice. "Okay so the deal is Tom's father was, like, a self-made billionaire. He built hotels from the ground up. So, Tom tried to be a professional golfer, which the press speculated didn't make his father so happy. But when that didn't pan out, Tom tried to go work for his dad and he kicked him to the curb. Like, cut him off, no money, no job offer sort of thing. There was an insider in the company who said his father told Tom he had to make it on his own but offered him to come up with a business plan and pitch it to his board, or whatever." Cassie waved a hand. "So, Tom did that. He wanted to design golf courses or something. But a week before Christmas his father turns him down and, like, humiliates him in front of the board, saying it's a half-baked idea and he doesn't know what he's doing."

"That's awful." I could only imagine the shame of that, with an audience no less.

"So, a week later they are in Whistler, the whole family for Christmas, and Tom and his dad go with a ski guide into the backcountry." Cassie paused and leaned in closer to me. "Father never comes back."

"What happened to him?"

"He fell off a cliff. The guide says he didn't see anything. He was leading them through a no-fall zone and just assumed the guy's ski got caught or he lost his balance and fell off the edge."

"And people think, what, that Tom killed him?"

Cassie shook her head vigorously. "Yeah. Destroyed his family, well what was left of it. He's an only child so it was just him and his mom, but she, like, had cancer and this whole ordeal I think was too much stress on her body and she just, I don't know, succumbed to the cancer I guess."

"That's awful."

"Then he went on a total bender, drugs, you name it. His father's company eventually stepped in with their PR team and sent him to rehab." She poked her head out of the changing room. "Now it looks like he's a golf pro here."

"Are you sure it's him?"

She reached into her bag, pulling out what she called her smut magazines and flips to one of the pages. "I thought I saw a blurb in here about him." She scanned the back pages. "There." She pointed. "It is him."

I squinted to read the caption. "*Tom Wilson was spotted being released from rehab*."

"He's really cute."

"What?" I said, shocked.

"I'm just saying, maybe you can vet him for me. If he did do it, you're a psychiatrist and would know the truth. Maybe you can cure him?"

"Let me remind you that you have a boyfriend."

She rolled her eyes. "Fine, but if I can't have him, then you should talk to him."

I walked out of the changing room with Cassie and he looked at us, knowing very well that we were talking about him. His expression showed he didn't know whether to be wary of us or not. I saw in him an insecurity that I saw in myself. Not fitting into the world we belonged in. I knew it was risky, but he intrigued me.

"Fine," I told Cassie, turning back toward her. "I will."

I look at Tom now, and despite everything we have been through since that first time I spoke to him, I still wouldn't take any of it back. Cassie was right: I was and still am the best person for him. Sometimes, he forgets that.

"How do you feel?" I ask.

"Like I'm in prison," he answers.

"You didn't go to jail," I explain softly. "I wouldn't let them. You didn't know what you were doing. You're not a bad person."

There's silence for a few moments, when I decide to share my memory with him.

"Do you remember when we first met?"

He doesn't say anything, so I keep talking.

"I asked you for a golf lesson but explained that I had never played before, and I was worried I was going to be a lost cause. Then you told me that there are no lost causes, just lost golf balls."

I see the hint of a smile creep along his face. "That was before I actually saw you play," he says.

I start to laugh. "True. But after a couple lessons I got better."

He lets out a sigh.

"Remember, no one is a lost cause."

Tom turns to me then, giving me the slightest hint of a smile. Finally, he's starting to see the effort I put in is all for him. I just want us to be happy.

I smile back and reach for his hand now. He leaves his hand limp, but he doesn't pull away. It's a start.

Our problems are now behind us; I can feel it. We just need to take it slow and be patient.

Chapter Seventeen

Natalie

"Surprise!"

A loud scream escapes my throat, as an earbud is pulled from my ear. The music I was playing loudly dies and all I hear is a deep-throated voice.

I turn to see Luke leaning over the couch, his face so close to mine he almost looks like a blur. I lean back to confirm that it really is him, smiling down at me.

I had been so determined to block out any images or audible hallucinations that I've taken to blasting music on my AirPods while doing clinical work, trying hard to keep everything that bothers me about this place out of sight, out of mind.

I push aside my laptop and run around the couch, hugging him harder than I intended.

"I'm so glad you're back," I say into his chest, smelling his cologne on his blue button-down, the top buttons already undone and his tie, I assume, still sitting on the passenger seat of his car along with his jacket.

I step back and straighten my spine as I pull the cardigan wrap tighter around myself, noticing a hole in it. Spending these past few days with Sadie, I've felt more self-conscious about how much I've let go of my appearance. My hair alone after the surgery was such a mess that I hadn't bothered with anything else. I find myself wearing the same things all the time to the point that my T-shirts have faded and my sweaters are pilling. I feel it only makes me stand out even more in a place like the Hamptons. The furniture and artwork are more expensive than anything I could imagine. I likely look more like a squatter than someone who can afford to live here.

He wraps his arms around me. "Are you okay?"

"Yes," I say, trying to keep the shakiness out of my voice.

"Are you sure?" He lowers his eyes to mine.

I nod, eager to change the subject. "Are you hungry?" I walk away from him into the kitchen where I open the fridge. "There are some chicken cutlets here I could heat up."

"Sounds great," he says, setting his duffel bag on the floor next to his suitcase by the door.

"So how come you're back so soon?" I ask while pulling out a head of broccoli to chop up as a side dish.

"So, this deal is accelerating faster than we expected." He enters the kitchen. "Which is a really good thing."

"Great," I say over my shoulder, waiting for the but.

"The problem is, it means that I have to fly out to Geneva to close and we are likely flying out Friday."

I feel my shoulders drop. "How long will you be gone for?"

"About a week," he says. "Which is why I suggested to my boss that I work remotely for the remainder of the week here."

I put on a brave face and turn around to smile at him. "That's wonderful. I'm so proud of you." I hug him.

"I'm sorry that it means me spending more time away from you out here."

"It's fine," I tell him, pretending that it isn't tearing me up inside. That I'm worried I'm going to lose my sanity. I was really hoping he'd spend more time here. Rationalize for me the crazy things I've been witnessing. A part of me wants to leave, but going back right now wouldn't help me. I'm slowly coming out of my agoraphobia. Sure, I haven't left the property, but I know I'd go back to just the way I was, which at this point is a step back in the wrong direction. Then I think about Sadie. I can't leave her like this. She really needs a friend right now and to be honest, so do I. "Sadie is really great," I say.

"That's wonderful," he says.

I think about what Sadie told me. Her friend Cassie was there for her when her father died, and everything came out. I saw it in her face when I gave her the picture I found of Cassie. How heartbroken she looked. Then she proceeded to tell me how they *used* to be best friends. That must've been the trigger that brought back all those difficult memories. Then to have a falling-out with the one person she considered as the only family she had left, no wonder she was in a state. Sadie is strong-willed though, I can tell. It was why she has seemed to pull herself back so quickly.

I hear a roar of thunder and look out over the ocean. A dark cloud is hovering, another storm surely coming. Through the open window in the kitchen, I can feel the electricity in the air, almost like Luke and I: fully charged and we could strike a lightning bolt right through our relationship at any given moment.

"Has it stormed the whole time here?" Luke asks, rolling up his sleeves.

"Just seems to come in the late afternoons and rolls through pretty quickly."

"So, you've had a chance to get out?"

I nod. "I've been doing a lot of swimming."

Luke turns on the oven when we hear a rap on the back door. I startle while he casually picks his head up and turns. I'm the first to approach when I see Sadie. She is in a pair of white shorts and a blue silk top with her hair in a ponytail.

"Luke, I thought I saw you were back." She smiles, but it feels strained. Then she turns toward me. "Tom is home as well, and I would really love it if you got to meet him." She turns and points to the house. "Can you join us for dinner?"

"We'd love to," Luke says.

"Great, we'll see you in an hour?"

"Sounds good," I add. "Can we bring anything?"

She laughs. "Please, just yourselves."

"That was easy enough—now we don't have to cook," Luke says, pulling at his collar.

"I'll go get freshened up then," I say, looking down at my yoga pants.

"I'm sure this isn't as formal as the other day," he tells me.

"For Sadie everything is formal," I tell him.

As I climb the stairs, I feel the hairs on the back of my neck stiffen. Should I tell Luke about all that is going on? At least what I think is happening with Riley? I reach the hallway and peer into the guest bathroom. The floor has dried and the message on the mirror has faded away. The only remains are some dried water spots on the mirror.

What good would it do though?

Again, my thoughts slide to Sadie. I am still worried about her, and feel I need to be there for her. That sudden shift of someone needing me again instead of the other way around fills me with a sense of purpose that I haven't felt in a long time. Whatever is going on here is mostly in my own head anyway.

It is settled then. The thing with Riley is all a misunderstanding and there is no need to blow it out of proportion.

Still, I can't shake this feeling that something is lurking just below the surface that everyone is aware of but me.

"You made it. Great!" Sadie lights up as we walk through the front door. She's still wearing the same outfit as before. I'm relieved she didn't try to change into something fancier. She looks around behind us. "Looks like this storm is holding off," she says, then brings her attention back to us. "You look great."

I have on a cheery yellow sundress that hasn't seen the light of day in over a year but seems to have held up well in my closet. I make eye contact with Sadie as if to do a silent check-in, but she remains her smiley self—forcing me to try to believe that nothing is wrong. But I can sense an uneasiness in her. She seems almost uncomfortable. I can't tell if it's because we are here or because Tom is.

"I think I just heard the back porch door open, so Tom is out there." Sadie smiles at Luke as she kisses his cheek.

Luke nods and makes his way out the back door. When the door closes behind us, I look at Sadie more closely.

"Are you okay?" My voice low so no one else can hear.

"Of course." She almost looks confused. When she sees my serious expression not let up, her face finally falls. "I'm just a little nervous is all."

"Of what?" I ask.

"Tom can be a bit unpredictable at times."

"Should we leave?" I ask, unnerved by the thought that on top of Riley, Tom was someone I had to worry about as well.

"No." Her hand extends to my arm, gripping it tightly. I notice her desperation and again I see the look in her eyes that I saw the night I pulled her out of the ocean. The look that shows she's barely holding it together.

"Please stay. It would make things easier. It was my suggestion to have you both over."

The last thing I want is to be pulled into whatever this is, but if she's as scared of Tom as I think she is, I need to see this for myself.

"Okay," I give in, then remembering, "Oh, I'm not going to tell Luke about Riley breaking into the house. I don't want him worrying about me here, so do you mind if we keep that between us?"

"Of course," Sadie agrees.

I'm relieved I had a moment to talk to her alone.

"Good, then come on, let's join the men on the porch."

I follow Sadie but then I stop, noticing a shadow in the dining room. A clash of lightning flashes and the figure lights up. I jump back, letting out a startled screech.

Sadie turns back confused, but then grimaces when we realize it's her maid. She pulls my arm and leads me down the hall.

"What was your maid doing in the dark?" I whisper.

Sadie doesn't say anything, just shakes her head and lets out a huff of frustration.

On the back porch there are two swinging love seats suspended from the wooden ceiling. Tom is lounged and relaxed on one with a cigar hanging loosely from his fingers. His shirt has the top three buttons undone, exposing his tanned, hairless chest. Luke is on the opposite side of him leaning forward, his elbows propped on his knees. The storm has cooled the air to an icy chill, but it feels like more than just the weather that's causing this.

As Sadie and I step outside, I watch as the smile on Tom's face fades. He's looking directly at me as if I'm some sort of apparition. Like he knows me and wasn't expecting to see me. His gaze shifts from me to Sadie, a subtle communication between them, before seeming to recover. "The women have decided to join us," Tom says over Luke's shoulder. He sits up, taking a puff of his cigar. "Come sit." The cigar dangles between his teeth as he pats the cushion next to him.

"Anyone for a cigar?" Tom asks both Luke and me. I shake my head, while Luke agrees, though I've never seen him smoke a cigar before. There have been a lot of subtle changes I've noticed in Luke since he started this new job. His choice in expensive scotch the last time we were here, his fancy new suits, which I can understand he needs for work, but now with the cigar. Knowing the real Luke, it just comes off like he's auditioning for a part.

I turn my attention toward Sadie while Tom points at his cigar's label and describes the location and taste of this brand, while Luke pretends to know all about it.

"So, Tom, where are you from?" Luke asks, as he lights his cigar.

Tom pulls the cigar from his mouth and blows out a ring of smoke. A party trick he's obviously been doing for some time. "California."

"LA, right?" I ask.

He turns his attention to me and smiles. "Beverly Hills."

"So, I heard you were traveling this past week. That must've been nice," I say.

Tom draws a long pull of his cigar, then blows it out. "My wife told you that, huh?" He looks at Sadie and smiles.

I watch as Sadie shifts nervously. *Was that a lie she told me?*

"So, you're a golf instructor, right?" Luke asks.

"Yeah," Tom answers matter-of-factly, taking another puff of his cigar.

"What's your favorite course?"

Tom looks at his wife again, another message passed between them. "Augusta."

"Great course," Luke says. "I've never played, but I heard it's really hard."

I squint at Luke. Since when does he know anything about golf?

Tom gives a shrug. "It can be." He stubs his cigar out.

As the men continue to talk about golf, I look at Sadie, who seems almost like she is supervising the conversation. I try to branch off to something that Sadie and I can talk about, but I can tell she's only half listening to me.

"Is this a safe enough topic for you, dear?" Tom asks.

Sadie stiffens. "Of course, darling."

Tom turns back to Luke. "Apparently, according to my wife, I must be supervised."

"I never said that," Sadie says.

"No, of course not, we are the perfect couple, right? That's what you like to tell everyone. We have a happy marriage?"

"Tom," Sadie says. "Please."

A bolt of lightning strikes over the ocean in the distance, and I find myself jumping in alarm, not sure what I was expecting. As if in that moment Tom might jump up and do something irrational. I'm still trying to understand what Sadie meant by Tom's unpredictability, when I hear a low rumbling of thunder.

Tom stares at her for a long minute. Luke and I exchange a glance, Luke's head tilting, asking if we should go. I want to, but Sadie needs me to stay. It's as if she wants to show me something. Could Tom be the cause of her attempted suicide?

"Why don't you fix me a drink, sweetie, and see if our guests would like anything."

"I don't need anything, thank you," I try to say quickly, but then Luke speaks up.

"I'll join you in a scotch."

I clench my teeth and look at Sadie apologetically. It was stupid of me not to tell Luke that Tom has a drinking problem.

Sadie plasters on a smile. "Of course."

"I'll help you." I jump up, following Sadie back into the living room, closing the French doors behind us.

"I'm so sorry I didn't tell Luke about Tom's drinking issue. We can go. I don't want things to get worse."

"Tom's going to do what Tom's going to do," she states in a way that shows the night will not get any easier on her. I turn toward the back porch, wondering if I can somehow signal to Luke that I need to speak with him, but his eyes are fixed on Tom, deep in conversation.

I hear the shake of a pill bottle and turn to find Sadie crushing a tiny blue pill with a muddler from the bar.

My eyes widen. "What are you doing?"

"It's Klonopin. His doctor prescribes them to him but he never takes them. When he gets agitated, I slip it in his drink to calm him down."

I stare at her dumbstruck, not sure how I'm supposed to react. As a nurse, I know the dangers of mixing drugs and alcohol. But if I lived in fear of my husband, maybe I'd be doing the same. I can already sense the aura of hostility wafting off of him.

"Did he do that?" I decide to come out and say it, pointing to her shoulder. If he did then I can be more understanding with what I'm witnessing. Otherwise, I can't stand by and let it happen.

She looks down at her shoulder, embarrassed. "I guess you saw that, huh?" Sadie's fingers lightly touch over the fabric of her blouse where the gauze remains hidden.

Her gaze shifts from me to the floor and it's then I have my answer.

An exasperated sigh escapes from me.

"What were you two conspiring about?" Tom says as we walk out. My spine straightens like a rod.

"You think everything is about you," Sadie says in a subtle mocking tone. She's clearly had more practice at this than I have.

I watch as she hands the drink over to Tom, who seems to knock almost half of it back in one gulp, eyeing Sadie the whole time as if he knows what she's done.

I notice Sadie swallow nervously.

"I'm going to use the restroom and get some water," I say, handing Luke his glass and rubbing my sweaty palms on my legs. "Excuse me for one moment."

I go back inside, retreating to the bathroom. I pass the kitchen and smile at Marla, Sadie's cook, who gives me a soft wave with an oven-mitt-covered hand.

My body feels flushed with heat. I run my hands under the tap and dab the back of my neck. I hear a knock at the door, which surprises me. This house has at least three bathrooms on the main floor, surely the closed door indicates someone is in here.

I steady my breathing and open the door but freeze when I see it's Tom. It's like he purposely followed me here.

"Sorry, all yours," I say, gesturing for him to come in so I can get around him, but he doesn't move.

"So, I understand my wife rented the guest house to you both." His frame towers over me, and I feel myself shrink back.

"Yes," I say with trepidation.

"How long ago?"

I try to think back to the conversation I had with Luke. "It was quick. I think my husband found it online the middle of last week. We came here a mere two days later."

He seems to laugh inwardly and shakes his head.

"And my wife, she told you I was traveling?"

I nod, afraid that I somehow will get Sadie in trouble for something—something she'll wind up paying for later.

"What else has Sadie told you?"

I feel my throat constrict. I shake my head. "Not much else. Like I said, we just got here."

He lets out a slow breath and I can smell the liquor on it. I try to keep my nose from crinkling with disgust.

"Well then," he finally says. "Welcome to The Overlook. Just as eerie and just as isolating as the fictional one."

I realize that The Overlook name is not lost on him. In fact, maybe he was the one who came up with it.

Then he smiles at me and walks away.

"So, that was an interesting night," Luke says as he throws a decorative pillow off the bed.

I contemplate telling Luke the truth. How I found out that the bandage on Sadie's arm was caused by Tom, though

I doubt he noticed it. She made a point of keeping it concealed all night.

But is that true? She never answered me, just left me to believe that was the case, so I would agree to letting her drug him. Or is it from some sort of accident like when her head hit that rock in the ocean. In that case though, it was only a minor gash that she can easily cover with her hair.

It also sounds like Tom had no idea that Sadie rented the guest house out. I'm realizing more and more that it was purposeful, so she wouldn't be alone with him.

Luke crawls on the bed toward me. I meet him halfway, kissing him. He lowers his head to my neck and I turn toward the window, when I see a light on at the other house. I jump back when I see Tom, staring eerily at us through the window, though it's not close enough for me to be sure. I just see the shadow of a figure in the other house, but it's a masculine stature.

"What is it?" Luke asks.

"It's Tom," I say, pointing out the window.

But when Luke turns, he's gone, the curtain still swaying.

I try to get the image of Tom staring at us out of my head. Maybe he just happened to be looking out the window or maybe it was my imagination again? I can tell Luke seems to think so.

I may not know for sure if Tom hurt Sadie, but there was no mistaking her behavior tonight. She had a deer-in-the-headlights look about her all evening. It's clear Sadie is afraid of Tom. The question is, should I be as well?

Chapter Eighteen

Sadie

"I think that went well," I say to Tom who is still sitting in the dining room after I see Luke and Natalie out the front door. The dessert dishes are still in front of everyone's seats. Half-eaten and now sunken chocolate soufflés with brown fudge oozing from their centers. It is Tom's favorite, and I wanted tonight to be good for him.

"Sure," he says, seemingly indifferent. He wipes his mouth with his napkin then, throwing it down on the table, he stands up.

"Still, it must be nice to have another guy to talk to about golf," I press, standing in the space that divides the front hallway from the dining room. The rooms are similar with the rich mahogany spilling into the coffered ceilings of the dining room.

Tom ignores my statement as he walks toward me; now that the room is quiet, I can hear the echo of his heels against the wood. He gets a mere few inches from my face, and I can feel his hot breath on mine. I find my body standing erect, ready to decide if I should be in flight or fight mode.

"Was this all meant to be some sort of an apology?" He sneers, but without waiting for a response he walks past me and starts to tread up the stairs.

I look nervously as the door to the kitchen swings open and Marla comes in to clear the dishes.

Luckily, she seems oblivious to the exchange.

"Everything turn out all right, Mrs. Wilson?"

I nod and plaster a smile on my face. "Perfection," I tell her. "Thank you again so much."

Then I hastily make my way up the steps. When I reach our room, I see Tom staring at the guest house from our window.

"Was this all on my account?" he asks me again, his voice starting to sound slurred.

I look toward the guest house, even though from my position I'm only looking at a wall.

"What?" I ask.

"You told me the new neighbors were coming over for dinner," he clarifies. "I didn't realize it meant that you had rented out the guest house and so quickly after . . ." He lets the rest hang in the air.

I swallow, trying to keep my voice steady.

"I thought it would be best for all of us," I say.

He shakes his head, before he closes the curtain.

"You know I didn't do it."

You're responsible for all of this, I think.

"Tom." I keep my voice even. "You don't know what you did."

"What am I to you, anyway?"

"What do you mean?"

"What's more important to you: the money or the control? At this rate, I'll give you all the money."

The comment feels like a slap. "You." I stammer. "You are the most important. I love you, Tom. My whole life revolves around you. But you, you continue to act like a child. You don't take responsibility for your own actions. You did this to yourself." My voice rises in indignation.

"Yeah, it is my fault. I'm the monster." His voice is sarcastic but also knowing there is an inkling of truth.

"Tom, you're not a monster." I soften, easing myself onto the couch in our bedroom, trying to act casual and hide the fact that my nerve endings are firing off like warning bells.

"You're always trying to control people, Sadie. You literally made it your life's work. But some people . . ." He trails off. "Some people should be left alone."

I reach for him, urging him to come sit next to me, but he continues to keep his distance like there is a vast black hole between us and if either one gives in, we run the risk of inescapably falling into a place that we will never come back from.

"People change," I say. "You have grown."

"Into what?" Tom says angrily. "What have I become?"

Tears start to build behind my eyes because I don't know what has become of any of us anymore.

My heart beats so hard it feels as if it's going to break my rib cage. I stand and leave, needing some fresh air. I sneak down the stairs, past Marla, hoping that she doesn't see me. When I spot her, her back is to me and she is scrubbing the last of the dishes in the sink.

I sneak outside onto the back porch with a quiet click of the handle. Then I sit on the rocker, the balls of my feet slowly pushing me back and forth. I hear the faint squeak of the metal above me, but it starts to creak louder and louder as my pace kicks up. The clouds finally break, and the rain falls heavily around me. The pace of my swing trying to keep up with the pace of my mind that is racing in all directions.

Whose fault was all of this, really?

I think back to the afternoon last week when I saw Owen splashing around in the pool and walked over assuming Cassie wasn't too far away.

She was nowhere to be seen.

"Owen?" I called. He seemed to struggle as he swam to the edge of the pool. Barely able to catch his breath.

"Where's your mom?" I asked.

He shrugged his shoulders.

"Does your mom know that you're in the pool?" I asked, slightly concerned.

He shrugged his shoulders again.

I sucked in a breath. Typical Cassie, leaving her son to fend for himself. I heard the loud whir of a car engine, that brought me to the front of the house. I gave one last look to Owen, who seemed to have taken a break and was sitting on the steps.

When I reached the front of the house, I saw Riley and Cassie sitting in the front seat of her car.

"Cassie?" I called out, holding a hand over my eyes to block the sun.

I couldn't see her expression, but she came out of the passenger seat laughing. Riley couldn't have gotten out of the car any faster.

"I have to get back to work," he said to Cassie or myself—I'm not sure. Then he awkwardly walked away.

"What were you doing?" I couldn't keep the irritation out of my voice.

"I couldn't get my car started." She put her hands up in defense. "Riley was just helping me jump-start it."

As she said this, I notice that Riley's truck is parked in front of hers, both hoods open.

"Did you know your son is in the pool by himself?"

She looked at me strangely. "Yeah, he can swim."

I looked back behind me. "You don't think he's too young to be unsupervised?"

"You need to give kids their independence."

"What if he drowned?"

"I told you, before, I'm teaching my child resilience. He needs to teach himself how to survive. He needs to know I may not always be there to save him."

"That's a really warped idea," I told her. "It's not like he's eighteen, he's six."

"Are you okay?" She looked at me curiously.

I wasn't okay, I realized.

I turned my head and caught Riley pretending to do something in the rose garden, but really, he was just watching Cassie.

She flipped her hair and jutted her hip to show that she knew he was watching her too.

"I need to speak with you," I told her, steering her toward the backyard where we would be out of earshot of Riley, and she could at least keep an eye on her kid.

"I asked you to leave Riley alone," I said quietly.

She turned back around as if looking for him, then gave a mischievous smile.

"What?" She shrugged. "I'm just having fun with him."

"I know," I said sternly. "That's my problem."

She rolled her eyes at me, and I felt a tingling sense of rage build up in me.

"Riley suffers from PTSD," I explained.

"So, I can't talk to him?"

"Not in the way that you are," I explain, unable to keep the edge out of my voice.

Then I see Cassie's face register my anger. This isn't the first time that she's been privy to it and she knows where this will lead if she keeps going.

This was just like Cassie. Always taking things that were mine and messing with them. It was like that time she took my favorite Barbie to play with. She decided to give it a makeover with permanent marker. I was never able to get it off again. Then in summer camp, I told her I had a crush on Thad Stevenson, and I caught her skinny-dipping with him. Or the time I had caught my roommate Jackie in college making out with one of her professors. I told Cassie in confidence, but it had somehow managed to slip out of her mouth when she came to visit me. The rest of the year Jackie and I roomed together was horrible and awkward.

Subtly though I found ways to even the score over the years.

I knew if she got into Riley's head, something bad would happen, because with Cassie, it always does, and I'd lose Riley.

I took a beat, suppressed my anger and spoke more like a psychiatrist. "These are emotions he's not entirely familiar with and I'd rather if he were to experience them, they would be with someone more genuine and not someone who will break his heart."

"He is still a grown man. I'm sure you're babying him too much like you do everyone."

I swallowed what I really wanted to say down my throat. What I wanted to tell her was that Riley doesn't always express a lot of empathy, and I wasn't sure how he might react to someone if he found out they were simply "having fun" with him.

I'd seen what happened when he was angry.

"Want to camp out tonight like old times?"

I looked at her, confused. "What?"

"Owen wanted me to take him camping. We have sleeping bags. It's supposed to be a clear night. I thought maybe we could use the firepit over there to roast marshmallows and sleep out under the stars. What do you think? You want to join us? Pretend like we are at camp again?"

I glanced over toward the corner of the property where we had paved out a section. On it was a driftwood gas firepit surrounded by four white love seats. I hadn't remembered if we had ever used it before. I wasn't even sure it still worked.

And yet, I couldn't keep the smile off my face. I realized this was what I needed. Some girl time, with my oldest friend in the world. "You know something? Yes, I will join you."

That night, Tom insisted on joining as well, helping Owen with his stick when he looked like he was getting too close to the fire. Cassie insisted he was fine, but we ignored her. Tom still drank, but he seemed less malicious tonight, though I kept seeing Cassie and Tom exchange glances with one another and I wasn't quite sure what to make of it.

Shortly after, I said goodnight to Tom and lay out on a blanket, staring up at the stars. After an afternoon of swimming Owen had fallen asleep relatively quickly.

"Do you remember that summer in camp when Parker Grant stole your bra?" She pulled out a bottle of white wine I didn't even know she had from her sleeping bag. She unscrewed the cap and swigged straight from the bottle, before handing it over to me.

"You really are making it like old times," I joked. "And yes, I do. I also remember how you retaliated."

"Come on, you have to admit breaking into his bunk, stealing all of his clothes and throwing them in the lake was a great idea."

"We were only supposed to get my bra back, but you took it to the next level."

"Tell me he didn't deserve it."

"He did." I smiled. I had been one of the few girls that summer to grow breasts, which was already awkward enough. Then to have Parker Grant steal my only bra and laugh about it with his friends had been enough to put Cassie on a rampage.

"Nobody treats my best friend that way," Cassie told me.

I reached for her hand, and she squeezed mine back.

After a generous swig, I handed the bottle back. She in turn took another drink then stood up. "Come on, let's go for a swim.

"What?" I looked over at Owen who was still asleep. I expected Cassie to head toward the pool but instead she walked in the direction of the beach.

I chased after her. "Where are you going?"

"To the ocean," she called over the loudness of the waves as we descended the steps to the sand, bottle still in hand.

"What about your bathing suit?"

Cassie put the bottle down and took the ends of her orange cotton dress, lifting it over her shoulders.

I stopped. "Oh no," I tell her.

"Come on, just like that time in Barcelona. We skinny-dipped in the ocean after we left the bar."

"You thought it would sober us up before our flight, which was in an hour."

"It worked, didn't it?"

"Because it was winter, and the water was freezing. We were lucky we didn't die of hypothermia."

Cassie was now submerged in the water in nothing but her underwear. "But it was fun!" she called to me.

I let out a sigh, but gave in. I missed this part of me. The part that used to be fun, that would follow Cassie to the ends of the earth for a good time, always leaving with stories of our adventures that I knew would stay with me forever. But being with Tom, always having to be one step ahead of what he might do, has worn me down.

I stripped down and swam out to her, the water slightly chilled but not too bad.

"At least it's not as cold as Barcelona," Cassie said when I got to her.

She leaned back, spreading her arms and legs to float. "Not a bad way to look at the stars," she said.

I joined her, doing the same. The weightlessness made it feel as if I were in a sensory deprivation tank.

"Why did we ever stop?" I asked Cassie.

"What do you mean?"

"You left me," I said. "Right after my wedding, you left, and this is the first time I've seen you since then." There was silence as I waited for a response. "Was it something I said?"

"No." Her voice was soft. For some reason I was afraid to look at her. So, we continued to float, staring up at the stars.

"What happened?" I asked once more.

"I was in love with your husband."

Chapter Nineteen

Natalie

"Danny," I hear myself call out. I see Danny on the beach. He's trying to build a sandcastle. I go over to try to help him, but something is stopping me. I'm not sure what. I see the waves crashing, the tide getting closer and closer to him. I try to call out to him, but he doesn't hear me. I can't get to him, then suddenly a wave topples him.

"Natalie!" His voice a high-pitched shrill cry as his tiny arm stretches to me.

"Danny!" I scream, still unable to get to him.

He cries out again as the wave drags him into the ocean and he disappears.

"No!" I wake up sweating, yet my body is freezing. I swallow hard and sit up in bed, wiping tears from my eyes.

"Are you okay?" Luke comes into the room holding a cup of coffee. He's got on athletic shorts and a shirt, sweating like he just got back from a run.

"I'm fine," I say, rubbing my face. "Just a bad dream."

He puts his coffee mug down on the end table, sitting on the side of the bed. "Could it have been one of your hallucinations?"

"I stopped taking my pills. I don't have hallucinations anymore," I lie.

"Did you tell your doctor?" he asks, concerned regarding the pills.

"Of course." I try not to roll my eyes as I stand up out of bed. "He told me it was okay."

"Okay," Luke says, satisfied. "I know you know what you're doing. I just worry."

"I know," I say, feeling guilty now that he has to always walk on eggshells with me. Not sure how I'll react. I soften. "I know."

I leave him to his shower as I go downstairs to the fridge, the air chilling my perspiring face like a cooling mask. I reach in and pull out a yogurt container, noticing now there is only one left. There had been several in here before.

I shudder, thinking of Riley again.

I peel the top off, catching my finger on the aluminum. "Ouch!"

"You okay?" Luke asks, coming around the corner, scaring me. I had thought he had gone to shower.

I look down at my finger. A small red spot balloons on the side of my index finger. I instinctively bring it to my mouth. "I'm fine," I say, mad at myself. I finish tearing the lid and open the garbage when I have to do a double take. There are several rotted banana peels in the garbage.

I thought we didn't have bananas, I think to myself.

It was also strange because they look like they had been just placed there, sitting right on top with nothing else covering them. I scratch my head, feeling the grooves of my scars.

Please keep it together. I have to remember my brain is healing. I shouldn't be overthinking this.

"It looks like I have a two-hour meeting from noon to two," I hear Luke say as he peers at his laptop screen on the kitchen table. "Would you rather do a breakfast picnic?" He turns to look at me.

I shrug my shoulders. "Might as well just eat here, then let's go to the beach for an hour. I haven't swum in the ocean yet and my first virtual appointment is at ten."

"Great." He smiles. "I have to be back by ten to prep for this meeting anyway." Luke turns back to his laptop and types out a few emails as I go upstairs to put on my bathing suit.

Twenty minutes later Luke and I are basking in the sun overlooking a calm ocean with a blue sky. I've thrown on a pale-yellow bikini for the occasion with a long white terrycloth dress.

"Wow, what a wonderful morning." Luke props himself up on his shoulders, spread out on a beach towel. His toned muscles are accented by the oily sunscreen he's just put on.

"It really is," I say holding a hand over my sunglasses so I can look at him.

Luke looks back at the house. "Have you left the property since you've been here?" His voice is serious.

I fall back onto my towel and close my eyes. "No car."

"What about with Sadie?"

"I plan on it," I lie.

"I'm glad you have a lot more room to breathe out here," he tells me. "Just don't forget to take the opportunity to make those baby steps. We wouldn't want another regression when we go back to the city."

"I know you're right," I say. I should be making more of an effort. "Maybe we can drive into town for dinner tonight," I suggest.

Luke smiles. "That's my girl."

"I'm going to go for a swim," I tell him, standing up. "I'll be right back."

"Okay, I'm going to relax for a bit." He lies back down.

I make my way into the surf. The distinct memory of pulling Sadie from the water flashes through my brain and I push it away, submerging beneath the waves. The coolness revives me with a sort of energy that immediately makes me start to swim my freestyle strokes. I eye the two buoys, making sure to stay between them. The beach is relatively quiet. Over by the public beach I can see a cluster of umbrellas, but they are still a way down. When I feel my muscles start to ache, I remind myself that I'm also here to spend time with Luke and should swim back. I swivel my head in search for him, when I see him a little further down from the guest house, talking with someone.

I swim in closer and realize that it's a woman with a little girl playing in the surf next to him. I make my way toward them before climbing out of the water.

"Hi." I smile sweetly.

Luke turns back. "Marissa, this is my wife, Natalie." He extends a hand in my direction.

I give a small wave.

"Hi, Natalie, it's nice to meet you." She shakes my hand then places it on the back of the small girl beside her. "This is Charlotte."

"Hi, Charlotte." I grin.

"Hi," she answers, not looking up but continuing to draw pictures in the sand with the stick she has found.

"I love your bathing suit," I say. "You look like a ballerina." I note the pink suit with shimmering ruffles.

"Charlotte loves to dance," Marissa says, adjusting her large floppy hat. "Luke tells me you are staying at the Wilsons'?"

I nod. "Yes, just for a few weeks."

"Oh, how nice. Wonderful people," she says in a way that sounds noncommittal, then she turns and points. "We're next door."

I look beyond the dunes.

"Where is the boy?" the girl asks.

My heart stops beating. "What?"

"Don't you have a boy? I've seen him."

"No boy," Luke says. "We don't have any children." His voice drops on the last part, and I pick up on it.

"But I've seen him," she insists.

"That was a while ago, sweetheart," her mother reminds her.

"No, I saw him today."

I stare intently at her. "You did?" Is there a part of me that isn't crazy? But if not, what does that mean for both of us? There is no boy.

"Well, it was lovely meeting you both. I'm sure we'll see you around." Marissa gives a light wave and gently guides her daughter with her hand on her back, toward their own house.

I find myself staring at them dumbfounded. Not sure how to make sense of it. Is she really seeing Danny too?

By the time I come out of my trance, I turn and see Luke picking up seashells and skipping them along the surf.

When he sees me approach, he shakes his head.

"We never did finish that conversation," Luke says. "Or did we?"

I know exactly what he's talking about.

"Luke." My voice is soft and lost in the wind.

"I've been patient," Luke says, throwing a shell hard into the water. "But this is important to me. I want to have a family." He turns to me this time.

My eyes begin to water. I knew this moment would come; I just didn't know when. Only that when it did I still wouldn't be prepared for it. I try to rationalize what to say, but if I tell him about my childhood now, then it would show that I'd lied to him. He'd lose his trust in me. But now given the fact that I keep seeing my dead six-year-old brother, I'm even more against the idea of children. But there is no way to say that.

"I love you so much," I start. "Isn't that enough?" My voice cracks.

"I love you too." He looks down at the sand. "But I want more." He pauses. "Is that so bad?"

"That I'm not enough?" I try to keep the hurt out of my voice but it's obvious.

"You are enough," he says, "but I want more out of life."

"I'm sorry," I say. "I just . . ." I hesitate. "I just can't."

"What are you afraid of?" He grabs both of my hands now, his eyes desperately looking into mine.

This is it. I should tell him the truth, but I can't. He'll be upset I never told him before, and he'll start to wonder what else I'm lying to him about. Before I know it, he'll wonder if he even knows the real me at all.

I want to say that I'm afraid of being a parent. But he'll just try to reassure me that I'll be great. He has no idea.

"I'm sorry this isn't enough for you," I say again, pulling away from him. I grab my towel and start to head back to the house.

"Natalie," I hear him faintly call behind me, but I must keep going. I feel the tears coming and I don't want to break down out here.

I traipse up the steps, walk over the dunes, then increase my pace across the lawn, past the pool. The wind has picked up, carrying the crashing waves of the ocean in my ears.

I stop for a moment under a large sycamore tree just outside the house and catch my breath, trying again not to cry. I hear a loud buzzing noise before a snap comes from above me. Suddenly, I am tackled to the ground.

"Natalie," Luke cries, his voice loud in my ear.

I turn my head to see an oversized branch on the ground where I was standing. The loud whir of the chainsaw is still buzzing.

Luke helps me stand up. "Are you okay?"

I shake my head still confused by what just happened.

"Hey!" Luke yells up the tree.

The buzzing continues for another moment before it finally stops.

"Hey!" Luke yells again.

It's then that I notice a ladder on the back side of the tree trunk. Riley climbs down holding a chainsaw.

"What do you think you're doing?" Luke yells at him. "You didn't bother to look and see you could've killed someone!"

Riley towers over Luke, his eyes possessing the same vacancy as before. He looks almost warningly at Luke then proceeds to walk past him.

"Hey, I'm talking to you!" Luke starts to follow him.

"Luke, no," I say, nervous. "Stop, please."

But I can tell Luke is angry and rather than take it out on me he's going to try to take it out on Riley—an even worse idea.

"Luke, stop!" I give one more call of warning.

Luke catches up to Riley and grabs his shoulder to spin him around. Riley, in one swift motion, pushes him to the ground.

"Luke!" I yell, stumbling up and running toward them. Riley pins Luke down and grabs him by the shirt collar.

"Let him go!" I yell, pulling on Riley's shoulder, trying to break him free of Luke whose arms and torso are trapped under Riley's weight. Riley doesn't even flinch as he stares straight into Luke's eyes, a smile creeping across his face.

"Please let go!" I start to cry now, thinking about the dove that Riley so easily killed.

Luke's eyes bulge in fear.

In an instant, Riley releases his grip, then turns and walks away, smiling. He didn't hurt him, but he made it pretty clear he could've killed him if he wanted to. And next time, Luke might not be so lucky.

Chapter Twenty

Sadie

I'm about to go for a walk on the beach to clear my head after my fight with Tom last night. I had ordered a charger for the burner phone I had found in Tom's drawer, but when I went to retrieve the phone from my blazer pocket, it was gone.

He might've figured out that I found it, but how would he have known where I had put it?

Again, I don't want to bring it up without having any sort of proof. I need to see what's on the phone first before I attack him. Our relationship is walking a tightrope as it is.

My fingers are on the railing of the porch when I spot Natalie already on the beach with Luke. They appear to be fighting. Natalie's arms are folded into herself, while Luke looks upset, throwing shells into the ocean.

I should go back inside, but I'm intrigued. She's clearly not in a happy marriage either.

Natalie storms away and after a slight hesitation, Luke starts to follow her.

I retreat inside.

I can't help the smile that edges across my face. I shouldn't be happy about it; I know that. It's like that German word, *schadenfreude*, taking pleasure in other people's pain. It's not that I enjoy seeing Natalie upset, but rather that misery loves company. It's nice to know that you aren't the only person suffering in a marriage. Especially when you are surrounded by happy couples. You start to think it's your fault all the time. I was raised to think everything was my fault, but I'm trying desperately not to be like that anymore.

I noticed the neighbors earlier, walking along the beach. That woman and her little girl. I remembered overhearing her in town. I was in one of the aisles of the grocery store when I saw her and thought I'd go and say hi, but another woman had recognized her and walked over. Both pushing shopping carts with their little girls sitting in the front of them.

I waited, debating whether I should go join them or wait for the other woman to leave.

"So how are your new neighbors?" the one asked the other.

"Oh, I don't know," she said. "I wish a family would've moved in. She seems nice enough, but they don't have kids, and I just don't know how you relate to someone like that. They don't get what you're going through."

"I know what you mean," the other one agreed.

I bit my lower lip so hard I could taste blood. How dare they judge me like they know anything about me? But in the end, I took a deep breath and walked away.

She had come sniffing around when they spotted Owen playing on the beach, but she was disappointed to learn that they were just my guests staying only temporarily.

Meanwhile I was the one stuck talking to her while Cassie, in her hot-pink bikini, had decided to take a walk along the beach, leaving me to supervise Owen.

As she walked in the opposite direction, she pulled Tom up from his beach chair.

"Tom, come for a walk with me."

I couldn't say or do anything in that moment, and it was almost as if Cassie knew this and that was her plan.

An hour had gone by, and I hadn't heard from either of them. Neither one had their phone on them.

Eventually the neighbors left, and it was just Owen and me on the beach.

Despite my job as a therapist, I don't know what it was about kids, but they made me nervous.

"Can I play in the ocean?"

I looked back down the beach, hoping to see Cassie. The truth was, I didn't want to go in the ocean, but I didn't trust Owen going in by himself. He wasn't a strong swimmer at all.

"Can we wait for your mom to get back?"

After another half hour of Owen getting bored with the sand and picking up on how pink his shoulders were getting, I finally suggested we go inside.

I left the chairs for Tom to clean up and I took Owen into the guest house where I fixed him a snack and put on some cartoon that he suggested.

I stared out the window in frustration, growing more and more angry.

Eventually I saw them climb the stairs from the beach and I immediately went out to meet them.

"What the hell happened to you guys?"

Tom looked on edge, but Cassie didn't bat an eye. "We just went for a walk to catch up," she said. "Oh, and Tom agreed to watch Owen so you and I can go out for some girl time tonight."

I was surprised then. Suddenly I wondered if I was over-reacting. But I still had her words stuck in my head from the night before. *I was in love with your husband.*

I asked then why she came back.

"I don't have feelings for him anymore and the truth is, I missed you so much. I had to see you again."

She held my hand and we continued floating in the water as we stared at the stars. I wasn't sure what to think in the moment. Just that it felt like Cassie was truly a loyal friend. She did the right thing by leaving.

But I could see my jealousy getting the best of me.

Did she steal him for a walk to tell him about her past feelings? Would he leave me for her? The way things have been going between us, I felt nauseated at the thought. It wouldn't do me any good to have it out with them right now. I would only look hysterical despite having a good reason for it.

If I was going to manage this situation properly, I needed to look like the calm and rational one, which shouldn't be hard next to Cassie.

He chose me over her once. I just have to do what's necessary to make sure that happens again.

I softened my shoulders and looked to Tom. "Thanks. On that note, why don't I go get ready?" I told Cassie. "Owen is inside. He just ate and he's watching TV."

"You're the best. Thanks." She kissed my cheek, and practically skipped inside.

I turned back toward Tom. "So, what did you two talk about?" I asked, trying to keep my voice light and not accusatory.

He shrugged his shoulders. "Just telling me about her crazy life."

I noticed he said it in a way that made him seem almost envious. I knew the feeling. I felt that way when Cassie told me about her life too. How she makes you feel like you wish you were there with her when it happened.

"Have you told her about our life?" I looked at him cautiously.

I had tried to explain to him that his mental illness was not his fault, but he didn't see it that way.

"No," he answered quickly, which made me think he was lying. I wasn't sure why he wouldn't want to tell me. What was there to hide from me? I've been there and seen him through all of it. Still, I didn't see any reason to press him, so I let it go.

It wasn't until later I learned the reason why.

That evening, Cassie and I pulled into the Southampton Publick House.

It's a white structure right off the main drag, tucked in next to a stream of storefront buildings.

"I don't think I've ever been here," I admitted to Cassie, though to be fair we never went out.

"It's cool. Owen and I stopped here before we met you." Cassie stepped out of the car in a thin pink halter with ripped jean shorts that, in my opinion, went too far up her behind for a woman her age, but maybe that was just because of how long her legs were. Cassie could've been a model if she had tried. She certainly had the body for it. The halter hugged her in a way that accentuated all the right parts of her.

I looked down at my own white cotton sundress. It was only standing next to Cassie that I realized I don't own any pink clothing, or anything of color really. Like my life, everything is beige.

Cassie walked in like a regular, waving to a bartender on the left side of the restaurant, then headed out a back door, bringing us to an outdoor bar with a blue awning.

"What are you having?" she asked me as she perched on a brown barstool, reading the laminated menu.

"Just a glass of wine," I told her, trying to see what kinds of white they had.

"Let's do a shot of tequila."

I put my menu down. "No." I practically laughed. "I really don't drink like that anymore."

"What happened to you? You used to be fun." She waved the bartender over. "Two tequilas."

"Cassie," I said again. "No."

She stared at me as if she was daring me to do it. To give in to her like I always did. The truth was, I drove there.

"At least a margarita," she said to me. "Remember when we used to drink those?"

I nodded. "That time in Ibiza we drank them at the beach all day."

"Wasn't that so much fun?"

I smiled, remembering the soft white sand, the cool breeze and the hot men next to us who we thought were flirting but turned out to be gay. It didn't stop Cassie from trying to flirt with them. But then I also remembered the mixture of lime juice on our lips and how I developed a rash that stung like a sunburn.

"Just a Pinot Grigio, please," I instructed the bartender.

He nodded and turned around to tend to our drinks.

Cassie fluttered a disapproving hand at me.

"So, what did you and Tom talk about on your walk?" I asked, propping my elbow on the sticky bar.

"Nothing really, just catching up. Why?"

"I'm wondering what I have to update you on versus what you already know."

She shrugged. "Just that life has been a bit of struggle over the past few years, for both of us." She left it at that.

The air felt thick between us. We used to know each other so well. Our tells were obvious but time had changed us both. I'd reached a point in my life where I was tired of games.

The bartender returned with my wine while Cassie looked down at the two tequila shots in front of her. She looked at me one more time as if giving me one last chance to reconsider joining her with a shot.

I stared at her. I wasn't even going to shake my head at this point. Then she rolled her eyes as if it was my fault that she now had to take two shots.

"Bottoms up." She held one tiny shot glass up and I toasted her with what looked like a fishbowl of wine compared to her small shot of liquid.

"What shall we toast to?"

She looked up, her blue eyes reflecting the overhead lighting. "Let's toast to freedom."

"Freedom?" I questioned.

But she never answered me. Instead, she clinked my glass then downed both shots, one after the other, then bit at the lime wedge sitting on a paper cocktail napkin.

"Whoa." She made a face.

It took me some time to realize, but you can never recapture your youth. Even if you don't change your habits and you act like a perpetual twenty-two-year-old, it doesn't make you stay young. For one thing, your body can't keep up like that in your thirties. Cassie is beautiful, but she has constant dark circles under her eyes and dry patchy skin that ages her a good five years older than me. Now stress can certainly age a person as well and I've had my fair amount of it. But Cassie and I look older in different ways.

"How do you plan on getting your life together?" I asked bluntly.

She bit her lime again and I'm not sure if it was my question or the sourness of the lime that caused her to make the face she did.

"I told you already," she said, wiping her sticky fingers on a cocktail napkin. "My plan is now that I've left that dirtbag behind, I'm starting my life over. I'm going to create a stable life for Owen and me."

I nod at her rehearsed line. "But how exactly?" I pushed. "What are you going to do for a job?"

She shrugged her shoulders then called out to the bartender. "Margarita, please." When she saw I was still waiting for an answer, she turned back to me.

"I'm looking into it."

"Where?" I asked. "Where are you going to live? Where is Owen going to go to school in the fall?"

Her gaze fell on mine and suddenly she was very serious.

I shook my head. "No, Cassie." I was already reading her mind. "You need to stand on your own two feet. I can't support you anymore."

"I've never made you support me," she said angrily. "Jeeze, I haven't even seen you in seven years."

A few of the patrons around us turn their heads slightly in our direction.

I was taken aback. "Cassie, I didn't mean it like that." My words fumbled over themselves. "What I'm saying is you need a plan. You need to get a job; you need to find a proper place to live with your son. You need to think of him."

"I am thinking of him." Her voice was even louder then.

I cringed and sunk into my chair at the scene she was making. "Just calm down," I said, my voice low.

I saw the white-hot embers of anger burning behind her eyes. I could tell there was more that she wanted to say to me about the subject, but then I watched her blue eyes turn cool again. Her body softened into her stool, and she smiled.

"Let's not talk about this tonight," she said, her fingers rubbing the salted rim of the margarita the bartender had put in front of her, then she brought it to her lips. "I wanted tonight to be about having fun with my best friend. Can we please just focus on the good times we've had together?"

I surrendered and I smiled in agreement. In the end I let us live the night out like we were young again. We stumbled out of the bar and Cassie managed to find a karaoke bar where we sang and laughed until it closed and they finally kicked us out. And the truth was, I did enjoy myself. I did miss Cassie and a night like that with her was exactly what

I had needed. I just wished that I could've been my dumb twenty-year-old self again. Because after so many experiences with Cassie, I knew that there was a catch to all of this. Cassie had a motive for being here and it was going to make this the last fun night we would ever share together.

Chapter Twenty-One
Natalie

"Are you okay?" I sit next to Luke on the couch as he continues to stare out the window, his mind seemingly somewhere else.

"I'm okay." He coughs. "Are you okay?"

I realize that Luke is referring to when he had to tackle me to escape a falling tree branch.

My elbow feels a bit bruised, but I ignore it, telling him I'm fine.

"I don't know what that guy's deal is, but I don't trust him around you."

If only I had told him the half of it.

But again, I look at Riley's actions. He's not a social person, he isn't exactly aware of his surroundings and when threatened, he'll defend himself. I think back to when I saw him that first day we moved in.

"Sadie told me he suffers from PTSD," I explain. "He means well, but he's been through a lot and if you threaten him . . ." I trail off. "Let's just calm down and I'll talk to him."

"No, I don't want you anywhere near him." Luke points in the direction that Riley had walked off.

"You forget that I'm a nurse first," I say sternly. "I've dealt with worse people. He didn't mean it."

"Yeah, I'm sure he didn't," he says sarcastically.

"You started it," I remind him. "You put your hands on him. I know you were upset because I almost got hit with a branch but that's my own fault. I know what I'm doing," I assure him, rubbing the back of his head.

His eyes meet mine sadly and for a while we don't say anything. "Don't you think you'd make a great mother?"

I hesitate and close my eyes, feeling his hand wrap around mine as he pulls it toward him.

"There's something I have to tell you," I finally admit.

"What is it?" He sits up, looking at me more seriously now.

I take a deep breath. I owe it to him to tell him the truth. I've got to give this marriage a fighting chance.

"I never told you about my brother Danny."

"Danny?" He looks at me, confused. "I thought you were an only child?"

"I was from the age of eight," I admit. "Danny and I were in a car crash. He died and my parents blamed me."

"When you were eight?" he says, befuddled.

I nod, realizing how ridiculous that sounds now, but when I was eight, it felt like it was my fault.

"I had been in the back seat fighting with him. I took his bear, and my father turned around to get the bear back. That's when he ran a red light, and a dump truck crashed into Danny's side of the car. He was six years old."

I don't realize that my eyes are wet with tears until Luke pulls me into a hug. "Oh my God, Natalie," he says.

I'm waiting for him to say to me, *why didn't you tell me*, but he doesn't.

"I'm so sorry. That had to have been so traumatic. I understand now why you don't have a relationship with your parents."

I nod, wiping my cheeks.

His eyes narrow onto mine. "It's not your fault," he tells me. "I don't care about the circumstances. You were eight;

you were not the one driving. It was not your fault. You were a child."

"Thank you for saying that," I say, my voice cracking.

He gives me another hug and I bury my head in his shoulder. "Losing Danny was so hard. I can't help but feel, especially after this recent accident, that I'm not meant for happiness. Like the other shoe is going to drop."

"What do you mean?"

"You are right. I am afraid." I clench and unclench my fists. "I'm afraid of becoming my parents and acting horribly to our child. I'm afraid of having a child with you and God forbid losing them. Danny's death was so hard on me. I loved him so much. I feel like Karma will come back and I'll suffer all over again."

"Nat." Luke rubs the side of my cheek. "You can't think you deserved any of that."

"Whether I deserved it or not is irrelevant apparently. I'm already terrified of losing you. I almost did."

"But instead, you sacrificed yourself for me and I almost lost you."

I look at him. "It's because I knew I wouldn't survive without you, so I might as well fight for your life."

"Nat." He runs his fingers through my hair and kisses me. "You are not your parents. You of all people know what they put you through. You'd never do that to our child."

"Still," I insist. "What I see in the emergency room. The horrible accidents these children suffer. I just don't know what I would do if it were my child."

"You can't think like that. You can't live in fear of everything, or you never will live your life."

What he says makes so much sense. But I still can't find it in me to overcome that fear. "I don't know how," I admit.

"You will, I promise you." He hugs me again. "We can table this discussion," he finally says. "I'm glad you told me what was going on so that I could finally understand what you are going through. I want to work with you to figure this out and get through it. Together." He wraps his hand in mine.

"Really?"

"Of course." He shakes his head at me.

"I thought you were running away from me. I thought you didn't want to be with me anymore."

Luke lets out a sigh. "I should've told you."

"Told me what?" My stomach clenches, like it's waiting for a punch.

"My boss came to me a few weeks ago. He told me that my performance is not what he thought it would be. He understands our situation, but he told me that I need to be more focused, or they are going to have to find a replacement."

"I'm so sorry, Luke. You could've told me," I say, knowing just how hypocritical I sound.

He tilts his head, his hand over his mouth. "How am I supposed to tell you something like that?"

"I'm sorry for putting so much pressure on you."

I watch his jaw tighten; the muscles clenched. "It's not your fault." He shakes his head.

"I love you so much," I say.

"I love you too." His forehead on mine. "Let's just promise to be honest with each other from now on, okay?"

I nod, closing my eyes tightly. I realize now is the time.

"I'm still seeing things," I admit.

When I open my eyes, he's looking at me, confused.

"I went off my medication because I was seeing my brother Danny. But despite being off it for several days, I still see him."

"It's okay," he assures me. "The important thing is you know that the images aren't real. It's your body still healing."

"But what if it never goes away? What if I can never be normal again?"

"Look at me," he says, noting the high pitch of my voice. I lower my eyes to him.

"You are perfectly normal and rational. This is part of the recovery process. And if it becomes somewhat permanent, we can figure out the right form of treatment. The good thing is that you don't let it scare you."

"Right," I say.

He rubs my head again. "You don't have to be tough for me, you know."

"I know but I want to be," I answer.

His head falls to the side. "I know, but you must be honest with yourself as well. You can't force yourself to heal faster than your body is ready to."

I nod in agreement.

"Now I expect an honest answer," he tells me.

I sit up straight.

"Are you unhappy here? If you are, we can go home. I should've never forced this on you. It's an unfamiliar place, but I should trust that you know yourself and what you are capable of. If you don't want to stay here by yourself, we can go home."

I smile and reach for his hands. "Thank you for being so understanding. I don't know how I got so lucky with you."

His lips form a partial smile.

"But I do want to stay."

"Are you sure? I'm not so sure I trust that groundskeeper."

"Like I said before. I'm going to talk with him. I know how to properly evaluate someone. And if after speaking with him I'm still uncomfortable, then I will let you know and we can leave, okay?"

Although not happy about it, Luke finally agrees.

"Besides, I think Sadie needs me."

"Sadie?" He's surprised now.

"She really is going through a hard time right now and I want to be there for her. She doesn't have many friends."

"Okay. If you feel safe."

I don't know if I feel safe, but Luke has enough to worry about. He just told me he's on the verge of being fired. The last thing I want is to put any more pressure on him. I can handle this situation on my own.

"I do," I lie.

A few hours later, Luke is on his call when I hear a knock at the door. I'm fortunately in between appointments.

I hurry over, cutting the corner too fast and almost knock over what is probably an expensive vase sitting on a round side table. "Shoot," I call out, managing to get a grip on it before it slips. I'm surprised at just how heavy it is. I turn and see the shadow start to leave so I quicken my pace to get to the door.

When I open it, I see Riley still in his brown Carhartt pants and button-down holding a grocery bag of fresh fruit.

"You should keep bananas in your house." He hands it to me. His face looks worried, like he knows he's in trouble but trying to apologize.

I soften my face into a smile. I step aside for him to come in, but he looks around and shakes his head.

Now I know that Sadie must've have told him not to go inside the guest house again while we are here.

I feel for him in that moment. I'm sure he relies on this job, and he's worried about losing it. I find myself not wanting him to get fired either. It was never my intention. I just wanted him to understand the boundaries.

When he won't come in, I hold the bag up as a thank you and place it on the floor in the foyer. Then I close the door behind me, standing out on the porch with him.

"I'm sorry if we have upset you," I say softly.

He keeps his head down, shifting from one leg to the next.

"Luke worries because I just got over a bad accident." I part my hair to show him the rigid skin of my scars.

His face looks intrigued. Then he shyly looks away.

"I had an accident too," he says, looking down again.

Part of me wants to ask him about it, but I don't want him to become uncomfortable. I nod instead to show I understand.

"I want you to know not to be afraid of us. We don't want to cause you any harm. But while Luke and I are staying here we would appreciate that if you want to come in, you knock first and ask permission?"

His eyes shift but he still avoids eye contact as if slightly embarrassed. "Okay."

"It's not a big deal," I assure him. "Maybe we can be friends?" I suggest.

He looks up then, surprised, and I can guess that no one has ever said that to him.

It breaks my heart.

"I'm not afraid of you," he says. Then he turns and looks at the bigger house, where Tom and Sadie are. "It's them I worry about."

I look at him confused and his face becomes worried again, like he's said too much. He slowly starts to back away from me and makes his way down the porch.

"Keep fruit in your house," he says again.

"I will." I smile.

As he walks down the path and out of sight, I find myself looking over at Sadie and Tom's house. Why would he say he's worried about them? They are in fact the ones who hired him and from what I gather from Sadie they are very understanding and almost protective of him.

But then I think about how I asked Sadie to talk to him. I can't help but wonder what she said to him. Did she threaten him somehow?

I can't imagine Sadie doing such a thing and with Tom back I wouldn't have been surprised if she had him talk to Riley.

He's right about one thing. I worry about Tom too, but maybe I should worry more than I realize.

Chapter Twenty-Two

Sadie

I hear the click of the front door and a pair of keys being tossed onto the front entryway table.

"Tom, is that you?" I call out, coming down the stairs. I wrap a blue cashmere robe around my white silk camisole. It's nearly eight at night and Tom has been gone all day.

"Welcome back, Mr. Wilson." I hear Shar's voice in the front hallway as she gets ready to leave for the night. There is always a warmth in her tone when she addresses Tom.

"Thank you," he answers. Their rapport is always so pleasant, like they are purposefully trying to anger me.

I continue to hear shuffling in the hall, and I stop on the last step, waiting for Shar to close the front door behind her.

"Where were you?"

"Out for a drive." He keeps walking until he gets to the living room, not bothering to turn the lights on, the moonlight outside casting dark shadows across the floor.

I follow behind, standing in the hallway. The room feels cold; I reach for the remote for the fireplace and turn it on, then with my arms folded, I face him. "Are you okay?"

He shrugs. "You're the doctor, right?" He goes to the liquor cabinet now and pulls out a bottle of whiskey and a rocks glass.

"Tom, don't go down that road."

But he ignores me and makes a generous pour, lifting it to his lips and downing it instantly. I watch his shadow from the fire dance on the wall like something tribal.

"Tom, you just left the hospital." I keep my voice calm and even. "I don't want to see you go back."

"Is that a threat?" He laughs, his grip tight on the glass.

I continue to stare at him to show him how serious I am.

He bites his lip and looks up, smiling for a moment before slamming his glass hard into the fireplace. The flames flare up as the glass explodes.

I instinctively jump and a grin emerges across his face. He enjoyed scaring me like that. The shadows on his face from the fire make him look sinister, but I can be just as intimidating.

"Is this all because your precious plan didn't work out the way you wanted?" I say, referencing the burner phone. I may not know what's on it, but clearly, he was conspiring about something.

He looks at me with a genuine expression of surprise.

"You don't think I know what you've done?"

He swallows.

"Please sit." I try to soften our standoff. The truth is, I don't want to fight.

We both make our way to the couch. I tuck my legs underneath my sleeping gown while he keeps a distance from me, legs spread wide with his elbows on his knees.

"Sometimes in life, we do things that are rash. We all make mistakes, and we can be forgiven."

He looks at me warily. "What did you do?"

"It's not about what I've done," I say. "It's about what you did. What you can't forgive yourself for."

"What are you talking about?"

This will certainly hit him where it hurts.

"I need to tell you the truth about your father's death."

He squints at me. "How would you know about that?"

"Because under hypnosis you told me the truth about that day."

"You've never done hypnosis," he challenges me.

"I have actually, with my clients' permission. But I didn't think you'd let me because deep down you know the truth."

He swallows again. "I don't know what you're talking about."

"I was worried you wouldn't be able to live with yourself, but I can see now the damage I have done. It's allowed you to simply suppress any wrongdoing on your part, so you don't have to take responsibility for anything you do."

"Tell me." His voice hardens to stone.

"When you took me to Whistler, to your family's home before you sold it . . ." I swallow. I know I'm going too far but I can't seem to stop myself. "I could tell you were struggling and if I'm honest with myself I wanted to know the truth."

Tom leans in closer, urging me to go on.

"You were half dozed on the couch. You were in a twilight state and didn't know I had turned off the TV. I started to ask you questions about that day."

"You did what?" he asks, his voice sounding betrayed.

"I know the truth, Tom. I know that you killed your father."

Tom stands up now, pacing the room. "That's not true."

"But it is," I say gently. "You told me about the guide taking you on a run called Singing Pass."

Tom stops dead in his tracks.

"You were angry with him. You had picked up more speed than him and you were coming on him fast. You slammed into him. You knew you should've waited until he was farther ahead, but you didn't because you were mad and part of you wanted to send him off that cliff."

"That's not true. I was nowhere near him." His voice breaks, unsure of himself now.

"That's what you've told yourself."

He puts his head into his hands. I come over to rub his back, like a supportive wife.

"I know you didn't mean it," I say. "Just like I know you didn't mean what you did with Cassie either."

Chapter Twenty-Three

Natalie

"Are you sure you'll be okay?" Luke whispers in my ear.

"I'll be fine," I murmur.

I feel him kiss my cheek. "I love you."

"Love you too," I say dreamily. I turn and check the clock. "It's almost four in the morning. I know his flight to Geneva is at eight and he's got a long drive ahead of him. "You better get going."

I feel his lips press to my forehead one more time before I hear the faint fall of his footsteps.

My mind sleepily falls back to dreaming about Danny. I don't know how to make him go away, but then a part of me doesn't want to. I don't want to ever forget Danny. I hear what sounds like whimpering, and I groggily open my eyes.

My heart catches in my throat. It's Danny standing in the door frame. He's scared and clutching a teddy bear against his chest. The same one I remember from all those years ago.

"I'm scared," he says in a soft voice. "I had a bad dream."

My chest feels heavy. This echo of Danny sneaking into my room at night. He was always afraid of going to my parents because they would send him back to his room, but he knew if he came to me, I'd lift the spread and let him come in with me.

I swallow my urge to fight this. To try to rationalize the experience in some way. Right now, I just want to be with Danny. "Come here," I sigh sweetly.

He comes to me and snuggles his back up against me in a spooning position. I wrap my arms around him. It all feels so real to me. I can smell the faint strawberry scent of his hair, the softness of his skin and the bones of his back pressed against me.

I feel the tears start to come. It's like reliving a precious moment in your life. I don't see this hallucination as a bad thing. For once, I welcome it. I welcome the ability to relive this moment. One of my favorites. I want to stay awake, I want to hold him forever, as if I can somehow stop what will happen. Like I have the ability to turn back time and all I have to do is never let go and he'll be alive today.

I wake a few hours later, the image still fresh in my mind as if it only happened moments ago. But as I had suspected, the room is empty. I'm the only one in my bed. There is no Danny. Not anymore.

I sit up, wiping my eyes, wondering if maybe Danny himself had come to me in a dream to let me know he's all right. It's what I would like to think, but I'm rational to a fault and given what I've seen of the world, I don't believe there is one after this.

I stand up, facing the morning sun as it rises above the ocean. It reminds me that each day is a chance to start afresh. We start over again and we do the only thing we can do, which is keep moving forward. You can't change the past; we just have to move on with our lives.

I stretch and decide to go for another swim. As I continue with each long stroke I wonder if maybe accepting Danny as a part of my life will be a good thing. This whole time I've been fighting it, but why? He is a part of my life that's worth remembering and if I get a chance to see him every once in a while, then I want to welcome it, because I love Danny, and the truth is, I'll never stop loving him.

It's in that moment that I feel my heart surge. I stop swimming mid-stroke, standing in the shallow end of the pool. I realize for the first time what I want. I want someone to love and care for like Danny. I just always worried about the idea of replacing him. I think about what Luke said yesterday. If Luke and I have a child, it would have me and Luke and a little of Danny in them. I think about how much I loved Danny. I was young, but it was unconditional. I can do that again. I can love someone like I loved Danny.

My mind skips again. What if after all of this I realize that I can't have children? Would it be the same? But my heart catches up shortly with my head and I realize that of course it's not about having a child with our DNA. It's about having a child to love and look out for. Someone we can protect as best we can and give them the life we've always dreamed of for them. It doesn't have to be about history repeating itself. I find myself looking up at the sky. It is a new day and in it, a new beginning. We have the power to be the person or parent we want to be.

Luke is right. I will be a good mother, because I know what I want. I am not my mother, nor will I ever become her because I've spent my life fighting that. I can be me.

My heart is so full I want to cry and laugh at the same time. I want to call Luke and tell him my revelation. Tell him that I do want kids and that as far as our jobs and everything else, we will make it work. If we are a team, we can make it work.

I climb out of the pool then, reach for my towel and dry myself off. I'm about to turn and wrap my towel around my waist when I freeze at the blue and red flashing lights in front of me. They are in front of Sadie and Tom's house.

A deep chill runs up my spine. Something has happened.

Everything in me wants to race over there and find out what's going on, but I can't. I'm afraid. Afraid of what I might find out. I take a few more steps toward the driveway, when I notice that there is only one cop car. A police officer is leaning against his squad car, lazily checking his watch. His partner is likely inside.

I debate about calling out to him and asking if everything is okay. But as I look around, I realize there are no ambulances, no additional cars. Whatever this is it looks routine of some sort. There is no sense of urgency, which means this is no emergency. Still it feels like something big must've happened. I look over toward the main house, trying to peer into the windows to see if I can see anything, but on bright mornings like this, all I can see is the sun's reflection off the glass panes.

I take it as a sign to go back and shower. I will certainly talk to Sadie once the car leaves, but no one could've hurt themselves or this would be a much bigger scene. I would've heard sirens. Whatever it is, I will find out soon enough.

I head back to the house, thinking about Sadie trying to kill herself, Riley's attack on Luke, and I know something is going on. There has been what feels like an undercurrent of some sort, one that will rip you under and wash you away. The fact that I don't know what it is keeps me on my toes. I had thought it was because Tom had come home, but the truth is, I've been feeling it all along, from the moment we arrived. I just don't know who I'm trying to help or who I'm trying to protect myself from.

After my shower, I throw on a green jumpsuit—a new online purchase, in an attempt to improve my wardrobe—and make myself a cup of coffee to get ready for my clinical work. I read a couple of emails, but my mind is too distracted by what is happening next door. The cop car is still there, so again I need to wait it out.

I look up at the blank screen of the television and decide to turn it on. Maybe if I can find the local news, I might have some sort of idea what might be happening.

The TV blares loudly, causing me to grimace at the noise as I quickly try to lower the volume.

I flip through the channels before I find the local news station. So far nothing much to talk about other than that the weather for the next few days is looking clear. After realizing I'm zoning out on news coverage of a local animal shelter, I decide to mute the TV and get back to work.

My laptop's FaceTime starts to ring, and I look at the time. "Oh shoot." I realize I have my meeting with Dr. Warton.

"Dr. Warton." I smile.

"Natalie, how are you doing?"

"I'm doing very well."

"Just wanted to check in with you," he says.

"I nod. Everything is going very well for me personally," I say, not wanting to elaborate.

"Any more hallucinations?"

I take a moment to consider. "No," I tell him. "No more." I realize that if my only hallucinations are of Danny then I accept that. I don't want him to go away anymore.

"Very good." He makes a note on the notebook that is sitting next to him.

"So did you return to the medication?"

I shake my head. "I think I'm done with it."

He looks at me cautiously.

"I feel better without it, honestly. I think the best medicine for me right now is fresh air and exercise."

His jowls lift lightly to a smile. "Believe me I'd much rather that be the case," he says. "I'm glad to hear that things are improving. I can tell you even sound a bit better. Less wary."

I shrug. "I was getting used to a new environment before."

"That's true." He writes something else down and I can overhear an announcement being made for a doctor on the PA system. "Are there any other sorts of updates that you would like to bring me in on?"

But his voice trails off in my head, when my eye catches the image on the TV. It's a picture of Cassie, Sadie's friend. The news is showing a different image, but it's still of Cassie—I know it.

"Natalie?" Dr. Warton's voice returns.

I shake my head. "I'm so sorry. Yes, everything is fine, but I'm sorry I have to go."

I slam my laptop down without a second thought and quickly lean over toward the coffee table to grab the remote. I unmute it with just enough time to hear: *the body that washed up two days ago on the Shinnecock inlet has been identified as Cassie Dune.*

Chapter Twenty-Four

Sadie

I wake to the sound of loud banging on the front door. I look over at the clock. Tom is sleeping soundly next to me. It's nearly eight in the morning.

I sit up, the room shifting on its axis as I stand up and reach for my robe hanging on the back of the bathroom door. I creep to the guest bedroom toward the front of the house and peer out the window. My heart seizes when I see a police car in our driveway.

I hear the door open. Shar, apparently on time, as usual, answers it.

I hear her start to pace upstairs. Quickly I scurry back to our room, closing the bedroom door.

"Tom!" I yell in a harsh whisper. "The police are here!"

His eyes open in alarm and he quickly sits up. "What?"

"The cops are here!" I say in another harsh whisper, and I tilt my head to the hallway where we can hear footsteps.

I hurry into the bathroom to brush my teeth and fix my hair. The last thing I want is to look like a train wreck.

"Get in the shower," I say, raking a brush through my hair. "I'll find out what they want."

Just then we hear a loud knock on our bedroom door.

"Mrs. Wilson?"

I continue to apply my mascara as she repeats her rap on the door. By the third time, I have managed to pull my hair into a sophisticated bun, apply lipstick and foundation, and a soft blush. "Be right there," I finally call.

I rush to my closet, finding a cream-colored, three-quarter-length dress with cap sleeves.

I smooth out the bottom as I look into the mirror.

"The police are here." Her voice seeps in through the door.

"Be right there," I say, a little more annoyed now. I look again at the mirror. My breath is shaky, and I take a few calm breaths to try to steady my fast-beating heart.

"You've got this," I say to myself.

I grab a pair of white heels and put them on. I'd like to give the impression that I'm on my way out the door.

When I open the door, Shar is staring at me for the first time. She hasn't looked me in the eye for some time now, but in this moment her icy blue eyes pierce into mine, a smile creasing her cheeks like she knows something I don't.

I hurry past her down the steps, quickly changing my demeanor when I see a rotund uniformed police officer, standing in my hallway. His hat is tucked against his chest, his arm holding it inward sitting on top of his protruding belly.

I cock my head in surprise. "Hello, may I help you?"

He looks up at me then, his thick eyebrows rise. "Mrs. Sadie Wilson?"

I nod and smile. "Yes."

"I'm Officer Tomlin, I have a few questions I'd like to ask you in regard to Cassie Dune."

I give him a puzzled look. "Oh, of course." I gesture him into the living room. "May I get you a coffee, tea, water or anything?"

He considers this for a moment. "I'll take a coffee actually—that would be great."

My body feels lighter. If he's taking coffee, he's not here to arrest anyone. I peer over his shoulder at his partner, much shorter and skinnier who is standing outside, leaning against the car. "How about your partner?"

"I can check with him," he says, stepping back out onto the porch to call to the other officer.

I take my time, preparing a fresh pot, stalling for as long as I can.

I eventually come into the room with a tray that has three cups of coffee along with a creamer jar and a bowl of sugar cubes. I plaster a smile on my face as I enter the living room. The sun is shining brightly through the windows, revealing tiny dust motes floating in the space between us.

"My partner is fine, no coffee for him," he says as he pours milk into one of the cups and brings it to his lips. "Is your husband home?"

"He's in the shower," I say. "Does this concern him?"

The officer considers it for a second. "I guess that might be for you to decide," he says.

I tighten my jaw and take a seat across from him on our white couch.

"So how can I help you?"

Officer Tomlin shifts in his seat as if trying to get comfortable. He takes out a balled-up napkin and pats at his forehead.

"Hot out today?" I ask.

"Gonna be a scorcher," he answers. "Was Cassie Dune staying at your residence these last few days?"

I pull at my ear and straighten up. "She was, but she left on Friday. I had renters coming to stay at the guest house on Saturday." I point toward the house, which he leans off his chair to see through the far window.

"Do you know where she might've gone after she left?"

I shake my head. "Cassie is a bit of a free spirit," I explain. "I've known her my whole life, and she sort of just comes in and out of it without so much as a hello or goodbye. But this was planned. She knew she had to leave by Friday."

"Did she tell you where she was going?"

I shake my head. "She just said she'd figure it out. She lives her life flying by the seat of her pants."

His face grows grim then. "I'm afraid I have some bad news."

I brace myself. "Oh?"

"Cassie's body was found washed up on the jetty in the Shinnecock inlet."

My hand goes to my mouth and my eyes begin to fill with tears. "Oh my God," I say in a shaky breath. "Can you be so sure it's her?"

He drops his head sadly.

I keel over my lap, suddenly having a hard time breathing, the truth of it settling over me.

He waits patiently for me to compose myself.

"How?" I ask.

"That's what we are trying to find out. We found her car abandoned at a marina near the Ponquogue Bridge, not far from where her body washed up. The death is currently ruled as a drowning as there didn't appear to be any blunt-force trauma." He looks up from his notes. "Was Cassie suicidal?"

I shake my head. "No, but . . ." I shrug. "I also haven't seen her in the better part of a decade. I know that her life wasn't going all that great, but she never told me much."

"We know she had a son, Owen," Officer Tomlin says, reaching for his coffee to take a sip.

"Oh God," I say. The thought of Owen comes to the forefront of my brain. My tongue becomes thick, and my head starts to spin with nausea. "Where is he? Is he okay?"

"We don't know," he says. "We were hoping you did."

"Oh God." My head falls into my hands. "That poor boy," I say, crying now. "I can only hope that whatever Cassie got herself into that she didn't take Owen down with her."

Officer Tomlin gives me a minute to compose myself.

"We were hoping you could walk us through the days leading up to the event. Forensics put the time of the death sometime late Friday night, early Saturday morning."

I nod, my eyes reddening. "She had already left by then," I say.

"A witness at the Southampton Publick House said that you two were pretty intoxicated the night before."

I feel my eyes prick with tears again, but I hold them back. "It was her last night here and so we wanted to go out with a bang. I hadn't seen her in seven years, and I didn't know when I'd see her again."

"Was there any altercation?"

I think back to Cassie's raised voice and the other patrons looking around at us. There was no point in lying—surely, they heard us.

I nod slowly. "I had started the night off on the wrong foot. I knew she'd have to leave soon, and I was trying to figure out what her plan was. Where she was going to live, what she was going to do for money . . ." I trail off. "She got angry and told me that she'd figure it out. Then she told me not to ruin the night and just let us have fun, so I did." I shrug my shoulders. "That was it though."

"Was there any argument from her about leaving?"

"No," I say almost too quickly, crossing my legs.

"Was there anyone who might've wanted to hurt Cassie?"

"She had told me that she had a boyfriend who was abusive. She had called the cops on him, and when he got arrested, she came to stay with me."

Officer Tomlin leans forward now at this lead. "Did he know where she was?"

"I don't think so." I shake my head. "I only knew she was coming the day before when she called me. Before that I hadn't heard from her in seven years."

"Is there anything you can tell me about this boyfriend?"

"I wish I could," I tell him. "The problem is Cassie was very elusive when it came to details. I didn't even know where she was living before she came to stay with me."

He leans into his back pocket and pulls out a notepad, writing down this new information. "Was this man the boy's father?"

"I'm not sure," I say. "When I asked who the father was, she told me she didn't know, though she could've been lying."

"So, this could be a situation where the boyfriend was the father of Owen, came and found Cassie, pushed her off a bridge and took Owen."

"Oh God." My head falls into my lap again, and I suppress another sob.

"I'm sorry," the officer says. "I didn't mean to upset you. We just want to try to figure out what happened to her son, try to get a sense if he's alive or not. Time is of the essence in situations like these."

I pull myself upright and reach for a tissue on the coffee table in front of us, and I dab my eyes. "You're doing your job. I understand. And of course I want you to find Owen as well. I hope he's okay."

"Can you walk me through the Friday she left?"

I crumple up the tissue in my hand. "It was all very amicable. I had told her that I had renters coming Saturday afternoon and cleaners scheduled to come beforehand, so they would need to leave by Friday night."

"What time would you say they left?"

"We said our goodbyes that afternoon, around four. I'm not sure what time they left."

"Thank you," he says. "This has been helpful."

Relieved for it to be over, I stand up. "Is there anything else I can help you with?"

"Actually, there is," he says, standing as well. He takes the pen that was in his hand and points it at my left shoulder. "That bandage on your arm."

I freeze. It must've shown from my sleeve when I reached for a tissue.

"Can you explain to me the details of how you came to get that injury, and why the cops were at your house the night of Cassie's death?"

Chapter Twenty-Five
Natalie

My body stiffens. Cassie Dune is dead.

I shove my laptop off my lap and stand up. I need to know what happened here.

I step out of the house, just as one of the officers is approaching the front door. I stop in my tracks.

"Hello," I say.

"Hi." He slows his stride. "I'm Officer Tate. My partner Officer Tomlin is speaking with Mrs. Wilson now."

I nod, but my face still shows confusion. Then I take it I should introduce myself. "I'm Natalie Copper. I'm Mrs. Wilson's tenant."

Officer Tate hooks his thumbs into his belt and arches his back, his chin lifted as if this will add more height to his short stature. He's barely taller than I am. I notice his upper lip is dimpled with sweat and I wonder how long he's had to wait outside on such a hot day.

"Can I get you something cool to drink?" I ask him.

"That won't be necessary," he says in a tone that is all business. "Can I ask when you arrived?"

I nod. "We got here Saturday around two-thirty, likely?"

"We?"

I stumble over my words. There's something about the presence of an officer that is always intimidating. You feel as if you did something wrong even if you didn't.

"My husband Luke and I."

He looks over my shoulder. "Is he here now?"

I shake my head. "He had to fly to Geneva early this morning. He's due to come back next week."

"So, it's just you?"

"Yes," I admit.

"Are you certain of the time you arrived?" he questions. "You seemed a bit unsure."

"It was between two-thirty and three o'clock. I remember because Sadie—" I stop myself. "I mean, Mrs. Wilson came by to check on us and invite us for dinner. We wanted to get unpacked and settled, but we also wanted to make sure we had time to run into town and bring flowers and wine over as a hostess gift."

Officer Tate's eyes glaze over as these details aren't necessary.

He ushers me along. "So, you have been here at this residence since Saturday afternoon."

"Yes." I nod.

"Just you and your husband?"

I nod again. He looks up at the guest house as if assessing it. He seems satisfied. I think he's about to turn to go when he stops himself and turns back around.

"Did you know the Wilsons before you rented this house?"

"No," I say.

"How did you come to discover the house was for rent?"

"My husband found it, on some renters' website. I'm not sure which one, but I could ask him once he lands and get back to you."

Officer Tate puts a hand up. "That won't be necessary—we should be able to get that information. Would you happen to know how long it had been on the market for? Or at least when you booked it?"

"We booked it last week."

"Really?" He seems surprised. "It seems odd that anything would be available for rent in the middle of July. How long are you renting for?"

"A month."

Officer Tate lets out a whistle. "Even more rare," he says.

Suddenly the oppressive heat of the morning is getting to me. I'm sweating more than normal. Somehow, I feel as if I've done something wrong.

"My husband believed we must've seen the listing as soon as they had posted it. Within hours likely."

Officer Tate sucks in his cheeks as if he's literally chewing on this information. Then he gives me a slow nod. "Thank you for the information."

"You're welcome," I say.

As he turns to leave, I stop him.

"Do you mind me asking what's going on?" Even though I have a sense of it, I'd still like to hear it first-hand.

"The body of Cassie Dune was found in the Shinnecock inlet. She had been previously staying in this house." He points up. "From what we gather, until Friday."

My body stiffens.

"She had a son," he adds. "Owen. We are trying to locate him."

I feel a hard lump build in my throat. "Do you have a picture of him? In case I've seen him?" I ask.

He pulls out a picture that looks like it's a school photo. "We found it in her wallet," he says.

I take the picture from him, the corner edge creased in a way that it might just tear off.

My body seizes as I stare at the picture. The boy in the photo is Danny. But upon closer examination I see it's not

Danny. But a boy the same age who looks like how I remember Danny.

"Do you recognize this boy?" he asks, seeing my reaction.

My eyes start to well with tears and I shake my head. "No. He just looks a lot like my brother, who died at his age."

Officer Tate's expression softens. "I'm sorry," he says. "Nothing worse than the loss of a child."

I nod and slowly hand the picture back to him.

He looks at me sympathetically. "Well, if you think of anything or find anything that could help us with this case." He reaches in his back pocket and pulls out a business card and hands it to me. "Just let me know."

"I will," I assure him, the sadness still in my voice.

I watch him as he walks across the lawn and straight into the Wilsons' house.

I hear their front door snap shut and it breaks me out of my trance.

This isn't making sense. What if the boy I was seeing was Owen? I turn on my heel, running into the house. I burst through the door so abruptly that the door swings loudly on its hinges and cracks against the wall. I slam it quickly behind me.

"Owen!" I call out. "Owen, are you in here?" It doesn't make sense that he would be. Although I have had visions of seeing him, where would he be the rest of the time?

I start checking all the doors and closets, under the beds, but there's nothing. Nothing indicates that there is a child here. I rush out the back door, checking under the deck, through the dunes, my breath heavy with determination.

What is happening here? What does this all mean?

I make my way to a chair on the back porch, and I sit, taking in a deep breath. I've never been one for paranormal. I don't believe in ghosts. I do believe in my hallucinations though. Which made sense when I thought they were Danny. That was my childhood trauma reappearing in the forefront of my mind. But they didn't start until I came here. I thought it was the change of scenery.

But now, now I'm not so sure. This boy—Owen. He looks like Danny, and he went missing the day before we arrived. But if he were alive and in the house, then I'd know it.

So, what the hell is going on?

My body starts to shake with . . . I don't know what. Adrenaline, nervousness, or just the understanding that not everything has a rational explanation the way that I would've hoped.

What if he's alive, but not here? I think, but at the same time I'm calling myself crazy.

Whether I'm crazy or not, I need to do whatever I can to find him. I couldn't save Danny, but maybe I can find a way to save Owen.

Chapter Twenty-Six

Sadie

I must confess.

There is no getting around this point. "Would you like some more coffee?" I ask as my eyes flick upstairs.

"I'm just fine, thank you," the officer says slowly, treading lightly so as to not scare me off.

"I don't want my husband to hear," I say more softly.

"Officer Tate?" he calls the other officer from the front hall.

Officer Tomlin looks back at me and nods understanding. "Just a moment."

I sit back as his footsteps retreat into the hallway. The front door closes so the voices I hear are faint and muffled.

My heart feels as if it's going to beat out of my chest. There's a pounding in my head, but then I realize it's footsteps. Tom's footsteps coming down the stairs.

I worry about what my face will give away. I want to say I'm sorry and that I never meant for this to happen. But instead, I hear the front door open again.

"Mr. Wilson?" an unfamiliar voice asks.

"Yes?"

"I'm Officer Tate. I'd like to ask you a few questions. Do you mind stepping outside with me, please?"

"Um . . ." I hear Tom say with hesitancy. "Sure."

Once the door closes again behind them, I hear Officer Tomlin's footsteps become louder as he reaches the living room.

"Now," he says, sitting back down. "You were about to tell me about the bandage on your arm."

"My husband, he stabbed me with a knife. It wasn't his fault." I put my hands up. "He has DID—it's multiple personalities. It was an accident."

"What was your husband doing with a knife?"

"He was on some sort of drug. You see he's a recovering drug addict and I'm not sure how he obtained the drugs, unfortunately, likely from Cassie."

"So, where were you when this occurred?"

"In our living room. I was trying to coax him to bed, and he had the knife in his hand."

"That doesn't seem like an accident."

"He was trying to keep me back; he wasn't trying to attack me."

"So, he was threatened by you, like he needed to defend himself?"

I roll my eyes. "In his mind, yes. Listen, you can call Dr. Turner, and he can give you his full evaluation."

The officer leans in now. "We will be sure to do that. Now, where was Cassie at this point?"

"I assumed that she was gone by then."

"But you're not sure."

I shift nervously. "No, but the house was dark. It didn't look like anyone was there. Like I said, we said our goodbyes around four."

"Let me get this straight. Your husband stabs you, yet you allow for other tenants to move in just a mere twenty-four hours after this whole thing occurs. Do you think that was a good idea?"

I sigh. "It's something that can be triggered when he uses drugs. Something that Cassie gave him, and that he'd otherwise have no access to."

"Are you sure of that?"

I nod sadly. "Cassie's ex-boyfriend was into drugs," I say, remembering her tell me how he'd come home from work coked out and angry, so it seems rational. "I wouldn't be surprised if you find more of it in her car or even in her system." Suddenly I blink and consider the thought. "Had she taken a hallucinogenic Friday night? Could that be why she jumped?"

"We are still waiting on the toxicology report," he tells me. "Let's go back to your husband and the knife."

"I think I merely startled him, and he thought he was defending himself from danger. I'll remind you again he was on a hallucinogenic. He probably thought I was a demon or something."

"What did you do after that?"

"I called 9-1-1."

"Were you concerned he would hurt you again? Do you think maybe he killed Cassie before she left?"

"My husband did not kill Cassie," I say angrily. "I called the cops because I knew I couldn't try to contain him. They came and I advised them of his condition, and they brought him to the hospital for a psychiatric evaluation. He was released on Tuesday. He's fine now."

"When you called 9-1-1, where was your husband?"

"In the living room."

"Where was the knife?"

"Lodged in me."

"Before that. Could he have used it before on Cassie?"

"Did she have stab wounds on her body?" I counter.

"No."

"Then I think we are done with this line of questioning." I cross my arms.

I watch as he takes this all into consideration, then closes his notebook. "All right then," he says, giving in. He stands up, going over to his partner and returning with a Ziploc bag.

My mouth goes dry when I see the contents.

"It appears that this burner phone was found by your maid in one of your coat pockets. It called only one number, Cassie's burner phone, which was found in her car. There were calls multiple times a day for several months leading up to her arrival, yet you told me earlier you didn't know she was coming until a day in advance and you hadn't heard from her in seven years."

I try to swallow but it feels like sandpaper. "I don't understand. That isn't my phone. I found it in the back of my husband's drawer." I look at the floor confused, trying to make sense of it. "Tom is the one who brought Cassie here?"

"I think another lead is that Cassie was blackmailing your husband in order to get money out of him. Then she shows up here to put the pressure on him and he kills her."

"Why would she ask my husband for a loan?" I say. Why wouldn't she just ask me? "He couldn't have given her one," I clarify. "Due to his condition, I'm in control of the finances."

"We found an email on Cassie's laptop asking your husband for a loan."

"What?"

"His response was to ask if she still had the same number. There are no further emails from what we gathered and given these two burner phones . . ." He trails off, but he's made his point.

"I think you should see yourself out." I harden, sucking air in through my nostrils.

"We will look into all this information to confirm its accuracy, and we will be in touch."

"You do that," I say tightly.

"I'll see myself out," he says. He gives me a nod and retreats to the front door.

Chapter Twenty-Seven

Natalie

I've been trying to get a hold of Sadie, but she's not answering the door or responding to text messages. It occurs to me only now, that she might be at the police station or maybe identifying Cassie's body.

I can only imagine how upsetting this all must be for her. She's officially lost her best friend for good. I realize now that she's going to be very fragile and that I'm going to really have to keep an eye on her.

The rest of the day I try to concentrate as I continue with my clinical work and virtual appointments, but I'm constantly one eye off the screen. Searching for I'm not sure what. I don't know if I'm waiting to see Sadie outside so I can talk to her or if I'm trying to summon another vision of Owen.

But my heart stops when I see Riley's red Ford truck, crunching along the gravel of the driveway.

Could he have had something to do with any of this? Riley gets out of his car, with the same demeanor as always. Could he have killed Cassie? I think about the dove whose neck he snapped, that expression of amusement on his face when he had Luke pinned down. But what about Owen? What if Owen is trapped somewhere? Maybe Riley killed Cassie and then took Owen and is holding him captive? The idea constricts my ability to breathe.

I toss my laptop to the side of the couch. I have to do something. But what? I can't exactly run up to Riley and accuse him of murder and kidnapping.

I think about the food and him showering here. Maybe he didn't want to go home because he would see Owen and it would remind him of what he'd done? I think back to hearing Sadie tell Marla to make Riley a plate of food because he lives alone.

"You have to do something," I say out loud to myself.

I wait for Riley to appear from the shed and see him come out with the lawn mower. I smile with relief. I'm going to need to make sure that I'm not heard, and the loud engine of the mower will do just that.

Riley puts on his headphones, and I wait until he's on the other side of Sadie's house. I need to look in his truck, but fear paralyzes me. I think of the car crash with Danny, being crushed beneath the metal, the loud buzzing of the scary machine that had to cut us out. I think of my body cracking on the windshield to save Luke. I start to feel dizzy as my chest tightens, nausea getting the best of me. I swallow it down, fighting back against myself. I have to get to his truck; I have to save Owen.

I muster up the courage and kickstart my adrenaline, making a beeline to the car. God forbid the car alarm goes off; he may not hear it right away, but he would eventually. I take my chances and pull on the driver-side door handle.

It swings open with a loud creak, and I breathe a sigh of relief. I lean in searching the center console and the glove compartment, trying to find his address somewhere. I sit fully now in his driver's seat and that's when I notice a black bulge wedged in the side door. I reach for it, realizing it's his wallet.

I open it up and pull out his drivers' license.

The whir of the mower gets louder, and I turn to see Riley is coming around the side of Sadie's house, headed toward me. I need my phone. I curse myself. I need to take a picture of his address.

The motor gets louder, and I know it's only moments before Riley notices me.

Thinking fast I close the driver-side door shut and duck under the window. If his door isn't open, he shouldn't suspect anything right away.

While my head is ducked, I take the paperwork that I had pulled out from his passenger seat and shove it back into his glove compartment. I hope that he doesn't pay as much attention to the detail of his paperwork as he does the roses.

With my body still lying along his front seat, I reach back into my jeans pocket for my phone. I hear a loud bang, which almost makes me yell. I feel the weight of his car slump and realize Riley has climbed into the bed of his truck.

My heart jumps. I'm completely frozen, afraid of what he might do if he sees me here. The truck bends and rocks as I feel Riley pull something from his truck and toss it off to the side. As he climbs off the truck, it rights itself.

I try hard not to move and hope that he doesn't need anything out of the front of his truck.

After what feels like an eternity, I peek my head up, but I don't see him anywhere. I remind myself to breathe, my body covered with sweat. I need to at least do what I came to do.

I pull my phone out of my pocket, but my hand is shaking so badly that it drops into the well of the car.

Panic sets in, but I fight it, reaching around feeling for it until I finally get a grip on it. I open Riley's wallet again and hold my phone in front of it, snapping a picture of his license.

"What are you doing in my truck?"

I let out a scream as I look up and see Riley, red-faced and angry, staring at me from the passenger-side window.

He opens the door and I quickly right myself and open the driver's side door. I throw his wallet at him as a distraction and run as fast as I can into the guest house.

"Hey!" he yells. I turn and see him slam his passenger door shut and start to chase me. My lungs are burning but I keep going. I reach the front door and slam it shut before locking it, then I quickly run to the back door, locking it as well.

I hear a loud banging from the front door. "What do you want?" he yells. "Why were you in my truck?"

But I don't answer. I don't want to see his angry face again. Because the last time I saw it, it nearly killed my husband. I scramble for my laptop on the couch and run up the stairs. Between that and my phone I can lock myself in a room and call the cops, if need be, though I am the one who broke into his truck.

I try to ignore the insistent hammering on the front door and steady my breathing. "You need to find Owen," I tell myself. "Concentrate on finding Owen."

I sit on my bed with my legs folded in a meditative position, as if I could somehow summon Owen. I open my laptop and pull up Riley's address.

Based on Google Maps, I notice he lives near the Ponquogue Marine Basin.

I google Cassie Dune and find an article saying that her body washed up near the Shinnecock inlet. I pull up the map again, running my fingers along the water, then put a hand over my mouth.

Cassie's body was found not far from where Riley lives.

The pounding has appeared to stop, and I wonder if Riley has given up or found a way in. He has a key, I remember. That was the only explanation to how he was breaking in all the time.

How stupid could I be?

Terrified to come out of my room, I quickly reach into my pocket again and pull out Officer Tate's card.

The card quivers in my hand as I struggle to read the number.

"Officer Tate," the voice booms through the line.

"Officer Tate, this is Natalie Copper. I'm Mrs. Wilson's tenant. We spoke earlier today."

"Yes." His voice fills with recognition. "Did you find something you wanted to tell us?"

"Yes," I answer. "The groundskeeper here, Riley Sterling. He has a history of violence. He's been breaking into this house, eating food, using the shower. And he also had an altercation with my husband."

"And did you report it?" he asks.

"No," I say regretfully. "Because I felt bad for him. I found out he suffers from PTSD. I think he was cornered and acted out of fear, but he's still stronger than he realizes."

"So, what does that have to do with Cassie's disappearance?"

"I looked up where he lives," I start. "It's right near the Ponquogue Marine Basin," I start, but he cuts me off.

"That's where Cassie's car was discovered."

My blood runs cold.

"Owen might be there," I say. "Can you get a search warrant for his house?"

"There is a set of fingerprints in her car that haven't been identified. Perhaps I can bring him in to run a match."

"So, you can come get him now?"

"I could. Do you know if he's home?"

I shake my head. "He's here, at the Wilsons' residence."

"Thank you for the tip," he tells me. "I'm going to look into it now and get back to you."

"Please hurry," I find myself saying, but the line is cut, and he's already gone.

My head starts to pound. I hope I've done the right thing. I hope that Owen is there alive and safe, and they find him. But if not, I've angered a potential murderer who I'm stupidly only now realizing likely has a key to this house.

And it's then that I hear another loud crash. Something that sounds like the breaking glass of a window.

Chapter Twenty-Eight

Sadie

My phone shrills, erupting the quietness of the room like the explosion of a grenade. I'm assuming that it's Natalie again, who I have yet to call back. But when I look down at the screen, it's an unknown number. The way my skin prickles across my whole body, I know it must be the police. Darkness settles over the room, like the shadow of the grim reaper, now that the sun is going down. I walk through the living room to answer it outside.

I see Tom sitting on the couch bleary-eyed, in some sort of trance of his own, lost in his own thoughts. He took a Klonopin after I had told him that I lied to the police for him, but they found his burner phone. The look on his face said it all and I couldn't bear to look at him after that.

I silence the ringing and step outside, the air still thick with humidity from the heat of the day.

"Yes?" I answer.

"Mrs. Wilson, this is Officer Tomlin."

"Hello," I say cautiously.

"I wanted to ask you about your groundskeeper. Riley Sterling."

A cold sensation runs across my arms, causing all the hairs to stand on end. "Sure, go ahead."

"Did he have any sort of connection with Cassie while she was staying there?"

At first, I'm not sure how to respond. "Connection?"

"Would there have been any reason for Cassie and Riley to interact?"

"Reason, no. But if I'm being honest Cassie tended to flirt with him a bit. I told her to leave him alone, but that doesn't mean she did."

"Would there be any reason for his fingerprints to be on the steering wheel of her car?"

"I can't imagine a reason," I say quickly.

"Well, we just discovered Riley's fingerprints in her car, which we have now learned was parked in a marina less than a block from where Riley lives."

A cold shiver runs up my spine. "Oh my God," I say with disbelief.

"Did Riley Sterling have a history of violence?"

"I-I'm not sure," I stumble. "He could get angry at times."

"We were speaking with your tenant, Mrs. Copper? She told us there were some instances of Riley breaking into the guest house and using the shower. She also mentioned an altercation with her husband Luke and Riley."

"Yes, she did tell me that. I spoke to him about going into the guest house, but he denied it. As for the situation with him and Luke, I'm not really sure what happened. I wasn't there. But I know Natalie was shaken by it."

"Could there have been a misunderstanding between Riley and Cassie?"

"I don't know." My voice is grave with guilt. "I don't think so. I hope not."

"Thanks for the clarification," he says. "I'll call you if we need any more information."

"Thank you," I tell him before hanging up the phone and letting it drop to the floor. I sit on the front stoop, clasping my fingers so tightly my knuckles hurt. I'm trying so hard to keep it together, but I'm not sure how much longer I can hold on for.

My mind goes back to Cassie and our last day together.

I was walking across the lawn, still hungover from the night before. The sun was beating down on me and I already had perspiration on the back of my neck, as if I wasn't dehydrated enough.

I wanted to talk to Cassie. Last night was fun, but I needed to make sure that she had some sort of plan. She couldn't hide out here forever. Whatever she needed, I'd help her, but she couldn't stay here. I could already notice a shift in Tom. He seemed very calculated in everything he did.

I was in love with your husband.

Tom wasn't next to me in bed that morning, but I assumed he went for a run. I'd been encouraging him to get exercise.

I got to just outside the rose garden, when I looked up at the guest house. I heard splashing and assumed that Owen was swimming again.

I was about to cut through the garden when I heard voices, muffled.

Riley and Cassie?

I was about to intervene, convince Cassie yet again to leave Riely alone, but I stopped dead in my tracks. The voice wasn't Riley's. It was Tom's.

"If this is going to work, you need to hold your end of the deal."

"Relax." I watched as Cassie pulled Tom in and hugged him. "We are going to get you out of this."

I stumbled backwards and headed quickly to the house, hoping that they hadn't seen me.

Cassie and Tom? Cassie was supposed to be my friend. My breathing became shallow as my anger boiled. I exhaled deeply.

Were they having an affair? What did he mean by *hold your end of the deal*?

Did they really think they could make a fool out of me? I was the rational one. Both of them would be nothing without me and here they were conspiring behind my back.

Well, they had another thing coming, if they thought they would get away with this.

Cassie was out of here and out of my life, for good.

I headed upstairs to my computer and listed the guest house for rent immediately. The photo shoot that was done on the house for the Wall Street article was only two years old and nothing had changed, so I uploaded those pictures. It was the Hamptons in July. Someone was going to snatch it up within the hour, I imagined. Then that could be my excuse as to why she had to leave. There would be no choice—someone else was coming in.

I heard the side porch door close and I stiffened. Tom was back, which meant they were done with their little rendezvous. They thought they could sneak around behind my back, but both of them forgot just how clever I really was.

I sent out a text to Cassie.

Can we talk?

I watched the three gray dots appear.

Of course.

My phone pinged on the desk next to my laptop and I looked over at it.

Can you come here? We can talk outside by the pool.

Three gray dots.

Don't want to be too far from Owen in case he needs me.

Okay, coming over now.

As I headed downstairs and then opened the front door, I heard the crunch of the gravel in the driveway. Riley had just come to work.

Three more gray dots appeared on my phone.

Not just yet. One hour.

Did this have something to do with Riley as well? Or was that a coincidence?

I jumped when I turned to go back inside and found Tom coming out through the door.

"Jeeze," I said. "You scared me."

"Sorry," he said, unfazed.

"Where are you going?"

Tom looked down at his athletic shorts and shirt. "I'm going for a run."

"I thought you already went." I was curious to see what he would say.

"I wanted to have my coffee in the garden first."

"See anyone while you were out there?" I pressed.

He looked at me oddly. "I think I saw Owen swimming but that's it. I'm assuming Cassie was somewhere nearby."

"But you didn't see her?"

He put his AirPods in his ears and smiled. "Be back soon."

Almost an hour later I realized that Tom still wasn't back yet. I looked out the front window and noticed Riley's car was gone. When did he leave?

I pulled out my phone and texted Cassie.

Can I come over now?

But I didn't get a response.

I waited about five minutes, then I texted her again, but she didn't respond.

I walked over there, but as I did I felt my pace start to slow and a weariness took over me. I couldn't explain why but I had a feeling, deep inside me, that something terrible had happened.

The back door was wide open, the wind rocking it on its hinges. Owen was nowhere to be seen.

I stepped nervously up the steps and stood in the door frame. "Cassie? Owen?" I called out. But the house was silent.

Chapter Twenty-Nine

Natalie

It's dark now. I'm getting hungry but I've been too afraid to leave the room. After hearing that crash I've been paralyzed, having horrific daymares that I would open the door and find that Riley has been patiently waiting outside my bedroom door for me to open it so he can kill me.

"Natalie?"

I jump up at the sound of my name being called. I realize that it's Sadie.

I open the bedroom door and see no one is there. I breathe a quick sigh of relief.

"Up here," I call but continue to make my way down the stairs.

"What happened?" she asks me.

It takes a second to see what she is looking at when I notice that there is a rock in the middle of the living room and a broken windowpane.

"Riley," I answer.

"Riley?" Her face is curious.

"I—" I choke on my own words. "I made him mad."

"What?"

I try to think of how to explain this to Sadie. These crazy visions—she'll think that I'm insane.

"When the police told me what happened," I start, "I had a hunch about Riley. When he had gotten into that fight yesterday with Luke it seemed like a possibility that he could've done something to Cassie. Then I got worried that her son Owen was maybe being held captive in Riley's house. So, I broke into his car to get his license, and he caught me doing it."

"He caught you?"

I'm not sure if her shock is that I did that or that he caught me. I nod slowly, then continue. "He chased after me but then I locked the door on him. I think he threw the rock out of anger."

Sadie swallows but her face is unreadable. "I see."

"I found something though," I tell her, urging her to sit on the couch, ignoring the possibility of shards of glass. I pull my laptop from under my arm and place it on the coffee table. "Look at this." I point.

She squints her eyes and leans in. "What am I looking at?" she asks.

"There—" I point "—is where Cassie's car was found." I move my finger over. "This is where her body was found." Then I move my finger over toward the final point I'm trying to make. "This is where Riley lives."

Sadie's eyes go wide, and she sits back on the couch, looking baffled.

She starts to tear up, and I realize that I've been insensitive. This was her best friend and I'm treating it like some sort of detective novel.

"I'm sorry," I say guiltily. "There is still hope for Owen," I assure her. "They will find him, and he'll be okay. I just know it."

Although I don't tell her that I'm not really so sure.

"You're right," Sadie says. "Let's focus on Owen, and just pray that he's okay." She wipes the tears from her eyes.

"Well, I'm sure there's something we can do," I encourage. "There has to be some sort of clue as to what happened, right?"

Sadie looks doubtful. "I told you I had the house cleaned before you got here. I just wanted the place to look nice for you. I didn't think I would be destroying evidence."

Sadie starts to hyperventilate, her nerves frayed. I try to calm her down. I go into the kitchen to fill up a glass of water for her and one for myself, now realizing just how thirsty I've been all day.

I hand the water to her and sit beside her. She gulps it eagerly as if she too has forgotten to take care of herself today. Everything has been focused on Cassie and the truth of what's happened.

"Let's try," I encourage. "We'll split up. I'll look upstairs more thoroughly now, and you down here. Then we can switch. Remember I found the picture of Cassie in the house, so even if the place was cleaned up, it doesn't mean they got rid of everything."

I see something unreadable wash over Sadie's face. "You're right," she agrees. "Let's do it."

I leave Sadie to it downstairs and climb to the top floor, though I'm not sure what I'm really looking for; then again, I might know when or if I see something.

I start in my bedroom. I check under the bed, then flip my mattress. I know when someone wants to hide something they'll sometimes slice their mattress and stuff the contents in there. I rip off my sheets and notice that there is a mattress protector that is fully zipped around the entire mattress. I unzip it and call for Sadie to help. She comes in perplexed.

"What are you doing?"

"If someone has something to hide, it's usually in the mattress," I say, tugging it out while Sadie pulls at the protector. The mattress then hits the floor with a loud thud. I come around the to the other side and flip the bottom of the mattress up.

Nothing shows up out of the ordinary. I continue a sweep around the rest of the bedroom and bathroom. So far, nothing. But maybe Owen had some secrets of his own?

I walk into the guest room, which I know now was Owen's bedroom, and feel my heart break a bit. I think about Danny's room and how my family left it preserved like a shrine. Although this room has already been cleaned out, still, it being the last place he slept, I feel as if I'm violating his space.

We have to find him though, a voice inside reminds me.

I let out a deep breath and start to do the same with Owen's bed. I flip the mattress, not finding anything. I check the drawers, feeling around for anything that might be taped to the top or back of anything.

I open the closet now, pushing back the empty hangers, in case there is anything else that might be on the wall of the closet. But when I sweep the hangers back, I notice something that I hadn't before. There is a dark line that runs along the back wall of the closet. It's too clean to be a crack. That's when I realize that it's not a crack. It's a door.

I push on it with a touch of force and, as I suspected, the wall pushes back into a crawl space. It's dark, other than a single pull-chain light bulb and a window that allows the moonlight in. It streaks across the space, and I fall to my knees.

The first thing I notice are drawings on the walls, taped up. In the corner is a stack of construction paper, markers and tape.

This must've been his hiding place. His safe place, when he was here. I allow my eyes to gaze over the walls and down to the floor where I find a pillow and a throw blanket as if he was setting up a picnic for himself.

I freeze, my heart nearly stopping when I see the brown teddy bear propped against the pillow. The same one that Danny had, sitting right here.

How? I think to myself. *How is this possible?* It was all so real, but he's not here now so it couldn't be. My eyes start to well with tears, a mixture for Danny and Owen, different children yet so similar, joined together by tragedy.

I hold back a sob and reach for the brown bear.

Then my eyes widen when I see something that's under the bear.

"Natalie?" I hear my voice being called from the hall.

"In here," I yell back.

"Where?"

"The closet." I allow her to follow my voice until I see her frame darken the space.

"What the—" Her voice cuts off as she stares in bewilderment. "I didn't even know this had a crawl space," she says in amazement.

"I think we might've just discovered what will help us find Owen," I tell her.

I hold it up to her.

"The bear?" She looks at me confused.

I shake my head. "No." I hold up my other hand. "This," I say, revealing a phone.

Sadie's eyes widen in shock. "Does it work?"

I attempt to turn it on. "It's dead," I say. "But I have a charger."

I find my charger in the kitchen and plug it in. We hear the beep of the phone confirming it's charging. I'm relieved to find that it's a match.

"What do we do now?" she asks.

"We wait," I answer.

As we sit in silence, I see that Sadie appears to be shaking. She must be a nervous wreck. I can only imagine how shot her nerves must be.

The screen finally pops to life and she and I both jump in anticipation, but my hope falls when I notice the password protection appear.

Sadie and I look at each other.

"Do you know what her password might be?" I ask.

Sadie looks at me like I'm crazy. "I couldn't begin to guess what her phone passcode was."

"Let's try her birthday. You know that, right?"

Sadie nods. Her breath is shallow. She tells me the date and I try the month and day, but it doesn't work.

"What about Owen's birthday?"

She shrugs. "I didn't know she had a child until she showed up."

I try an obvious 1-2-3-4 and 0-0-0-0 but after three tries we get locked out for five minutes.

"Maybe the police can get in," I suggest.

Sadie shakes her head. "I remember a news article about how there was a huge dispute between Apple and the FBI, I think, because they refused to hack into a terrorist's phone. They said that it was an invasion of privacy, and they didn't want to lose the trust of their customers."

My shoulders fall. It seems like we are onto something, and we are too close to lose now. The password screen comes back to life, but our hope is shot. Suddenly it occurs to me. The message on the shower. I distinctly remember the mirror saying *get out*, but then on the shower was a number: 6666. I had thought it was demonic but that would be three sixes not four. I look down and type 6-6-6-6.

The home screen pops up. Sadie and I look at each other in surprise. I smile, relief washing over my face. "We're in!"

I click on the text messages with Sadie looking over my shoulder, both of us scanning through and seeing if anything looks out of place. Each one I turn to Sadie for some sort of confirmation, but she shakes her head.

"Would you recognize Riley's number if it were on here?"

"Yes," she agrees as we continue to scan her contacts.

"Anything?"

Sadie's face falls in disappointment. She walks away now, looking out the window as if defeated.

"Don't give up," I tell her. "I'm sure there is something here that can give us some clue, even if it's the last call she made and finding out who it was to."

Sadie continues to look out the window and I watch as her head dips.

I feel as if I should give her a hug, but I also feel compelled to keep searching. We can't waste time. Any precious moment wasted could cost Owen his life.

I turn back to the phone, now opening the pictures. I scroll down to the most recent photos. They look like self-portraits of Owen, using some sort of filter to give himself bunny ears or bug eyes. There is one that I hover my finger over. I notice the image moves, showing me that it's a video of Owen.

I hesitate, then turn the volume up and click on it.

It's of Owen. He's in the crawl space as I recognize the pictures behind him. He's not saying much, just making funny faces and laughing at the image of himself as he brings the camera far away and then so close you can see the bottom of his nose. I'm about to click out of it, when a woman's scream can be audibly heard. I turn toward Sadie who is immediately by my side, leaning in over my shoulder.

Owen stops what he's doing and shifts the camera from his head, leading it over to the window.

Sadie and I are so engrossed in the video, terrified at what is going to happen next, that I don't hear the loud creak of the door or the footsteps approaching us. All I hear is the loud thwack of something against my skull before everything goes black.

Chapter Thirty

Sadie

I have no idea what's going on around me. Black spots appear in my vision, and I feel woozy. I'm having that same out-of-body experience that I had before. As if I have left and another person has taken over. For some reason instead of Natalie in front of me, I see Cassie and I'm brought back to those final hours.

Cassie, where are you?

I texted her again, as I pushed back and forth vigorously on the swing on the back porch.

Something came up. I'll be back tonight.

Where was she going that she would be away all day?

I checked my email and saw a notification regarding the rental.

I grinned as I scanned the applications. I'd priced it low for a reason, but I still couldn't get over how there were so many applicants in a single day. I started to research each one when I came across a couple in their mid-thirties, who could come as early as Saturday afternoon. I researched the names. Luke and Natalie Copper. I stared at the picture wide-eyed. The wife Natalie looked just like Cassie. A smile formed at the corners of my lips. Wouldn't it be lovely for Cassie and

Tom to learn that I'd replaced her with someone who was practically a doppelgänger?

Perfect, I thought. Cassie will have to be out by tomorrow. It gave her no time to try to follow up with whatever "deal" she and my husband had made.

I clicked *approved* on the application and told Shar that she would need to come in early Saturday morning to scrub the place down.

Adrenaline ran through my fingers as I typed a text out to Cassie, telling her she had to leave. A roar of thunder rolled off the ocean and I stopped to see a looming dark cloud in the distance. It looked much more threatening than anything I'd seen before and wondered if this storm would be the worst yet.

Through the open window, I heard the front door open, and Tom appeared. He came in quickly, heading right up the steps. If he had been running at some point, then he would need a shower. There would be no more conspiring today. Whatever he thought he had planned for that night, I was going to drug him with so much ketamine he wasn't going to be able speak.

"Cassie?" I called out. It was dark and the rain had been on and off all day, cooling the air that felt like an icy chill coming off the ocean, which had an oily black color to it.

"Over here," she answered. She was wearing a pink zip-up hoodie with white yoga pants. Her legs were folded under her on a lounge chair that she had pulled close to the pool earlier while she was watching Owen swim.

"I left the door open in case Owen needs me." She tilted her head back toward the guest house.

I pulled another lounger next to her, the metal legs scraping loudly against the pavement.

"Where were you?"

"Owen hit his head on the side of the pool. It was bad enough that he had a concussion, so we went to the emergency room to have him checked out." She rolled her eyes. "We were there forever."

"How is he?"

"He's okay now."

"That's good to hear."

She looks at me sadly, then begins to speak. "Listen, if it was me who did something to offend you, I'm sorry. I don't want to leave on terms like this."

"It's fine." I tried to shake it off. "I really forgot that I had rented the house out."

She squinted at me in confusion. "Why would you want to rent the house out? It's not like you need the money."

"It's a great way to meet new people."

"Did Tom know you were renting it out?"

"Of course," I lied. "He must've forgotten."

Cassie gave me a sad smile. "Are you doing okay?"

"I'm fine," I said defensively. I'm not the one in the hot seat. In our relationship, I've always been the doctor while Cassie has always been the patient.

"This is me," she told me. "I know you're not okay. This has to do with you and Tom, doesn't it?"

"It has to do with you and how despite having a child you still don't have your life in order," I spat back.

"Tell me again, what happened with Tom?" she said, ignoring my comment.

I looked at her, confused. "You knew his history before I did," I reminded her.

She continued to stare at me before I finally started speaking again.

"The first few years of our marriage were great, but then he started to spiral again. The drug use increased, he started online gambling, and he acquired a massive amount of debt. Then two years ago he accidentally overdosed on fentanyl. That's when I decided to get him out of Los Angeles and move here."

Cassie stared at me in a way that made me uncomfortable. Her eyes narrowed in on mine.

"Sadie," she said slowly. "Tom doesn't have a gambling problem."

"Yes, he does," I scoffed. How would she know?

She shook her head. "Remember that time in Atlantic City?"

My nerve endings started to fire off.

"We had gone to that wedding, Jen and Steven's, I think. Tom and I had to pull you several times from the blackjack tables. You wouldn't stop. You'd lose money and you kept adding more chips, saying that if you played big, you'd win big. Tom was the one who tried to explain to you the house always wins, which is why he never liked to gamble."

"He said that, but then eventually he must've changed his mind."

Cassie shook her head again. "It was always you who had the gambling problem," she said. "Not Tom."

"What are you trying to say?" I asked, now offended.

"Why did you move to Southampton, Sadie?"

I was starting to get agitated. "I just told you; Tom was spiraling."

She shook her head at me again. "I recognized Laney."

That stopped me dead.

"Why?" she said in disbelief. "Why would you hire Laney, the woman who your father had a second family with, to come and clean your house every day? Why would you move across the country for that?"

"Don't call her Laney," I said, disgusted. "I can't even associate her with that name. Her real name is Charlene. She called herself Laney because it makes her sound innocent, but she's just Shar to me now."

"Sadie," Cassie pressed.

"Because she deserves it!" My voice rose in anger. "It felt good to come back here with all that money. I knew she was still out here and when her son got cancer and had blown through what my father had left her, she was forced to clean houses. I sought her out and hired her, overpaying her so she wouldn't refuse. With my last name changed and her not seeing me since I was ten, she had no idea. I waited until she got comfortable, until she realized that she couldn't turn down the paycheck, and then I told her who I was." I smiled, thinking about that day that I finally told her. Laney had turned ashen. "The look on her face is a priceless moment I would never take back," I said triumphantly. "Letting her see that I won. Despite all that she had done to our family, how she destroyed it, I still won. And you have no idea the pleasure it gives me to watch her clean up my messes every day, even though it would never make up for what she did."

Cassie's face was a mixture of shock, disappointment and confusion, like she didn't recognize me. Then she looked up at me, her voice shaking. "Tom's not sick, is he?"

"What do you mean?" I asked. "What does me hiring Laney have to do with Tom's sickness? Of course he's sick. It's why we moved across the country. I'll admit I had my reasons for choosing here, but the main reason for leaving didn't change."

"This is me," Cassie said, shaking her head. "You can't lie to me. I'm your best friend."

She swallowed hard then, looking down as if giving herself some sort of courage for what she's about to say.

"I know the change started when you lost your job."

"I didn't lose my job," I argued. "I stepped back after Tom got sick."

"I ran into one of your colleagues a few years back. They told me about Jason."

I stiffened.

"The sixteen-year-old who swindled you into believing his parents were monsters, when in fact he was orchestrating all of it."

"He did pull the wool over my eyes," I finally admitted, but then narrowed my gaze onto her. "Rest assured, I'll never let that happen to me again."

Cassie inhaled deeply through her nose, holding my eye contact.

"While Jason used it to get away from his parents, you used his methods to trap Tom."

"What on earth are you talking about?" I'd started to sweat. She knew more than I thought. She knew everything.

"Two years ago, Tom wanted a divorce. He felt suffocated by you and your need for control. He told me you would throw lavish parties despite his addictions, all in an effort to social climb. He said you became someone he couldn't even recognize. Money had changed you and you were no longer the person he fell in love with."

Tears started streaming down my face then.

"Sadie, you've been using your therapist training to manipulate him and other people into thinking he's something he's not. You've been keeping him a prisoner to keep him from leaving, haven't you?"

"How dare you!" I stood up then. I felt myself flush with heat. "Why don't you tell me the real reason you're here, Cassie? Is it so Owen would finally get a chance to meet his father?"

Cassie stared at me; her mouth gaped open. Not sure what to say.

"You told me you were in love with Tom," I said. "You tried to steal him from me, but you didn't win. That's what you meant on my wedding day when you told me the best girl won. You left after he chose me. Then you found out you were pregnant with his baby, and you stayed away, but you made a big mistake by coming back."

Cassie was still at a loss for words.

I put my arms out. "The math adds up," I told her. "I haven't seen you in seven years. Seven years, Tom and I have been married, and here you are showing up with a six-year-old boy."

Cassie finally opened her mouth then, a hand up in defense. "Sadie, I came because Tom asked me to help him."

I started to cry, my voice loud and unstable. "I vowed I would never become my mother. I would never let Tom do what my father did to my mother. And yet no matter how hard I tried—" I caught a sob in my throat "—it did happen. Tom does have another family and it's with my best friend in the whole world." I broke down then, my head in my hands.

Cassie stood up. She tried to hug me, but I flinched.

"You of all people know how hard it was on me. You, more than anyone else, saw how it destroyed my mom and me. You were the one who told me that you would always be my family."

"Sadie," Cassie said softly. But I cut her off again.

"But you couldn't stay away, could you? Your life is such a mess that you didn't know what to do with yourself. Here you are with a six-year-old boy, and you can't give him a stable life. So, you decide you'll come here, tell Tom—the man you've always been in love with—that he has a son, so you could just push me out and move right into my life and give yourself a fairy-tale ending. Am I right?"

Cassie shook her head, slowly approaching me. "Sadie, it's not like that," she repeated.

"Don't tell me it isn't. I know the truth!" I yelled at her. "I heard you in the garden with Tom, telling him how you were going to help him get out of this. Out of what—his marriage to me?" My voice is high-pitched.

"We are going to get you the help you need," she said slowly and cautiously.

But those words set off an explosion inside me.

Cassie reached her hand out to me.

I felt all the rage that had been building up inside me coming out. I pushed Cassie hard. She let out a scream as she fell into the pool.

After that it became that out-of-body experience again. I saw myself from above while someone else stepped in to do the job I couldn't.

I watched myself jump in after her. She let out another scream but this time it was stifled as I held her underwater. I saw through the water her eyes wide with terror. She had water in her lungs and she grabbed at my hands that were holding her down. She tried to free herself, but I found a strength inside me that I didn't even know I had. An adrenaline rush surged through me. I couldn't stop at that point, even if I wanted to.

I held her there for a long time, even after she had stopped thrashing. Her large blue eyes were still open, staring back at me, but there seemed to be a sense of peace in them. She could stop fighting back against this life.

It's then that my mind came back into focus. Despite how loud the wind had picked up, despite the rain that had begun, there was a quiet stillness in me as my mind thawed like a frozen block of ice at what I'd just done.

I'd taken a life. The life of my best friend. A gasp escaped my throat, and I felt my legs go weak. I hunched over, a hand over my mouth. I just killed my best friend. I thought about the life that we had together. All the good times. The times that we laughed and cried, the sentimental moments that I would cherish forever. But then something hardened me into stone. The Cassie I was mourning was dead a long time ago. This person wasn't Cassie. This was a money-grubbing, husband-stealing opportunist who abused her relationships to get what she wanted. This person never cared for me. This person just wanted me out of the way so she could take what she thought was hers.

And I refused to become my mother. I'd kept that promise to myself. I saw the threat and I handled it. I took care of what needed to be done to preserve my marriage and my happiness.

I heard crying start behind me, which brought me out of my trance. I turned around and found Owen was standing there, innocently in his green pajamas, his eyes wide with terror. He was staring at his mother's body floating lifelessly in the water.

And I came to the horrible realization that Owen had been awake this whole time and he'd seen everything.

Chapter Thirty-One
Sadie

Owen and I stared at each other for a long moment. His face was full of confusion, like maybe what he was seeing in front of him was not real. I swallowed hard.

"Owen," I said slowly.

A crack of lightning broke above us. Owen went wide-eyed and started to run.

I found myself scrambling out of the pool, the water sloshing loudly, making Cassie's body slowly rock with the waves.

"Owen!" I called more loudly now.

He kept running toward the dunes. It was hard to see him as the rain had really started to pick up. I held a hand over my face as I squinted. I saw him duck under the boardwalk. I slowed my pace, trying to think of my next move. I softened my voice as I got closer. "Owen, honey. Your mommy fell in the pool," I called to him. "She was struggling. I tried to save her, but it was too late." I did my best to convince him. "I'm so sorry, sweetie. Please come out. I'm not going to hurt you."

Another flash of lightning struck, lighting up the sky and I saw him hiding under the boardwalk. "I saw you push her," he told me, and my face hardened as my stomach tightened. "I saw you hold her down."

I realized now that he did see everything, and he would tell everyone. And I couldn't let that happen. I'd worked too hard to lose it all now.

I lunged for him, not sure what I was going to do, not really trusting myself. He ran from me, down the boardwalk toward the beach. The waves were kicking loudly, and I was surprised to see him run straight into them. I ran in after him.

"Owen," I called. "You don't know what you saw." I tried again, but my voice was lost among the waves. I saw a head bobbing and swimming farther out.

Wherever he thought he was going, he wasn't going to make it. I remembered him on the beach the other day. He wasn't that strong of a swimmer and the water was ten times more dangerous now with the storm. A roar of thunder rumbled and a clash of lightning struck somewhere in the distance. I looked for Owen in the darkness when I saw his luminescent skin in between the waves. I went in after him.

"Owen, come here," I called out, paddling my arms. I was narrowing the space between us when a large wave toppled us, spinning me to the point where I didn't know what was up or down. I tried to breathe, but another wave slammed over me, pulling me back. I tried again, but another wave crushed down, like the jaws of death, trying to drag me out to sea. My lungs were getting tight as I started to panic. I needed to find the surface, but it was too dark. Eventually, I felt my feet against the bottom and I pushed with my legs as hard as I could to the surface, gasping for air. I frantically swam out of the surf, falling onto the beach on all fours, coughing and trying to catch my breath. I looked around for Owen, but he was nowhere to be seen. If the same riptide had hit him, then he likely wouldn't have made it.

Relief washed over me. I didn't want to kill a child. But I was sure happy that the problem seemed to have resolved itself.

I stood up, my clothes weighing heavy on me. I stayed on the beach for some time, waiting to see if he appeared anywhere, but the waves must've swallowed him up.

I needed to work out my next move.

I walked over to the garden shed where we kept all the essentials that Riley needed for landscaping. I pulled out the wheelbarrow and brought it over toward the pool. I pulled Cassie's body out. She was heavier with her clothes soaking wet, but I managed to angle her into the wheelbarrow.

It was fortunate that Cassie, after receiving my text, had already packed most of her things in the car. I wheeled her over to her car and then ran inside her house to find her car keys, which were sitting on the sideboard next to the front door. I unlocked her car, then eased her into the passenger seat. Luckily from there, it looked like she was sleeping, though I didn't worry about anyone stumbling upon her. I put the wheelbarrow back, wiping the handles and the inside with a damp cloth, making sure there was no evidence left behind. I made sure I placed the wheelbarrow just as I found it, then I closed the shed door.

The rain had stopped, and I took advantage of it clearing up a bit to see if I could spot Owen anywhere. The way the tide was pulling, I didn't think he'd get washed up on shore. The ocean was still kicking and, after a few moments of surveying the beach and the water, I was satisfied the ocean had pulled him out. I ran back to my house, stripping off my wet clothes for new ones. I checked on Tom, still passed out on the couch. The glass of scotch I gave him with the crushed-up ketamine was empty. He would be out for the rest of the night. I washed the glass and put it away, then walked back over to the guest house and gathered up the remaining items I saw that were Cassie's and Owen's. She did pretty much take care of everything. It was the first time since she had gotten here that I hadn't seen an explosion of toys and bathing suits and towels haphazardly strung everywhere. All that was really left was a duffel bag in Cassie's room that had clothes for her and Owen that they likely had planned on wearing when they left the next day.

Still, I combed through the place, checking for any trace of their existence, any Lego pieces, clothes in the dryer. Which reminded me to grab their bath towels and wash them. By the time the renters came, there would be no trace of anything. I was sure of it.

Now I needed to decide where to go with the body.

Part of me debated dragging her to the ocean, letting it swallow her up, but then there was the situation with her car being here. It led to a line of questioning that I didn't want to answer. Like why I didn't call the police when I saw her car still here and Cassie and Owen gone? That looked suspicious.

I looked at a map on my phone, and I smiled. It was all too perfect. This was all meant to happen this way. It was just too easy how it all seemed to fall into place.

Maybe there was someone looking out for me. Maybe my own mother helping me clear a path to a brighter future.

I waited until three o'clock in the morning. The storm had subsided, and the roads were quiet. No one would have been awake. I put on gloves and drove Cassie's car thirty minutes to the Ponquogue Bridge. With the strong winds and the tide, I felt as if luck was on my side. I pulled over, making sure there was no one around. I got out and opened the passenger side. I stared one last time at Cassie. For a moment I looked at her, not as my betrayer, but as my friend.

"Goodbye, Cassie. Time to rest now—it's all over."

I reached in and got my arms under her armpits as I dragged her out. I was grateful that Cassie had always been on the frail side and she was lighter since her clothes had dried. As I pulled her out, her head fell to the side limply. I propped her on the edge of the bridge, then reached further down toward her legs before lifting her up and over.

I heard a splash moments later and I worried at first that maybe I should've weighed her down, but that would have looked like murder. This was going to look like a suicide. After a few moments she started to sink, and I felt a rush of relief.

I got back into the car and pulled it into the Ponquogue Marine Basin. I parked the car near several boats that were sitting on trailers. Then I did one more check of the car. I locked it and walked up toward the cluster of houses just across the street.

I took a play out of Cassie's handbook, and I knocked on Riley's door.

It took several heavy bangs on his door before he finally opened it, angry and half asleep. His hair was disheveled and he was in a white T-shirt and red plaid boxers.

He gave me a concerned look. "What are you doing here?"

I started to sway a bit, giving off an appearance of being drunk. "I wanted to see you." I ran my finger flirtatiously on the door. "I was lonely."

He looked around nervously. "You shouldn't be here."

I flung my arms around his neck and started to kiss him. As I had suspected he instantly pushed me away.

I stumbled back, embarrassed. "I'm sorry," I said. "I'm so stupid."

I crouched down on his porch step. The smell of wet concrete and salt filled my nostrils. I put my head in my hands.

His face softened a bit. "How did you get here?"

"I'm so embarrassed," I said, ignoring his question. "Can you please drive me home? You can stay in the guest house until tomorrow morning." I stood up and stumbled for effect.

He bit his lip but then shook his head finally. "Let me just change," he said.

He ushered me into his foyer, which really was just a small hallway taken up by a set of steps that led to what was likely a bedroom and a bathroom.

I didn't want any evidence that I had been here, so I stayed right where I was instead of wandering around.

A few minutes later, I heard the stomp of his heavy boots coming down the steps.

"I'm so embarrassed," I said again. "I don't know what I was thinking." I started to tear up.

Riley didn't know what to do, so instead he opened the door, and I followed him out to his truck.

I climbed into the passenger seat, reaching into my pocket for Cassie's car keys. I pulled them out and placed them under the seat below me before putting my head in my hands.

This time I really did start to cry. What I'd done hit me like a wave and I began to weep.

"It's okay," Riley said awkwardly.

That's when I remembered he was here. He was driving me just like I had planned. I swallowed back the rest of my tears, and I pulled myself together. I wasn't out of the woods yet.

Tom. He still had to pay for what he had done.

My mind went to Jason, the former patient of mine, who again gave me another idea. When I got home, I headed into the kitchen, blood pumping coarsely through my veins. I flexed and unflexed my fists, psyching myself up. I opened the knife drawer and pulled out a filet knife. One that was almost never used if ever and was likely still the sharpest. I wedged it between the cabinet and refrigerator door so that the point was sticking straight out. I took several quick breaths then ran my arm hard into it. The pain hit me like a shock wave. I felt nothing until it started to pulsate. I grabbed a cloth and pulled the knife out of its spot. My breath shallow as I worked through the pain. My one hand covered the wound to keep it from bleeding all over. I put the knife in Tom's hand and folded his fingers around it. Then I started to scream.

Chapter Thirty-Two

Natalie

I wake to a throbbing sensation on my head. *Where am I?* My vision is blurry and I'm trying to remember where I am and what's happened.

Then I see Sadie standing over me and it all comes back to me. I had found the crawl space in the back of the guest bedroom closet. I discovered a phone in there and I was able to charge and unlock it.

The video.

There was a video of Owen; he was playing with the different app filters on the phone, playfully making himself look distorted when suddenly you hear a terrifying scream. Owen runs to the window, and you can see Sadie drowning Cassie in the pool.

I swallow hard, my eyes wide. Sadie is standing over me with a large vase in her hand.

She's breathing heavily like she's been running. "I'm sorry," she says. Her voice is filled with regret. "I didn't want to have to do this."

She raises the vase, and I try to get up, but the pounding shock waves through my skull leave me partially blind and discombobulated.

I outstretch my hand. "Please, no," I say weakly.

Suddenly there is a loud crash, then something falls next to me. I blink to clear my vision, and I see Sadie on the floor, the vase shattered.

There is a wave of confusion that washes over me. I see a trickle of blood on the side of Sadie's forehead, but I can see from where it hit that it isn't fatal.

But who did it?

I turn my head, my vision spinning, and I try to focus. Standing over me is Danny.

I blink again in disbelief. It's not Danny. And then I realize it's Owen. The boy from the photo.

It can only be my imagination, I think. But then, how did Sadie end up on the floor?

Sadie is starting to struggle next to me. I look toward Owen. He's standing there, staring like the petrified child that he is, holding a heavy marble tissue box cover, the corner tinged with blood.

"It's okay," I assure him.

I don't know if I'm really talking to Owen, or Danny, or whoever, but I see now that Sadie is starting to come to. She turns and spots Owen as well, her eyes wide like she's seen a ghost.

Before she can do anything, I throw my body on top of Sadie's, doing my best to contain her.

"It doesn't end like this," she cries.

I grab her arms and try to twist them behind her back to prevent her from being able to fight. It's something we were taught in the ER with unruly patients. Only in my weakened state, I'm not as effective as I once was. She frees her hand and slams her head back, head-butting me. I fall backwards, my vision blurred. She sits on top of me, reaching for another vase. She's about to bring it down, when my reflexes catch up and I stop her motion, pushing the other side of the vase. We struggle against each other. I think about what happens if

Sadie succeeds. If she kills me then she will surely kill Owen, and I can't let that happen.

"Run, Owen!" I yell.

I hear his footsteps scatter.

Thinking of Owen, a sudden surge of strength builds within me. A strength that I have been trying to summon my whole recovery. Adrenaline courses through my body and with all my might I manage to grab the vase from Sadie's grip and swing it across her face. This time it shatters fully; shards of porcelain are spread across the floor in blue and white floral patterns.

It knocks her out, but I know it's only momentarily. I run upstairs to the utility closet, where I had found the toolbox earlier, when Luke had fixed the toilet. I pull out the zip ties, drop the rest of the bag and run back down to secure Sadie's feet and hands. That should keep her until the police arrive.

It's then that I look for Owen.

Was he real?

Once again, I search the house, looking downstairs, when I remember I told him to run.

I know where he is.

I climb the stairs into his bedroom and open the now-closed door to the crawl space in the back of the closet.

He's crouched in the corner, his arms around his knees.

"It's going to be okay, Owen," I say softly, getting to my knees. I'm making sure to keep some distance between us as I don't want him to feel cornered. "You're safe now."

I see his eyes fill with tears and he runs to me. I embrace him in a strong hug, my arms wrapped tightly around him as he begins to sob. He is real; it's really him. What this poor boy has been through, I can't even fathom. He witnessed the death of his mother and has been hiding out this whole time, not sure who he could trust. He must've been so alone and so scared.

"I've got you," I whisper to him. "You're safe."

I feel his body collapse into me.

A warmth spreads across my chest.

I bring my hand to his head and gently start to stroke his hair. His cries turn into soft whimpers.

There is so much that I want to do for him all at once. But for now, knowing that we're safe I can just hold him.

"Get these off!" I hear Sadie yell from downstairs. The interruption is like a boulder crashing through the house. I can hear her body thrashing against the floor. She lets out another loud shriek, causing Owen to jump.

I pull away, rubbing his shoulders.

"You are safe," I remind him, hoping my words can soothe him. "But I have to call the police. I will be right back." I look him in the eye, so he knows I'm telling the truth. "I promise."

He nods.

I go into the crawl space and get him his teddy bear. He squeezes it tightly against his chest. I softly rub his head one more time then go downstairs to deal with Sadie.

I pick up my phone from the counter.

"Please." Sadie's voice breaks. "I'm sorry. Please don't do this."

I ignore her as I pull the card for Officer Tate out of my pocket.

"She tried to steal my life," Sadie pleads. "She was my family. She knew how it tore me up what my father did and yet she still tried to take the one thing left that mattered to me."

I start to dial.

"Please," she begs. "You know what it's like. You never come back from that childhood trauma. It sits inside you forever. It's only natural you would do anything to keep yourself from getting hurt like that again."

I stop what I'm doing and stare at her.

She looks at me hopefully.

"There is never an excuse for taking another person's life. That is not your right. I don't care what she did. Whether you cared or not, she had a life outside of you. She was a mother to a child, and you took that boy's mother away from him."

Her expression darkens. "She was a terrible parent." Her voice slices the air like a machete. "I was doing him a favor."

I hold the phone to my ear.

"Please! I never wanted to hurt Owen, I swear."

"But you did hurt him," I say. "You hurt him in more ways than you can imagine. You did to him what you think Cassie did to you, what you think your father did to you. Your hate, all it did was spread more of it."

"Officer Tate here." A gruff man clears his throat on the phone.

"Officer Tate, it's Natalie Copper. I need you to come back to the house. I have the murderer of Cassie Dune with me."

"We have Riley in custody," he answers.

"Riley didn't do this," I say. "I have a video of Cassie being drowned in the pool here by Sadie Wilson herself. It was recorded by Cassie's son Owen who has been hiding out here in the house for the past five days. We found him and he's safe."

"I'll be right there," he tells me.

"Send an ambulance," I add.

Sadie bends into herself and begins to sob.

"We are nothing like each other." I shake my head.

I hear footsteps behind me, and Owen is at the foot of the steps.

I reach for his hand. "Come on," I tell him. "Let's wait outside."

Chapter Thirty-Three

Sadie

I'm restrained to a stretcher as an EMT examines me. There are blue and red lights flashing, blurring my vision. "Tom," I hear my voice calling urgently. "Tom."

Tom appears in front of me almost like an apparition. "Tom." I reach for his hand.

He pulls away and shakes his head at me. "How could you?"

"She was trying to destroy us," I plead.

"Sadie, you killed her." His voice is deep, trying to make me see the seriousness of what I've done.

"I did it for us," I tell him again. "She was going to tell you the truth. That she was in love with you and that Owen was your son."

"Sadie," he repeats. "I never loved Cassie; I never slept with Cassie. She reached out asking me for money, because she was embarrassed to tell you. She knew you'd judge her. I realized when she reached out that if anyone could get me out of my conservatorship with you, it would be her. She was helping me, Sadie! And you killed her for it," he says in disbelief as he stares at me, his jaw tight.

I had it all wrong. He didn't love Cassie, which makes me feel a momentary sense of relief. But he was trying to break free of me. I held on too tightly.

"Tom," I say, my voice catching. "I'm sorry." I look down at my hands. My own hands that killed my best friend. I think about the note I wrote Tom before I staged my suicide. The truth is, I never actually wanted to kill myself. I merely wanted to get close to Natalie. I knew that she'd save me and we would become friends. She'd replace Cassie and I'd have the friendship I deserved, with someone who was just as traumatized as me, but looked enough like Cassie to remind me to always keep my guard up. But if things got out of hand and I did die in that ocean, I owed Tom the truth. "There's a letter for you in the safe upstairs. It explains everything."

I look over at another ambulance where Owen is wrapped in a blanket as Natalie and the EMT talk. I am grateful that Owen is okay. I really never wanted to hurt him. Several other police cars pull up. The most excitement this town has probably had in a while, and among the red lights I think of Riley.

I put the pieces together one by one in my mind. It all makes sense now. That night that I had told Riley he could stay in the house, Owen had managed to sneak back in.

He must've been terrified, but Riley knew he was there. He's known this whole time.

I imagine Tom upstairs. I gave him the code to the safe and he's likely reading the letter now. I go over in my mind what it says as if I'm reading it to him.

Dear Tom,

I'm so sorry for everything I have done to you. I never wanted it to come to this. I merely wanted us to be together and stay happy.

You were starting to pull away from me. I could sense it. You thought I only cared about the money, but it was you I wanted more than anything else. I needed you to see that. See that I would go to the ends of the earth to take care of you. You decided to drown your sorrows in drugs and alcohol the same way you did after your father and mother died. I didn't want to risk you going into rehab. The distance it would create between us while you were away made me fear that you would decide to divorce me. But I couldn't let you continue to do this to yourself, so I drugged you, wanting it to look like an accidental overdose so that you might scare yourself into getting straightened out. But instead, you seemed to plunge into a deeper hole.

I never wanted to hurt you, Tom. I just wanted you to realize what you were doing to yourself. With your inheritance, I was worried that an endless bankroll would not be healthy for you. I accumulated a sizable debt in your name from online gambling. That and your overdose allowed a judge to appoint me sole controller of our finances. Then I moved us away, hoping once again that you would appreciate a healthier lifestyle. But instead, you resented me when all I was trying to do was save you.

The last time that I had you admitted was more out of anger, I'll admit. You remember Jason, the one who got me fired. I took his lead and made it look like you had hurt me. But I had to punish you. I found out that you had slept with Cassie, before our wedding. What she never told you was that she was carrying your child. Owen is yours. And I'm sorry, but I could not let Cassie come in and take you away from me the way that Laney took my father away from my mother and me. I couldn't let you go and start another family, leaving me to rot away until I fell into a deep depression like my mother. That's why I had to do it. That's why I had to kill Cassie. I didn't mean for Owen to die and I'm sorry that he did. He didn't do anything, but he saw the whole thing. It wasn't planned; it just happened. I never had any intention of hurting anyone, until I saw no other way.

> *I know what I did was wrong, but don't forget that her blood is on your hands too. It never would've happened if you hadn't cheated on me with my best friend.*
>
> *Now that I am gone, I want you to know that I did and still love you. Everything I did was for you, for us and for the hope that one day we could be happy again. I'm sorry that I have failed you.*
>
> *I hope this letter exonerates you and allows you to live a life of freedom. Promise me that you will steer clear of your former path and prevent yourself from ending up like me.*
>
> *All my love,*
> *Sadie*

When I turn, I see Tom coming back out of the house with the letter limp in his hand. His jaw is slack. His face unreadable. I'm not sure what sort of reaction I was expecting from him. Anger, sadness, regret. Maybe all those things.

He looks at me like I'm a stranger. Someone he should recognize but doesn't.

"Tom." I try to reach for him again.

"I can't." His voice catches in his throat. "I can't believe you'd do something like this."

"It just happened," I try to explain. "I didn't mean to."

He puts a hand up, stopping me. Then he looks up as if remembering something.

"You said you hypnotized me and that I admitted to pushing my father. That's not true either, is it?"

I look down in shame; there is no point in keeping up with the lies. "No, Tom. You didn't kill him. I did hypnotize you but you told me instead how you watched in horror as he fell, and the only guilt you hold is that you weren't close enough to try to save him."

He clenches his jaw as his eyes blink back tears. He looks at me one last time, shaking his head, and then walks away.

I want to call to him, but I know it won't do any good.

Maybe Tom will one day forgive me. I hope that Owen can too. One day when he's old enough to understand everything.

I realize this is what happens when you let yourself into the eye of a storm. I gave in to that initial thrill and let it carry me away. But I realize there is no peace in giving in to your urges. Only more pain and suffering. And like the hurricanes I always seem to be chasing, I too have left irrefutable damage in my wake.

I just need to get some help and take back control. I'm going to be all right. One day, everything will be all right again.

Chapter Thirty-Four

Natalie

The sky has bruised from a pink to a dark purple, as night falls, making the lights of the emergency vehicles become that much more blinding. The air has cooled and at least now it's bearable to sit outside. Owen is crouched next to me on the porch as we watch police officers pass us to go in and out of the house.

"Owen," I say gently. "Can I ask you a question?"

His round blue eyes look at me warily. "Okay."

"Why didn't you call the police after what happened? You had your mom's phone."

"I was scared."

"Why?" I ask. "Didn't you learn that police can help you?"

Owen shakes his head and looks around nervously, then he lowers his voice to a whisper. "The cops took away my mom's boyfriend. I was worried if I called them, they would take me to jail."

"Oh, sweetheart." I edge a little closer to him, slowly so as to not overwhelm him. "I don't know about your mommy's boyfriend, but police only take away bad people. And you're not a bad person."

"Okay," he says but not very convinced. "It's just sometimes I misbehave."

I shake my head. "Police don't arrest little boys for misbehaving. They arrest those who hurt other people. They arrest people like Sadie who hurt people. You did nothing wrong. None of this is your fault. Do you understand?"

He looks up at me and shakes his head again. I lean in to hug him as he nuzzles his head into my chest, and I bring him in closer to me.

"Riley," I call over to him when I notice he's done talking with one of the officers. After he was released, he must've come directly here.

Riley walks toward me, his gait heavy. I can see the dark circles under his eyes like he hasn't slept in days. I'm worried he's still mad at me but he looks at Owen and I see relief wash over him.

I stand up, and Owen does as well. "I'm so sorry for everything," I admit. Then I look down at Owen. "You knew he was here, didn't you?"

Riley looks at Owen and drops his head, then nods.

"You were trying to protect him," I realize. I think about Riley peering into the windows, and about what he had told me earlier. *Make sure there is fruit in the house.*

"Thank you." I embrace Riley in a hug. He stiffens, not sure what to do. I step back and this time Owen hugs him as well. Riley smiles and puts a soft hand on Owen's back.

"You're a good man, Riley, and I'll make sure everyone knows it."

Riley smiles shyly, his dark hair falling over his right eye as he drops his head.

An officer walks past us. "Can I go home now?" Riley asks him.

The rotund officer looks over Riley's shoulder and signals to another officer for confirmation, then looks back at Riley. "Yes, you're free to go."

I turn back to Owen, who has retreated to the porch, fingering a gap between his bottom teeth.

A tingling sensation runs up the back of my neck. The tooth. The one I had found when I was making the bed.

"Owen," I ask. "Did you lose a tooth?"

"Yeah," he says, pulling his finger out to show me.

"When?"

"A few days ago, but the tooth fairy didn't leave me anything. I thought maybe because she didn't know where I was hiding. So, I tried to put it under your pillow. But that didn't work either."

I try to keep my eyes from watering. This boy, with everything he's been through, and there's still that sense of innocence that I'm so glad he didn't lose. "Well, she did actually. I just didn't know what it meant. Clearly now, I know it was for you." I walk inside the front door where I left my purse hanging on a hook. I reach into my wallet and pull out twenty dollars.

"Whoa." Owen's eyes go wide. "I've never gotten a twenty--dollar bill before."

I swallow my tears. "Well, she thought you have been exceptional lately."

I sit down next to him as he puts the twenty in his pocket, watching as some of the police cars start to pull out of the driveway, the excitement starting to die down.

My mind starts to race through all the weird experiences I had while staying here.

"Owen, did you write *get out* on the bathroom mirror?"

He looks up at me with a sad, guilty expression. "Yes," he admits. "My mom's boyfriend did that to me once, when I used the shower after him. It scared me. I was worried you and that man . . ."

"Luke," I clarify for him.

He swallows. "I worried you might try to hurt me too, so I wrote that to try to scare you to go away."

I suck in a breath. "It did scare me," I admit. "But I promise that no one will ever try to hurt you again."

He studies my face, then switches his gaze back to the activity around us.

"Thanks for letting me snuggle with you when I got scared."

A wave of realization hits me again. It was Owen who had crawled into bed with me when I was half asleep. All this time, every vision of Danny was really Owen.

"Of course," I tell him, my eyes watering.

"Are you going to be my new mom?" he asks, a trace of self-consciousness in his voice.

I stiffen, worried if he's somehow read my thoughts. "Do you want me to be?" I find myself asking.

I feel his head nod yes against me and I bring him in closer. I realize then that I do want to be his mom as well.

"This place is considered a crime scene now," Officer Tate informs us. "I'm going to need to take you back to your apartment in the city."

I stare at the cop car, its lights still flashing blue and red. My chest starts to tighten, and that familiar fear intensifies. I can't get in the car.

"And I'm going to have to call social services for the boy."

Suddenly I feel a small hand wrap in mine. I look down and see Owen staring up at me. His eyes are sad but hopeful. "Please, can I come with you?"

I smile at him, giving his hand a gentle squeeze. I look up at Officer Tate. "Can he? He's been through so much already."

Officer Tate looks at the boy sympathetically. "I have to call social services, but perhaps they can meet you tomorrow at your apartment. I'll say I couldn't get a hold of anyone tonight."

My shoulders relax with relief, and I feel Owens arms wrap around me. I hug him back feeling the tension in his body release.

I take a deep breath and turn back toward the car. "Let's get you out of here," I tell him.

Epilogue

"Let's go, Owen!" I clap from the stands as Owen gets up to bat for his baseball team. Luke is on the sidelines, coaching third base. He claps hard, trying to psych him up. "Let's see it, Owen, you got this," he says before bending over and settling his hands on his knees.

Owen gives him a nod, adjusts his oversized helmet and sets himself up at bat.

The coach at the mound lobs a ball at Owen.

"Strike one!" the umpire yells. The opposing team starts to cheer, but our team is louder. The boys all stand up now, their fingers gripping the fence. "Come on, Owen, you can do it!"

Owen sticks his tongue out, a quirk of his that I discovered he does when he's really concentrating. It's mostly with homework, but when he does it, I know he's focused and he's going to hit it. It turns out that Owen is quite the athlete. After the adoption papers went through, we thought joining sports this year would be a great transition for him. It helped him get settled into the upcoming year and make a set of friends who immediately took to his all-star qualities.

The coach tosses the ball, soft and down the middle, and Owen smacks it with a force so hard you can hear the loud ping of the aluminum bat.

"Go, Owen, go!" the kids cheer.

Owen drops the bat and runs to first, catching the first-base coach who signals for him to keep going. The ball flies over the head of the outfielder who scrambles back to get it. Owen rounds second and Luke calls him into third. The outfielder throws it in, but the third baseman misses the catch. All the kids are still getting their bearings with the new sport.

"Go, go, go!" Luke yells.

Owen runs as the third baseman finds the ball and hurls it into home. Owen slides under the catcher who misses him.

"Safe!" the umpire calls.

The whole team is on their feet and running out toward Owen.

I run my fingers through my shoulder-length hair as I catch Luke's eye and we both smile. My heart blooms with pride for Owen.

It continues to surprise me how well he's been doing. Kids are resilient that way. It's been almost a year since Cassie passed and I know that date will be tough for him, but we have him seeing the proper grief counselors to help him. Something I wish my parents had done for me.

I may not be perfect every day, but we continue to try and that's the most important part. You do your best and you continue to love unconditionally. Which, when it comes to Owen, doesn't make it hard.

I finally see Owen's head pop up from the mosh pit that has landed on top of him. His face is beet red, his helmet has fallen somewhere on the ground, revealing a mess of straggly brown hair, but he's smiling. He's happy.

I'm sure he'll want to write about this to Riley. This year his teacher said he was struggling a bit with his letters and suggested he write to a grandparent or pen pal just to give him the motivation to want to write often. We knew he would want to write to Riley.

I will be forever grateful to Riley for watching out for Owen. When everything came out, I made sure everyone knew that Riley protected Owen the best he could, and he saved his life.

The city took him in then. The mayor even gave him an award for being an outstanding citizen. We all drove back for that. Riley smiled proudly with one arm around Owen for a picture that was front-page news that next day. People in town have finally learned that rather than being afraid of Riley, they need to understand him. Based on the letters that Riley sends back to us, he is doing well and gets a lot of jobs through the municipality, keeping the town square and parks beautiful.

I read in the papers not long after the incident that Tom had attempted to kill himself, but their maid, Laney, had found him on the ground, a bottle of pills and a bottle of scotch not too far away. She had thankfully been there in time to call an ambulance, and he went to rehab shortly after. I saw his name in the news again recently. It said that he moved to Scotland and is working with a company that designs golf courses.

It had compelled me to look up Sadie and see how she was doing. There is a part of me that wants to see her rot away in there for what she's done, but I'm left with a swirling mix of emotions. One being, if none of this had happened, I wouldn't have Owen, who is proving to be one of the best things, next to Luke, to happen in my life. I did like Sadie before I knew of everything that happened. I think she's a bit broken and was never given the right tools in life to help her become a better person. With any hope, the facility that she is in can help her find peace with herself.

We are settling into our new lives as well. We left the city, relocating to a small suburb, but still commutable for Luke. Although Luke's new position has allowed him to work remotely and essentially make his own hours, occasionally he has to go into the city and there still will be times when he has to travel, but he has the flexibility to be there for Owen. He had to make some sacrifices at work for that. It stunted his pay a bit, but after our experience this summer, we know that all the money in the world doesn't buy happiness. It's about prioritizing the people you love. I saw how quickly Luke took to Owen and just how much Luke was meant to be a father.

I've finally started to feel like myself, but I realize that Luke was right. Cutting back on my hours wasn't a bad thing. In fact, I have a good schedule now. I work in a doctor's office two to three days a week and two Fridays a month I work in the emergency room. The schedule has shown me that I can be there for Owen, and Luke, without sacrificing myself.

I will always be nervous about cars. But I've gotten significantly better about it, and I have started getting comfortable with driving again. I continue to swim at a local gym walking distance from the house, which is doing wonders for my mind and body from a health perspective.

I stand up and make my way through the crowd toward Owen and Luke.

"Great job, kiddo." I bend down, giving him a hug.

"Thanks, Mom."

My eyes tear up as I look at Luke, who smiles warmly. Owen has never called me mom. I never asked him to. I never wanted him to feel pressured. He had a mom and just because she died doesn't mean that she's not his mother anymore. We had discussed that with him shortly after everything happened. We wanted him to know that he didn't have to forget about her.

Still, my heart flutters as I choke back my tears, hugging him tighter. "I love you, and I'm so proud of you," I whisper in his ear.

"I love you too." His small arms try to wrap further around me. Then he turns to Luke and pulls at his arm, bringing Luke to his knees.

An embarrassed grin spreads on his face. "I love you too, Dad."

I watch Luke's Adam's apple bob in his throat as he pulls him in tight. "I love you too, buddy."

"So, who's ready for pizza!" the other coach calls out to the team.

"Me, me," the kids cry.

Owen once again gets swept up with the team, all hurrying to the pizza parlor across the street from the baseball fields. I reach for Luke's hand, and he interlocks it with mine.

"How did that feel?" I ask.

"It's indescribable."

"I know," I say, leaning into his arm.

"I told you you'd be a great mom," he says, leaning his head on mine.

"Well, I just hope I can be as good with two," I say.

He stops mid-step.

I give him a wry smile.

He looks down at my stomach. "Are you?"

I smile and he sweeps me up in his arms, spinning me around.

"Do you think Owen will like having a sibling?" I ask.

He runs his fingers along the side of my head, pulling my hair back behind my ear. "I think he'll love it," he says.

Acknowledgments

This book was a bit of a challenge as I came up with the idea for the ending before developing the story around it. Writing a psychological thriller can be intense. I had to make sure that I wasn't overdramatizing certain medical conditions, and I want to thank Tanya Santoro for all of her hard work and dedication in attending nursing school just so she could answer my questions. I also want to thank Monica Dobbin who helped me understand the process of admitting someone for psychiatric evaluations.

This is my second book with the team at Hodder and Stoughton. Thank you to my editor, Audrey Linton, for providing great notes to make this book as good as it can possibly be. Thanks to my agent, Nicky Lovick, for all of her continued support and behind-the-scenes work.

Thank you to Dana Kaye and her amazing team, Samantha Lien, Eleanor Imbody and Jordan Brown, who have done a wonderful job of helping me get myself out there.

To my husband Paul and our two sons, I couldn't do half of what I do without their encouragement.

Thanks to my parents, Ernie and Joan Muir, who have always supported me by reading my drafts and providing great notes. The same for my in-laws, Paul and Marylou Psak, who also are always willing to read and edit early drafts.

I also want to thank Britin Haller who has been championing my work this past year with her amazing introductions and for getting me a board seat on the Mystery Writers of America.

As always, to all the readers out there. Thank you so much for your support. None of this would be possible without you.

Don't miss *The Tutor*, another utterly thrilling read from Courtney Psak...

Letting her into your home was your first mistake...

RAISING READERS
Books Build Bright Futures

Dear Reader,

We'd love your attention for one more page to tell you about the crisis in children's reading, and what we can all do.

Studies have shown that reading for fun is the **single biggest predictor of a child's future life chances** – more than family circumstance, parents' educational background or income. It improves academic results, mental health, wealth, communication skills, ambition and happiness.[1]

The number of children reading for fun is in rapid decline. Young people have a lot of competition for their time. In 2024, 1 in 10 children and young people in the UK aged 5 to 18 did not own a single book at home.[2]

Hachette works extensively with schools, libraries and literacy charities, but here are some ways we can all raise more readers:

- Reading to children for just 10 minutes a day makes a difference
- Don't give up if children aren't regular readers – there will be books for them!
- Visit bookshops and libraries to get recommendations
- Encourage them to listen to audiobooks
- Support school libraries
- Give books as gifts

There's a lot more information about how to encourage children to read on our website: **www.RaisingReaders.co.uk**

Thank you for reading.

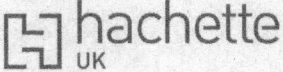

---

[1] OECD, '21st-Century Readers: Developing Literacy Skills in a Digital World', 2021, https://www.oecd.org/en/publications/21st-century-readers_a83d84cb-en.html

[2] National Literacy Trust, 'Book Ownership in 2024', November 2024, https://literacytrust.org.uk/research-services/research-reports/book-ownership-in-2024